MAFIOSA PRINCESS FAMILY

LIZA MALLOY

CHAPTER 1

Giada

The stillness around me contrasted sharply with the flurry of activity inside my head. Memories pinged into my consciousness faster than I could keep up, yet every time I dared open my eyes, I simply saw a cloudless blue sky. My brain told me there should be chaos, but there wasn't.

I tried to piece together the last few moments of my life, then realized I needed to rewind further for anything to make sense. There'd been Luca—first as a childhood friend, then as a crush at boarding school, then as my first love. Luca had broken my heart, and then there was Adrian. Adrian was good, but Luca was good for me. Yes, Luca was perfect for me.

And I'd had Luca, we'd had the perfect life, and then there'd been that stupid accident. My memories had been all scrambled and everything had been plunged into anarchy and it was all Julia's fault.

Suddenly I realized what had happened—my memories were back.

All of them.

I squeezed my eyes shut, then opened them, blinking again at the cerulean sky. My thoughts all seemed to be in order, right up until the last five minutes or so. That part confused me. My most recent recollection involved heading to the park with Luca to meet Julia for a hike, seeing her pull a gun out of her freaking purse, and then my brother materializing out of nowhere. I remembered hearing a gunshot and thinking Julia was dead, but none of that made sense.

I tried to sit up, needing to confirm that I'd merely imagined the horror around me.

"Don't," Luca said, his voice barely above a whisper.

His tranquil tone nearly convinced me that everything was fine, that he was only worried about my head. But then he added, "You shouldn't see this."

I wrestled my way to a seated position, expecting to see my brother looming over his girlfriend, gun still in hand. Instead, he was crouching beside Luca.

"Is she okay?" Angelo asked. I thought he was asking about Julia until Luca answered.

"I think so. She hit her head, so we need to go to the hospital after the cops get here."

Angelo nodded once, as if that were a perfectly reasonable response. Both men remained eerily calm.

I had to be dreaming.

I shoved Luca to the side and sat up. After one gaze to where Julia had stood, mere moments before, I regretted my stubbornness. I jerked my arm free and vomited all over the grass beside my husband. He patted my back, still fully composed and unruffled. When my stomach calmed, I motioned for Luca to help me to my feet.

Surprisingly, he did, keeping his arm around my back and supporting a majority of my weight.

"What cops?" I asked once I was stable, keeping my back to Julia. "Luca, we need to get out of here."

My brother and husband exchanged a glance.

"We can't leave yet," Luca said, his tone relaxed. "There was a shooting. The police are on their way."

"Right, so we need to hurry. Angelo too. If they find us here—"

"There's cameras," Luca interrupted.

I gazed around, wondering how he'd already ascertained such details amidst the craziness of the last five minutes.

Angelo nodded at Luca as if granting him permission for some task only the two of them understood. Luca slid his phone from his pocket, and calmly lifted it to his ear.

After a minute, he spoke, reciting our location, then saying with a clear voice, "There's been a shooting. A woman is dead."

I felt my eyes go wide, but when I turned to my brother, his peaceful expression matched my husband's.

"No, he's right here. He's not a threat. It was self-defense, er, defense of his sister," Luca continued on his call.

"Angelo," I began, my voice quiet.

"She was going to shoot you."

I opened my mouth to clarify that actually, she appeared to be aiming for Luca, but then I realized I had more important information to share.

"She was talking to an undercover cop. I saw them meeting. She knew I saw them. I told her I was going to tell Luca, but then..." my voice trailed off as I pieced together the timeline of the accident.

"You remember," Angelo said, a hint of a smile contrasting with the sadness filling his eyes.

"You need to sit," Luca said, apparently done with his call to the paramedics. "Let me walk you to the car. Once the police arrive, I'll drive you to the hospital. Don't say anything to anyone. Okay?"

I heard Luca's words, but then it hit me, the reality of what my brother—the brother who'd hated me since birth—had just done.

"You shot her to save me," I said, gazing up at Angelo.

He locked eyes with me for a moment, then turned back to the spot where Julia lay. I couldn't bring myself to look at her again. The patch of grass surrounding her had already turned a ruddy brown, soaked by her blood. I knew she was dead, there was too much blood for any other possibility, but I still couldn't fathom how everyone else was so calm.

I let Luca guide me to the car, then I watched from the passenger seat as he returned to my brother, the two of them seemingly shooting the breeze as sirens drew closer.

~

Luca

By the time Giada was settled into a bed at the ER, I felt like days had passed since we'd shown up at the park to meet Julia.

Yet somehow, it had been less than three hours.

The police had arrived at the park, arrested Angelo, and questioned me. After telling them the events of the morning, all of which would be corroborated by the security footage from the camera on the side of the park shelter, I insisted on driving Giada to the hospital for medical attention. They wanted to separate us, or at least to force us both to ride in the ambulance, but I resisted.

Finally, the cops settled for escorting us to the hospital.

I needed the time alone with Giada to review her story before the cops interrogated her. By the time we reached the hospital, the authorities would have figured out exactly who Angelo and I were, and that meant they'd have many more questions than they'd had initially.

I massaged my fingers into my temples, dazed by the crazy turn of events. Before this morning, I wouldn't have minded much if Angelo were locked up for the rest of his life.

But now?

I owed him everything.

Thanks to Angelo, Giada was safe. I was safe. And her memories were back.

I would do anything I could to keep him out of prison.

We told the cops exactly what had happened, and more importantly, precisely what the cameras would show. We explained that we all met up for a hike, and that Julia surprised us all by pulling a gun. Angelo had reacted quickly, shooting her to save his sister.

I was positive the cops would find the gun Angelo used was legally registered to him, with all permits in order. And they'd uncover absolutely nothing illegal or suspicious in his vehicle. This would be such a clear case of justifiable homicide that one might wonder if he'd planned it that way.

A spec of annoyance gnawed in the back of my mind, that awareness that Angelo could have—and should have— told me the moment he'd discovered what Julia had done. But I couldn't dwell on that. Angelo had taken care of the problem and without hesitation. So the moment they released him from jail, I'd thank him again.

Besides, I had my Giada back now. That was all that mattered.

"He should know what he did," Giada said, interrupting my thoughts. It took me a moment to remember she'd been talking about the FBI agent who had approached both her and Julia. "If he knows we're onto him, he'll back off."

"Sure, but another one will crop up to take his place."

"I won't talk to another one. I won't make the same mistake again," Giada promised.

"You didn't do anything wrong," I assured her, but it was a lie. Had she told me about this the moment the undercover agent had first approached her, maybe we could have avoided all of the heartache of the last few months.

"I need closure," she said.

I paused, pressing the pads of my thumbs harder against my temples to help me think clearly. I couldn't come up with a true downside to her plan. While I knew it would be futile to confront the guy, it might make me feel better, too.

"How would you even contact him?" I asked.

Giada pointed to the contact saved on her phone as "Gabby's brother." Her finger hovered over the name until I nodded. She clicked over to speaker, and the phone rang twice before a man answered with a nondescript, "Hello."

"Hi, it's Giada," she said. "I have my memories back. I'm at the hospital, in the ER at St. Mary's. Can you come?"

"Are you okay?" he asked, the worry sounding sincere.

"Yes. I hit my head again, but I'll be fine. I need to talk to you though. It's urgent."

He promised to arrive within the hour, then disconnected.

I did my best to distract Giada while we waited. I quizzed her about every little thing she'd previously forgotten, reveling at each regained memory. Much to my relief, she also still remembered everything since the accident.

"I can't believe you took me to a high school reunion when I had amnesia," Giada mused, a sleepy smile on her face. "That seems risky."

"I would've done anything to help you remember," I said.

Giada opened her mouth to reply, then gasped as a tall, lanky man appeared in the doorway.

The man stiffened sharply when he saw me seated beside Giada's bed, but he seemed to realize it was too late to turn around. I could almost see the gears in his head turning, trying to manufacture some plausible excuse for who he was and why he was coming to see my wife.

But then Giada spoke.

"Detective Grady?" she said, frowning. "Or um, whatever your name really is. Julia said you told her a different name."

His eyes darted from Giada to me, then back again.

"This is my husband, Luca Marino," Giada said. "I thought you two should meet."

I stood and extended my hand to the man and he shook it, albeit weakly. Then, I sank back into my seat at her bedside, signaling I wasn't a threat.

"I told Luca that you'd been asking Julia and I questions. Anyway, we thought you should know about Julia."

"What about her?" he said, not bothering to deny anything Giada had said.

"She's dead."

The man startled, his posture snapping to attention.

"She heard my memories were back, and she panicked. She came at me with a gun. She was going to kill me," Giada said. "But right before she could pull the trigger, my brother shot her."

I had to give him credit for staying calm, at least. His face portrayed no emotion. "Angelo?" he confirmed.

Giada nodded.

"Where is he now?"

"The police took him into custody and are questioning him. I assume he'll be released soon though. There were security cameras that recorded everything, so no one can say it wasn't done in defense."

"Convenient," the man mumbled, casting a glance at me.

I raised my hands defensively. "I wasn't aware of your existence or of your involvement with Julia until after it all happened. And really, if you actually understood me half as well as you claimed, you'd know better than to think I'd ever let my wife go anyplace where there was some untrained psycho with a gun."

I shuddered at the thought before continuing. "But Giada thought you should hear the news from her, that you should see firsthand what happens when you people meddle in someone else's business."

"Julia would still be alive if not for you," Giada said to him, her tone surprisingly harsh.

"She never would've lasted long in your family," the cop said.

"She never would've snapped and tried to kill me if you hadn't gotten in her head," Giada insisted. "I've told you all along, Luca is a good man. Angelo is a good man. You made Julia go crazy, and I would be dead if Angelo hadn't stepped in to protect me."

The cop dropped his gaze to the floor, waited a moment, then turned to me.

"You've made your point, Mr. Marino. I'll be on my way." He started to the door but glanced back at Giada. "Take care of yourself, Giada."

I pulled the curtain shut behind him, then turned back to Giada. "Do you feel better now?"

She appeared to consider the question, then nodded. I started to return to my chair and Giada frowned, patting the bed beside her instead. I perched on the edge of the thin mattress, then slowly scooted closer until we were seated side by side. I wanted to be near Giada, but I didn't want to get too comfortable as long as we were still in a small ER cubicle. Giada turned to her side, resting her head on my chest.

"What will happen to Angelo?" she asked.

I considered my response. The last thing I wanted was to give Giada false hope, but I didn't want her to be sad, either. Not when we should be celebrating the return of her memories.

"I'm not sure, but I think he'll be fine. The cops will want to follow all the proper procedures and do a complete investigation. They'll want to charge him with this if at all possible, and he might not make bail." I paused. "But I don't see how they could ever convict. It was a clearcut case of defense of another."

"Angelo's always had phenomenal aim. I don't understand why he didn't just shoot her hand? Or her knee?"

I smoothed my palm up and down Giada's back. Her question was rhetorical. On some level, Giada already knew Angelo could've saved her without killing Julia. She had to realize that Angelo aimed for the head intentionally because Julia had to die. Giada had to understand that, at the end of the day, there was no scenario where we could've let Julia live.

"Knock knock," trilled a female voice. Dr. Adams poked her head through the curtain. Her eyes widened at our position, but she recovered before I scooted back to my own chair.

"I heard you were here and that you got your memories back!" she said to Giada, reaching for the chart clipped to the foot of the bed.

"From who?" Giada said, frowning. She gazed at me as if expecting to hear I'd told people, but in the flurry of activity the last two hours, I hadn't told anyone anything except Marco and Alessio. I hadn't told either of them about her memory, though.

"Adrian," she said, jotting some notes on the clipboard.

"How did he hear?" Giada asked.

"I guess he's at the police station with your brother," the doctor replied, her tone nonchalant.

"Did he say how Angelo is doing? When can he come home?" Giada asked.

I rose to my feet, pressed a kiss to her head, then motioned to the curtain. "I'll be right outside in the hall, okay?"

Giada nodded, but worry clouded her eyes. I crouched down by the head of the bed, squeezing her hand. "I can stay. Are you okay? Does your head hurt?"

"No, I'm fine. I just…don't go far, okay?"

I hadn't planned on it, but now I wasn't sure if I should leave at all.

"I need to run some quick tests on you, Giada, so this would be the perfect time if Luca does need to make a call or something. He's welcome to stay while we're here, but we'll need to get you into CT before we discharge you."

Giada reached around my neck with her free hand, the one that wasn't clutching my hand, and guided me closer. She kissed me hard, then relaxed back on her pillow. "You can go now. Tell Alessio I do not want him to bring me any tacos."

I snorted a laugh as I released her hand. I loved the fact that she already knew I was calling Alessio, and that she remembered his determination to convince her Mexican food was superior to Italian.

My girl was back.

CHAPTER 2

Giada

$\mathcal{A}$fter a CT scan, another exam by the doctor, and a couple more hours of observation, I was released shortly before midnight. We still had no word on when Angelo would be released from jail, and the guilt over what he'd had to do because of me was weighing heavily on me.

I was beyond exhausted, but I was also far too stressed to sleep anytime soon. Luca clutched my hand the entire drive home, peering at me at every single stoplight.

"I promise I'm fine," I said for what felt like the millionth time.

Luca steered into the parking space and killed the engine. "You've been through a lot today."

I didn't answer, but let him guide me into the apartment.

"Are you hungry?" he asked. "Thirsty?"

I shook my head, then nibbled on my lip as I realized the one thing that would relax me enough to sleep.

"Does your head hurt?" he asked.

"No." It wasn't exactly a lie. My head felt fuzzy and heavy

from the influx of new memories, but I'd describe the sensation more as congestion and not pain.

I crooked a finger at Luca and he stepped closer, slowly pulling me into an embrace. "I know what would make me feel better," I said.

"Hmm," Luca mumbled against my hair. "You just finished telling me you felt fine."

"Yes, but it's going to take a while before I adjust to all these new memories. There are so many things I forgot and now I just want to enjoy my intact brain."

Luca's low chuckle made me smile.

"For example, I now remember how much it relaxes me to make love to my husband."

"Pretty sure I taught you that lesson again yesterday."

"Yes, but a lot has happened since then. And besides, it's different when I actually remember all of our history together."

Luca pulled back from our cuddle and grinned. "I'm not going to say no."

His lips brushed against mine so softly that I shivered. As we kissed, it all rushed back to me—the full impact of everything I'd forgotten.

"God, Luca, I'm so sorry," I said, pushing back. "I can't imagine how hard it was for you those first few weeks when I—"

"Shh," he whispered, kissing my tears. "You didn't do it on purpose, and it's over now anyway."

"I knew I was missing out on something while the memories were gone, but I really didn't understand how much I'd lost, and now…" I paused, too overwhelmed to even finish the thought. "What if I'd lost you today?" I said instead.

"You will never lose me. I'm right here," Luca said. He hoisted me onto the counter and kissed me harder, pausing only to lift my shirt up over my head.

I parted my legs so he could step closer, then slipped my hands up his shirt. His torso felt hot against my touch, so I nudged his shirt. He took the hint and removed it, then started kissing my neck, working his way down to my collarbone. By the time Luca unfastened my bra, his mouth caressing every inch of my sensitive flesh, I'd fully lost myself in the awareness of the moment. I pledged never to forget any second of my time with Luca, or any part of how beautiful and whole I felt when he touched me.

I clasped my legs together at the ankle, pushing Luca's pelvis harder against my own, and I groaned at his erection, suddenly desperate to feel more of him.

Luca knew exactly what I wanted because he knew everything about me. He hadn't forgotten anything, and I loved him even more for that.

"Okay baby, hang on," he said, clutching me tighter as he moved us from the kitchen to the bedroom. He lay me on the bed, finished undressing us both at record speed, then climbed on top of me.

His hardened length pressed against me, taunting me as he kissed me. He deepened the kiss, eliciting another sharp moan from me. Luca pulled back only to lick his fingers before pressing them against my own wetness. He growled his approval of how ready my body already was for him, then thankfully, positioned himself at my entrance.

I tilted my hips, welcoming him home as he thrust into me, filling me with an exquisite wholeness I hadn't felt since before the accident. Our bodies moved together like we'd synchronized the entire routine, but my mind whirled. I thought about our first wedding night, and the way Luca had looked at me when he realized I loved him no matter what he'd done in the past. I thought about the time he'd thought I might be pregnant, how he'd been so full of pure joy even when I'd betrayed him.

As my body sped towards a climax, I couldn't help but realize that I felt safest and happiest in bed with Luca. As long as we stayed here, wrapped in each other's arms, nothing could come between us.

I held back nothing when my orgasm crashed over me. I screamed Luca's name so loud that I couldn't even hear his moans a moment later when he succumbed to his own pleasure. He hadn't even pulled out of my body when I locked eyes with him and whispered, "Again."

Luca flashed me his adorably boyish grin, then worked his way down my body, licking and sucking everything in his path. Instead of protesting my impatient demand, or reminding me of the physical limitations of the human body, he simply worshiped my body for the next several minutes.

Once I felt ready for the next round, I rose to my knees, directing Luca to his back. I took him in my mouth, sucking his sensitive flesh until it reached its full length and hardness. Then, I positioned myself over him, letting my eyes drift shut in ecstasy as I sunk onto his waiting erection.

The new position offered totally new angles and sensations from our first round, while also freeing up his hands to pleasure my breasts. I didn't expect to come so quickly so soon after my last orgasm, but the combination of movements brought me right to the precipice far too soon. I was determined to ride the peak for as long as possible, but then I opened my eyes and saw the earnest look of love in Luca's eyes as he gazed up at me. In an instant, my innermost walls tightened, and wave after wave of delicious tingles washed over my body.

~

Luca

*I*t was after nine when my phone woke me. Beside me, Giada slept peacefully. I silenced the call and tried to extricate myself out from under her arm without waking her. I'd nearly succeeded when her fingers tightened against the flesh of my hip. I froze.

"Don't go," she pleaded, her voice raspy.

She lifted her head off the pillow, her eyes still filled with sleep. She was especially beautiful like this, without any makeup, and her hair messy from a night of lovemaking. I pressed my lips against hers, breathing in the warmth and willingness of her body to meet mine. Gratitude flooded me. Never again would I take this for granted.

"Never again," I whispered aloud.

She frowned, then repeated her earlier sentiment. "Don't go."

"I'm just making coffee," I said, confident the magic word would prompt her to release me. I was right.

While the coffee brewed, I brushed my teeth, combed my hair, and dabbed some aftershave along my beard without actually shaving. The instant the coffee was ready, Giada appeared as if summoned. I poured a mug for her, leaving ample room for milk and sugar.

"That's my sweatshirt," I said, my eyes wandering up her body. Her legs were bare, and the jersey cotton dipped just below her butt.

"You want it back?" she teased, lifting it just enough to show me her lower abdomen.

"It looks better on you."

"It smells like you," she said, snuggling against herself before accepting her coffee.

My phone chimed, this time from a text. It was Alessio, as had been the call. "Shit," I mumbled, right as a knock sounded at the door, mirroring the words of his text.

Giada raised an eyebrow, but made no attempt to move. "Alessio?"

I nodded. "How did you know?"

"Because I remember everything now. And he's always taking you from me."

I had to laugh at that assessment. I unlocked the door and motioned for him to come in.

His brows furrowed as he took in my appearance. I was naked aside from my sweatpants. "You just got up," he surmised.

"Give me five minutes to get dressed," I said. I was about to turn towards the bedroom when a feathery light touch skimmed my back.

"Don't go," Giada said, looping her arms around my waist.

Alessio crossed his arms, leaning back against the door.

I turned within her grasp, cupping her cheeks in my hand. "Amore, I have to meet with my guys. I won't be long, and I'll stay safe. I love you."

She thrust her bottom lip over the top one, her chocolatey brown eyes pleading with me. "Baby, don't go. I just got you back. I need…" her fingers stroked along my bare chest as she searched for the words. "I need more."

"More…?"

"You," she whispered.

Desperation filled her eyes, but not in a sexual way. I knew this woman better than I knew myself, and right now, she wanted to hold me for hours on end, not necessarily ravish me.

"Please," she repeated.

I struggled to remember how I used to say no to her.

"I'll handle it," Alessio said from across the room.

I turned to see him shaking his head, a slight hint of a smile on his lips.

"No, I can…" I began. I was the boss. I needed to explain to my men what had happened, to let them know where we stood and what would come next.

"Luca," he said, his tone sharper this time. "Stay."

I gazed back at Giada, half expecting her to thank him, but her eyes were still locked on me, and I wasn't even sure if she fully realized he was there.

"Grazie mille," I called to Alessio.

"Prego," he said. *You're welcome.* "I'll update you later."

I heard the click of the door shutting behind him, and I pulled my wife closer.

"Wait, you're really going to stay with me?" she asked, her eyes wide with surprise.

"You really don't remember?" I teased.

Her brows furrowed. "Remember what?"

"That I've never been able to say no to you?"

She grinned and did a mini happy dance.

"So, what do you want to do with me?" I asked.

Giada gazed at the ceiling, deep in thought. "Okay, well, first I need a shower. Then, I think you should do that thing with your tongue, just to make sure I'm remembering it correctly. And then…could we talk?"

I nodded in agreement with her plan. "That all sounds good, but what if we throw in breakfast before the shower?"

She gripped my hand and dragged me towards our bathroom. "No way. I need you hungry. I want to be the first thing you eat today."

~

Giada

By the time we got around to eating breakfast, it was already lunchtime. We sifted through the collection of baked pastas, casseroles, and miscellaneous cold salads that various relatives had dropped off upon hearing of my brief hospital stay.

"I hope they're feeding Angelo this well," I began, stopping myself abruptly and pressing my palm to my face. *What a stupid thing to say*, I realized. Angelo was in jail. He wasn't eating like a king.

Luca's warm body pressed against my back before I could

take another breath. He roped his arms around my waist and dropped his head to my shoulder. "Angelo will be home any minute now."

"Promise?"

He kissed the side of my neck and released me, whispering his promise in Italian. "Te lo prometto."

"Well, my aunts better have stocked his fridge with enough food to last all year," I said. "Otherwise I'll have to start cooking."

"Amore, no. Don't punish the man who just saved your life," Luca teased.

I swatted him, then selected a chopped green salad with little cubes of ham scattered throughout. Luca held up some pasta concoction that involved rotini, black olives, and tomatoes. I nodded eagerly, already feeling my mouth water.

We devoured the entire salad and most of the pasta, even though I suspected both dishes were meant to serve four. In our defense, we hadn't eaten much the previous day, and we'd apparently worked up quite the appetite with our overnight and early morning activities. We didn't talk much while we ate, both of us catching up on the plethora of emails, texts, and calls we'd received once news began to spread.

Nearly every relative had reached out, and I'd sent the same generic response thanking each of them for their concern. A couple coworkers had messaged me after I'd called to let them know I wouldn't be in for a couple days. And Melissa had texted to follow up after we left the hospital. But the only person I wanted to hear from was Angelo, and he was still unable to call.

The next best thing to talking to Angelo, I supposed, would be to talk with Adrian. As far as I knew, neither of my parents had even seen Angelo, nor had Matteo. But Melissa said Adrian had met with Angelo. Maybe he'd been to see him again. I gazed at Luca, debating asking his opinion before acting on my urge. His brows furrowed, and I assumed he was texting with Alessio or another guy about work. Emboldened, I decided a concise text wouldn't hurt anything.

I clicked on Adrian's name and typed, "how is he?" I hit send before I could rethink it.

A moment later, my phone rang.

Luca's eyes flitted up, and I tilted my phone towards him, showing the screen identifying the caller. Then I stood from the table as I answered, clutching the phone to my ear.

"Hi," I whispered upon answering.

"Hey," he replied.

"Melissa told me they let you visit Angelo," I explained.

"Yeah, my firm is representing him."

I waited for him to say more, but silence ensued. After a moment, I heard Adrian sigh.

"Look, you're a witness, so I'm not even sure I should be talking to you about it all, but—"

"I already gave the police my statement. There's nothing left to say. How soon can you get him out?"

"They're processing the paperwork soon. He should be home by dinner."

"Oh thank God," I said, relief flooding my limbs. "Is he…okay?"

Another silence followed.

"Adrian?" Suddenly, a terrible thought crossed my mind. "Did someone do something to him?"

Luca's gaze flitted to mine right as Adrian answered.

"No, nothing like that, Giada. He's been in his own cell any time he's not being questioned. No one has touched him. Physically, he's fine."

"So what aren't you saying?" I asked.

"Nothing. I don't know," Adrian replied. "I don't know the guy well enough to comment on his mental state. He doesn't even like me."

Angelo didn't like anyone, so that wasn't saying much. And

yeah, he and Adrian had more than their fair share of run-ins, but that had been ages ago, back when Adrian and I were still dating. Lately, they'd been friendly with each other. As far as I could tell, Adrian even did some work for my brother. Or maybe he worked for my dad. The line was blurry to me.

"He's been real, I don't know, stoic," Adrian finally said. "He isn't talking unless he has to, but that's smart."

"Has he said anything about…" I paused before saying her name, feeling guilty even though she tried to kill me. "Julia?" Her name felt like lead on my tongue.

"Yes, Giada. Almost all of the cops' questions are about her. He doesn't have a choice but to talk about her."

I winced, feeling stupid for asking now. "Right," I mumbled, trying to find a way to explain. "I just…well, I realize he's going to have to mourn her, and I don't want him to feel bad on my account if he's sad about her, because I understand it's all confusing. I mean, he has to be feeling so conflicted."

Adrian sighed again, louder this time. "It's not always about you, Giada."

Heat flushed to my cheeks at the insinuation. I stifled the urge to say nothing and instead retorted, "I know it's not always about me. But this time it absolutely is. I'm the reason Angelo did what he did, and—"

"Giada, I have to go. I'm glad you're alright, but I can't talk about this with you now. I'll send you a text when he's headed home, okay?"

"Yeah," I mumbled, right before a click signaled the end of the call.

I groaned and picked at my cuticles.

Luca

I turned to Giada as she let her phone drop to the counter, clearly dejected. I had no idea why she thought a conversation with her ex-boyfriend would help her feel better about anything, but I still hated seeing her sad.

I forked the last bite of rotini into my mouth and loaded our plates into the dishwasher before approaching Giada. She hadn't moved from the spot where she'd stood when Adrian, apparently, had hung up on her

Sensing my approach, she turned, shaking her head dismissively. "I'm fine. I…should just go lay down or something. Or maybe talk a walk. You should catch up with Alessio or something. I'm fine."

I bit back a snort. Two "fines" in under a minute. Yeah, she was just fantastic. I reached for her hand, then led her to the couch, tugging her beside me. I lifted her legs over my lap and ran my palm up and down her thigh. After a moment, Giada sighed and relaxed against me.

"You know this isn't your fault, right?"

Giada scowled. "Nope. I definitely do not know that, because it absolutely is. Look, I get how everyone apparently thinks I'm little miss self-centered and I make everything about me, but this is one hundred percent on me. Angelo killed Julia to save me."

"Right. Angelo did something. He chose to act."

"To save me."

"He could've let her shoot," Luca said. "She probably would've missed. Or I could've saved you, again. I've got a lot of experience at knocking you out of the way of bullets, you know?"

Giada laughed softly, betraying the next words out of her mouth. "That's not funny, Luca."

"Angelo also could've shot next to Julia, just scared her, you know? Or he could have hit her foot. Or hand. Your brother has many, many faults, but he's got decent aim. Aside from Enzo, I'd say he's the best in your family."

Giada shrugged.

"My point is that he could've stopped Julia and made sure you weren't hurt without handling things the way he did. Angelo chose to shoot that gun, not you."

"He had seconds to think. He just reacted."

I shook my head. "No. Because guys like Angelo and me—we think best under pressure. That may have felt like seconds to you but a whole slew of possibilities ran through his head in that moment."

Giada leaned against my chest, signaling she was done arguing with my efforts to comfort her, but I still didn't stop. She needed to hear the rest. She deserved to know the full truth.

"Did you think about what would've happened if Angelo hadn't killed her?"

Giada didn't answer. I assumed on some level that she had thought about it, but I couldn't be sure. And I wanted her to understand the full scope of what her brother had done for her.

"Come on Giada, think about it. Let's say he just scared her so she couldn't shoot. Or maybe he ran and tackled her. What would've happened next?"

"I don't know."

"I think you do," I countered. When she still didn't speak, I gripped her hips and pulled her onto my lap, forcing her to stare into my eyes. "If Angelo hadn't killed her, I would have. And I'm not sure I could've made it so quick and painless for her."

Sadness filled my wife's eyes, but she didn't look surprised at my words.

"Julia hired the men who tried to kill you the night of your accident. For that alone, she had to die. And if Angelo hadn't done it, any other man in your family would have, unless someone from mine got there first. No one tries to hurt Giada Conti Marino and lives to talk about it. Do you understand that?"

Giada nodded.

"Julia chose her destiny. She fucked up, and she paid the price.

She is the only one responsible for the outcome here, and I don't want to hear you blaming yourself or anyone else for this crappy situation."

Giada gazed at me a moment longer, then leaned forward, resting her head on my shoulder. I held her for a minute, nearly laughing at the realization that this was probably the only time she'd been on my lap that neither of us had attempted to initiate sex. Clearly, we'd worn ourselves out.

We were both quiet for several minutes, and then I nudged her upright. "Come on. We need fresh air. Let's take a walk."

Giada made no effort to move for several minutes, then slowly clamored off my lap. Nearly a half hour passed before we were both actually ready to leave, but by that point Giada seemed more cheerful.

CHAPTER 3

Adrian

The Conti family insisted I stay the night after successfully busting their son out of jail. They acted like I'd accomplished some sort of herculean feat, but in reality, securing Angelo's release had taken much longer than it should have. I didn't blame myself or my lack of experience for the delay though. Rather, I figured it was due to Angelo's well-known role in the mafia world.

Sure, the authorities couldn't substantiate any of the allegations against him, but they heard the same rumors the rest of us did. Anytime the cops managed to get their hands on a Conti, they'd hold him as long as possible.

The cops had commented on the convenience of everything taking place in front of the clearly visible cameras, but they couldn't connect the dots enough to pin anything concrete on Angelo. He had made sure of that. So ultimately, they had to let him go.

Eddie had driven us home, and Enzo met us once we passed

the gate to the Conti manner. He greeted Angelo, who'd been uncharacteristically quiet the entire drive, then turned to me.

"Marco is insisting you stay overnight. I can drive you to your place if you need to grab anything, but your room is stocked as usual."

I grimaced at the implication that I had a room at the Conti manor. Sure, I tended to occupy the same guest room every time I stayed there, but it wasn't *my* room. Other guests stayed in that room sometimes, too. Still, I knew the bathroom was stocked with every toiletry, and I kept a spare set of clothes in my car anyway.

"I have my own car here," I said, remembering as I pictured the bag in my trunk that I had, in fact, parked it at their house earlier in the day before heading to the police station with Eddie.

Enzo nodded in acknowledgment, but said, "Marco wanted me to drive you."

"Yeah, I mean, I have clothes in my trunk. And my sister can watch the dog."

"Cool. Well, just a heads up, you're kind of the man of the hour."

"I am?" I didn't have to feign surprise. Any celebration tonight should be focused on Angelo, the man who saved the beloved family princess.

Lorenzo quirked a brow. "It's not every day that a Conti walks out of jail a free man after taking a life. You're going to be a popular lawyer for a while."

I opened and shut my mouth several times without managing to formulate an intelligible response. I hated the implication that my skill was somehow responsible for getting Angelo off when he didn't deserve it. I didn't like anyone, especially the Contis, feeling like they could manipulate the law like that. The fact was that legally, Angelo hadn't committed a punishable crime. Yeah, he'd intentionally shot Julia, but he'd done so to save his sister.

And the irrefutable video evidence—as well as firsthand witness testimony—supported that fact and showed that he didn't have other options.

Legally speaking, Angelo's actions were excusable. There was nothing to prosecute relating to Julia's death. The whole incident was just another of many tragedies.

I appreciated the heads-up from Enzo, because the second I walked inside, I was mobbed. Leo and Stefano, some of Angelo's uncles, flanked me on either side, lifting me off the ground as they cheered in Italian. Marco rushed to me, thrusting a drink into my hands, then quieted the mob long enough to offer a toast.

I tuned out the words as the head of the Conti family spoke, instead focusing on the jovial faces around me. In the immediate vicinity, I saw only men, but just past them were their wives. Noticeably missing was Giada, but her absence could just as easily be explained by her marriage to the heir of the Marino family as it could be due to her connection to the events landing Angelo in jail in the first place.

Exhaustion riddled me. I hadn't slept well the night before, as I was stressing about how to get Angelo out of jail and what might occur if I didn't succeed in that mission. I'd powered through the day with the help of caffeine and sugar, but now those crutches were wearing off.

Still, an energized buzz filled the room, and by the time Marco finished his toast, the other men in his family were cheering my name. They raised their glasses in the air, chanting "Ad—ri—an" over and over like I'd just won the soccer match for the team. The excitement was contagious and my fatigue melted away by the time I downed my first drink.

As the men crowded around me and offered their congratulations, it hit me.

I was officially a mafia lawyer. There was no denying it now.

Glancing around, I realized Angelo was nowhere to be seen. That struck me as odd, but I didn't question it. He was probably showering. Or napping. Leo refilled my drink, then asked me what my "trick" was to getting the charges dropped against Angelo.

"Well, technically they never filed any charges," I explained. "They were considering it, but—"

"Ahh so modest," Marco's brother Vincenzo said.

The other men nodded in agreement.

"He didn't do anything wrong," I continued. I meant that Angelo was innocent in the eyes of the law, and wasn't necessarily making a statement about the morality of his actions, but Marco's men didn't seem to care about the distinction.

"Right?" Leo said, thrusting his hand into the air. "That girl had it coming. Bringing the feds into our business. What was she thinking?"

"And going after la principessa? Inexcusable," Giovanni agreed.

"Unforgiveable," Stefano clarified.

I plastered a smile on my face but shuddered inside. I'd tried not to think of Julia the past several hours. I tried not to think of the series of events leading to her death, and I really tried not to think about the pictures the cops had shared of the crime scene.

The aftermath of it all was gory, to put it mildly. By the time the forensic crime scene specialists photographed the body, Julia was unrecognizable. She no longer looked like a woman, and she barely even resembled a human. The gunshots had taken out the majority of her face and part of her torso. The parts of her that weren't immediately impacted by the bullet or its ricochet suffered from the pooling of blood internally, or the mess of dried blood coating her skin. Her previously lush hair now bore clumps of caked on-blood, interspersed with bits of foliage.

My stomach churned violently, and I turned away.

"Restroom," I mumbled to Leo, patting him on the back to excuse myself.

Once alone, I splashed cool water on my face and stared into the mirror.

I had done nothing wrong.

I followed both the letter of the law and its spirit.

My representation of Angelo Conti violated no ethical laws for an attorney, nor any greater principles of morality.

Yet, I still felt like shit.

And I knew exactly why.

In another version of the story, I was Julia.

Years ago, I'd been the innocent outsider, unlucky enough to fall for a Conti. The Conti family had pulled me into their web, just like they did with Julia. And just like Julia, I'd started to notice things. It hadn't taken long at all for me to realize who the Contis were, and what they were capable of.

I'd even shared my concerns with Giada. I'd encouraged her to trust me, to abandon her family for me. Even now, I couldn't believe my own gall. Had I actually expected her to forsake the Conti empire and run off with me? Maybe. Had I truly thought through it all—and realized what would have become of me had Giada actually gone along with my plan?

Absolutely not.

In no alternate reality would Marco Conti have let me steal away his precious daughter. Luca could get away with that crap. Me? No way.

And if they'd learned I'd talked to the feds? I wouldn't have just been shot in a park.

I had no doubt the very men who now praised me and offered me gifts wouldn't have hesitated a moment before breaking each of the bones in my hand, one at a time, crushing my kneecaps, and yanking out my toenails before finally leaving me to bleed to death.

A knock on the door startled me from my pity party.

"Dinner's served," called a familiar voice.

I opened the door and saw Matteo, Angelo's younger brother.

He smiled warmly but seemed to show a reasonable amount of joy, unlike the other men in his house.

"You okay?" he asked.

"I..." I gazed around and determined there wasn't enough time for a truthful response. "I'll be fine," I said, ignoring the way my stomach roiled at the mere mention of food.

Matteo chuckled, then led the way to the patio.

The dinner was pleasant enough, thanks to Valentina Conti insisting on no "shop talk" at the table. The food was amazing, as always. And Angelo had joined us for the meal, sitting at the head of the table beside his father.

A selection of desserts appeared right as we finished the main course, and the conversation turned to dating. The aunts never grew tired of teasing Matteo about his perpetual singleness, but this time, he was spared by the most unexpected comment.

"You don't need to worry about Matteo, Tina," Leo started, his mouth still full of cheesecake. "But we all know you about had your boy Angelo here married off and now he's back to square one."

Everyone chortled as though that hadn't been the least sensitive and most inappropriate comment imaginable. I caught Enzo's eye and noticed him cringing, but even Marco chuckled at the comment.

Luckily, the ladies began clearing the table a moment later, and I hopped up to help like I always did.

The women of the family seemed happy to be together, but less jovial about the occasion than the men. I wondered if they, too, felt the precariousness of the positions they occupied in this dark world.

It was late by the time the meal ended and the dishes were done, so I figured I was safe to sneak up to my room for the night. I charged my phone while I showered, relishing the feel of the hot water scalding my skin. I pretended I could physically scrub away my sins, but I soon grew self-conscious at the prospect of anyone in the house noticing I was showering too long.

I lounged on the bed and caught up on emails after my shower, then tried Melissa. She was working nights this week, so I didn't expect to reach her, but after hearing her brief voicemail greeting, I felt even lonelier than before. I was too restless to sleep and decided the fresh night air might soothe my nerves.

I tugged on a pair of shorts, then headed outside, grateful that the first floor of the house and patio area were quiet and dark. I treaded slowly over the patio, not wanting to trip but equally uninterested in drawing attention to my presence. It was too dark to walk around the property, and I didn't want to leave and come back and risk being shot on sight as an intruder. So instead, I made my way to a poolside lounge chair.

I selected the furthest one from the house, and was about to sit down, when a voice pierced the darkness.

"Can't sleep?" he asked.

I jumped two feet in the air, tripped over the lounger, and nearly fell backwards into the pool.

By the time I'd steadied myself and my breathing, my eyes had adjusted to the dark. I turned to see Lorenzo stretched out a couple of chairs down.

"Jesus Christ, Enzo. You scared the shit out of me. I didn't see you there."

"Clearly," he replied dryly. "Too much caffeine today maybe?"

I contemplated returning to my room since I apparently wasn't going to be alone out here. But, I never truly felt alone inside the Conti home anyway, and besides, Enzo was right. I'd had too much caffeine to sleep.

"Whisky?" he offered, lifting a bottle from the ground beside him.

I debated the invitation, then sat in the chair beside him. I raised the bottle to my lips and downed a healthy swig.

"How's Angelo doing?" I asked, genuinely curious.

"About like you'd expect."

I coughed to cover up my laugh. "Honestly, this whole scenario is so far out of my usual experience that I have no idea what to expect. I can't tell if he's enjoying being the hero or mourning his old girlfriend."

Enzo gazed at me, almost as if he couldn't tell if I was being serious. "No one is celebrating *him* as the hero."

"He saved the princess."

"Sure, and we're all really grateful for that, obviously. But he could've brought the Julia situation to our attention sooner and kept his sister out of it entirely."

I sighed and settled back into the chair. Enzo was right, of course, but I could never admit that out loud. Angelo's entire defense rested on him needing to act in the moment and not having advanced notice. I also remembered the way everyone in the Conti world went to extreme lengths to protect Giada, even though she'd shown us all time and time again that she didn't need the bodyguards.

"Has he said anything about Julia?" I asked instead.

"You mean about how she betrayed him and made him look like a complete patsy in front of the whole family?"

I downed another gulp of the whiskey. "No, I meant about how she was the love of his life and now she's gone."

Lorenzo swiped the whiskey from me and raised the bottle to his lips before answering. "She was not the love of his life. I'm not sure he ever loved her."

"Then why was he with her for so long?"

Enzo snorted. "Did Angelo never show you the nudes he had of her?"

"Eww," I said, repulsed more by the notion of a man showing others his naked girlfriend than the idea of Julia, in particular.

"Well, you might understand more if you saw. Angelo said the only thing hotter than the curve of her hips was her tight little..." Enzo paused, chuckling again. "Well, you get the idea."

I had no response for that.

"If he liked her more, he probably would've noticed sooner when she was acting strangely. Although, from what Giada says, it seems like Julia was more concerned about the Marino family business than ours."

"Really?" I turned abruptly to face him.

"Yeah. She was terrified of Luca, I guess." He paused, "Although, after what she did to Giada, she had reason to be scared."

I relaxed back against my chair. I knew exactly what Enzo meant. I didn't even want to imagine the shit Luca would've done to Julia if he'd known she hurt Giada.

Neither of us spoke for several minutes.

"Do you ever worry about what happens to people like us?" I asked finally.

"What do you mean?"

"Those of us who get close to the family but don't have that blood relation," I explained. "People like you and me. People like Julia."

Enzo cleared his throat. "If you think you're like Julia, you've got bigger problems than me."

"No, I mean, I'm not talking to the cops. I wouldn't do that. But I just worry that one innocent fuckup might be enough to put me six feet under."

Enzo gazed at me, "Then don't fuck up, amico."

Friend, I silently translated, wondering more about whether that was, in fact, our relationship, and less about when I'd started to pick up so many random Italian words.

"Marco is like a father to me," Enzo began. "And Giada is my… well, she's the principessa. She'll always be my princess. I don't agree with everything they do, but they're my people. If I have a problem with the family, I'm taking it to Marco, not someone else. And I trust him to resolve it appropriately."

I considered that, and supposed Enzo was right. He was safe.

He really was a part of the family. If not by birth, at least by blood oath. But I was still an outsider.

"I'm not family. I'm not a made man. I'm not even Italian. I feel like I'll always be on the outside."

Enzo took his time answering. "I think you're right where you belong, Patras. And don't sell yourself short. You understand a lot more about loyalty than you give yourself credit for. Marco rewards his friends very generously."

I nodded, even though he probably couldn't see me.

"I haven't heard yet what he's giving you for saving Angelo's ass. I bet it'll be good though."

I sighed again, the conflict I always felt over Marco's extravagant gifts bubbling to the surface. I understood firsthand what money could do for someone. My parents were both hard-working and gainfully employed. But when cancer had wiped out their savings, along with my mom's ability to work, Marco's sudden infusion of cash had been a lifesaver. Literally.

I'd had zero qualms about accepting a gift from Marco after doing him a little favor when it paid off my mom's medical bills. The other gifts from Marco had been small, well, aside from the car. But at the time, the car felt more like a gift to me as the man he thought would end up with his daughter and less like a bribe or hush money. Now I knew better, but now I also felt like I'd damn well earned that car after all the shit Giada had put me through.

And this? Well, I'd done an honest day's work. If Marco wanted to pay me more than my typical hourly rate, well, that was on him. If I was stuck with the pressures of this lifestyle, I might as well reap the benefits.

"Any idea why Marco wanted me to stay here tonight?" I asked.

"Yeah. You're family. Nothing makes Marco happier than being surrounded by the people he loves." He paused. "Same reason I get upgraded digs every time I talk about moving to my own place." He gestured across the pool, where the extravagant pool house beckoned to us. "I should probably get some sleep anyway. You good?"

I nodded. For once, I supposed I was.

~

Giada

The rest of the day was an exhausting blur. It had been Enzo, and not Adrian, who called to let me know Angelo had been released from custody. No charges had been filed, but they'd asked Angelo to agree not to leave town until the investigation had been closed in case they had any questions. The plan was for him to stay with my parents for a while.

By nighttime, I was exhausted, but couldn't imagine sleeping. I felt like I'd run the entire gambit of emotions since the day of the hike, and yet I'd hardly processed anything. At the moment, I was focusing on the amnesia and all of the things I'd forgotten since the accident. Most of the memories had fallen neatly into place over the past few hours, but other things still perplexed me.

Specifically, I recalled a conversation with Alessio at a diner. He'd told me some things about Luca's dad that had shocked me at the time, and now that my memory was back to normal, well, I was still shocked.

"Luca?" I didn't turn to face him, positive he was still awake even though his breathing was calm and steady. He lay behind me in our dark bedroom, one arm draped over my waist.

"Hmm?"

"Did your father ever hit you?"

"What?" he shifted behind me.

I rolled onto my back to meet his gaze. "It's just something Alessio mentioned when I had amnesia. I think he was trying to make me feel sorry for you."

Luca grimaced. "By saying my papà beat me?"

I tried to recall Alessio's exact words. "No, I think he said your dad made other people do it."

Luca held my stare for a moment, then flopped onto his back beside me.

I waited a moment, but when it was clear he didn't plan to reply, I pressed further. "So it's not true?"

"Yes."

I exhaled, relieved to know Salvatore Marino was slightly less of a monster than I'd imagined a few moments before. But then Luca clarified.

"It's true."

I swallowed the lump in my throat, scared to look at him and see the pain etched on his beautiful face. Fortunately, the room was bathed in darkness, and I could barely make out the shape of Luca's face, let alone the signs of any emotional scars.

"Well, he didn't exactly do it himself. He made his guys do it though."

I gasped, then tried to decide if that was any better. Ultimately, I reasoned Salvatore's way was actually a bit worse. Not that child abuse has a scale of awfulness, but maybe at least if he'd done it in a fit of anger, I could brush it off as a temperament thing. Something he couldn't control.

But ordering someone else to hurt his child? That was cold and calculating. Even less excusable.

"Who?" I finally asked.

Luca breathed a laugh. "Nothing good can come of me telling you that."

I sat upright. "You mean they're still alive?"

"Still alive and working for Papà."

"I've met these men?" I shuddered at the realization that they weren't even men. They were monsters.

"Yes. And they didn't have a choice. If they didn't do what the boss said, he would've punished them."

"So? They could've at least shown some integrity."

Luca's silence told me he agreed. After a beat, he spoke. "One time, my papà brought some guy into the office. An employee of the club, I think. He'd caught the guy stealing or something and wanted me to beat him."

Luca paused. My stomach churned.

"They gave me a baseball bat. When I refused to beat the guy, they hit me instead. And then I'm sure someone else beat him anyway. It didn't feel much like integrity."

A memory came back to me as he spoke. "Alessio said there was one time when I got mad at you. I accused you of getting in fights and lying about it. But you hadn't been in a fight. Your dad had some guys attack you."

"Yeah," Luca said. "I remember. It…sucked, but you were just reacting to what I told you. You didn't have any reason to trust me."

"You told me you weren't fighting. I should've believed you."

"I was covered in bruises. And sometimes, I did fight back."

"That's not the same."

We were both quiet for longer this time. I started to think he'd fallen asleep.

"I didn't want to burden you with the details at the time. And then he stopped, so it didn't matter."

"What made him stop? Was he afraid you'd fight back? That you'd come after him?"

Luca chuckled. "You think my papà could ever be afraid of me?"

"Yes."

"Hardly. It was Alessio. Alessio made him stop."

"How?"

"He talked to him. Told him he'd be a team player but that no one could touch me again."

"Wow. And your dad stopped, just like that?"

Luca snorted at that. "No, he beat the shit out of Alessio.

Broke bones and bruised his whole body. They dumped him by my car, half dead. I took him to the hospital and eventually, he healed. And after that, nobody messed with either of us."

"But you never told me any of that," I said, certain it was true.

"Why would I?"

"Because you trusted me. Because I loved you. When it was over, you could've told me. I could have supported you."

Luca took his time answering. "I didn't want you to think I was broken."

"I could never think that. You aren't broken, Luca. You're perfect."

He breathed a laugh. "Alessio always used to say that. The part about me not being broken, I mean, not that I'm perfect. Whenever I'd get stuck in my own head, which happened a lot, he'd pat me on the back and say No sei roto Luca. No sei roto."

"He's a good friend to you," I said. I hadn't always understood how Luca could tolerate someone like Alessio, let alone trust him the way he did. But the more I knew about their pasts, the more it made sense.

"He's a good man," Luca said, "and he gets me because he's like me."

At first, I thought Luca meant that he and Alessio had similar personality types. That was true enough, with both of them being detail-oriented control freaks who were surprisingly laid back about life-or-death situations. But then I read more into his words. "Do you mean Alessio's dad was abusive too?"

I half expected Luca to tell me that wasn't his secret to share, but instead, he whispered a pained "yeah."

"His mom was smart, kicked her man to the curb early on though."

I thought about that, tried to picture the myriad of feelings Luca must have for his own mom, the one who had to have known what his father did to him but never even threatened to leave. The one who never protected her son. But then again, what could she have done?

"I'm sorry you both went through that," I finally said. "But I'm glad

that you have each other."

"Me too. And now we have you," he said.

CHAPTER 4

Luca

Giada was still sound asleep when I left the next morning. I hated leaving her when I wasn't even sure where she stood emotionally this morning, but I'd missed too much work already. I'd check in on her often, and I could return to her if needed.

Alessio and I spent a couple of hours collecting payments, and then he dropped me off at the club to tackle some administrative work. I'd managed to focus without interruptions for nearly two hours when a hesitant knock tore my attention away from the papers in front of me.

I sighed, certain my concentration was ruined, "Si?"

"You have a visitor."

I recognized the voice as Lincoln's. He had proven to be fairly reliable, so far, but he was still the new guy and clearly, hadn't yet figured it all out.

"Giovanni is up front, right? He can deal with it."

Lincoln was silent for long enough that I started to hope he'd taken off.

"No, it's uh, personal," Lincoln said, his voice still uncertain.

Before I could respond, I heard another familiar voice.

"Jesus Christ, I don't have all day," Angelo Conti boomed before letting himself into my office.

I stood to greet him, unable to resist a snarky comment even given my gratitude over recent events. "Hi Angelo, come on it. Make yourself at home."

He rolled his eyes and plopped into the chair facing my desk. Behind him, Lincoln stood, wide-eyed and uncertain.

"Thanks, Linc. Shut the door behind you," I said.

"My father would like you and Giada to come over for dinner tonight if you're free."

I considered my schedule, then nodded. "I'll check with Giada, but that should work."

Angelo snorted at the notion that his sister might be able to veto the plans. But then, his demeanor changed. He dropped his gaze to his lap and began fidgeting with the band of his watch.

"He also thought I should come talk to you." He paused. "To, um, apologize."

"Apologize," I repeated.

Angelo shrugged. "For not, you know, mentioning my concerns about Julia to you earlier. I, um, well, I tracked her location and calls and everything, so I'm positive Giada wasn't at risk once I had any idea about what was going on, but my dad thought I should've told you the moment I had suspicions since it involved your wife."

"And your sister," I added.

Angelo shrugged.

"So why didn't you?"

He sighed, leaning back in the chair and crossing his legs at the ankles. He took his time answering. "Julia screwed up, big time," he finally began. "I get that. But I also… well it's my fault she got involved in all of this in the first place. And we were together for a while. So I didn't want to report anything to you and risk you going off half-cocked and—"

"I assure you I don't do anything half-cocked," I interrupted.

Angelo met my gaze head on, "You absolutely do, when it's anything to do with my sister. You'd burn the fucking world if you thought it would save her."

I shrugged, not disagreeing with his last assessment. "So?"

"So I thought you could understand that I didn't want Julia caught up in your emotional damage. And that's why I waited and took care of it when I did."

I swallowed back my annoyance, ready to reply, but he continued.

"Giada wasn't in danger. I never would've let anything happen to her. I hope you know that."

For once, Angelo sounded sincere. And I realized that, before he'd come here, I'd felt nothing but gratitude for Angelo anyway. I paused to collect myself, then nodded.

"I don't envy what you had to do, or the choice you made. I don't hold you responsible for what Julia did, and when push came to shove, you took care of it. You kept my Giada safe." I paused, then corrected myself. "Our Giada. I can't thank you enough for that."

Angelo gazed at me as if trying to gauge whether I was serious.

Finally, he spoke. "So we're good?"

I nodded. "We're good."

"Even?"

I wrinkled my nose. "I'm not sure I'd go that far, but let's just say you're certainly not on my shit list at the moment."

Angelo chuckled. "I guess I can live with that." He took a few deep breaths, then rose to his feet. "So, dinner's at seven, but come over before so everyone can gush over whatever dumb outfit Giada is wearing or whatever they do."

I nodded, and he started to the door.

"Angelo," I called, right as he gripped the knob. "I'm sorry for your loss. I wish there'd been another way."

He kept his gaze trained on the door, but his head bobbed up and down in agreement. "Yeah," he murmured. "Me too."

My concentration already shot, I waited until Angelo had shut the door firmly behind him, then dialed Giada. She sounded breathless when she answered.

"Hi. What are you doing?" I asked.

"Packing. My mom called and said you told Angelo we'd come stay at the house for a couple nights."

I blew out a sigh, training my eyes on the ceiling as if cursing the skies. "Dinner. I agreed we'd go to your parents' house for dinner, not overnight, and certainly not multiple nights. And that was literally ten seconds ago."

"Well, I don't know. My mom seemed excited to see us. Anyway, I know you're busy so I'm packing your stuff, too. Honestly, staying there will save you time because you won't have to worry about cooking or anything."

I nearly spit out the water I'd just sipped. "Yeah, because I spend so much time cooking our meals." To be fair, I cooked nearly as much as Giada, but we were both much more skilled at ordering food than making it ourselves.

"I guess I could call her back and tell her 'nevermind,'" Giada said. "I'm sure my dad can cope without his only daughter…"

I rolled my eyes. "Baby, it's fine. We'll go. Two nights max though, okay?"

She agreed, and we said our goodbyes.

∼

Giada

*B*eing back home was both chaotic and rejuvenating, as usual. The whole big family was there the first night, and the noise and busyness of it all kept my mind off of all of the darker aspects of my recent reality. Adrian joined us for dinner, which seemed weird, but then he left after the meal.

Each of my aunts managed to comment at least once about their disappointment that I wasn't yet pregnant, and I overheard a few of my uncles taunting Luca about it, as well. The teasing was mostly good natured, although now that I was the only Conti child in any sort of a stable relationship, I supposed I did have more pressure to produce a grandchild at some point in the not-so-distant future.

After dinner, all of us younger generation—my cousins, brothers, and Angelo's guys mostly, all headed out to the pool area. The bar was fully stocked, and Matteo and Giacomo were playing bartender. A few of my cousins had changed into their bikinis and were enjoying the hot tub, but I wasn't in the mood to be half-naked in front of family at the moment. I grabbed a drink for Luca and another for myself, then curled up against him on one of the lounge chairs.

Luca was quiet while I chatted with my cousin Mia and her husband about their recent trip to Sicily, but the soothing way he stroked his finger up and down my bicep while I talked made me smile. When I finished the last sip of my drink, Luca climbed out from behind me and stood. He made me a vodka cranberry with a hint of lime, then caught my eye as he approached with my fresh drink.

"I need to check in with Alessio," he said. "Are you okay here?"

I nodded to Luca. "Are you heading inside?"

"I'll probably just go to the front porch."

"Okay." I grinned as Luca leaned down to kiss me on the lips before walking off. A few of the drunker guys whistled at the brief show of affection, to which Luca responded with a bold middle finger raised above his head as he made his way towards the front of the house.

Angelo's best friend, Rico, was telling some story about the cat he brought to try to kill the mouse that was in his mom's apartment, so I scooted my chair closer, eager to have an amusing distraction from reality. The guys all took turns teasing Rico, then someone suggested he just shoot the mouse the next time he sees it. Then of course the guys joked about how that would lead to Rico accidentally shooting himself or, worse yet, his mom.

"Oh man, speaking of getting shot, my old pal Sebastian said that his buddy got shot in some drive-by gone wrong but they couldn't take him to the doctor because he has a record. So the wound like festered, and by the time they decided he had to go to the doctor, it was so bad they had to amputate."

The guys all expressed varying levels of disbelief and disgust at the story, and then Mia asked why they couldn't just go to the doctor. I suppressed an eye roll. Even I knew that. Doctors had to report gunshot wounds. Well, unless they didn't.

"I have a friend who's a doc, and she can handle all that stuff under the table," I said without thinking. I turned to see if Adrian was still there, ready to point out he was dating her but decided that was unnecessary info in his absence.

"How did you discover this little talent of hers?" Rico pressed.

"She's taken care of Luca a few times," I admitted.

"Ahh, so she's Luca's friend," Eddie said in a tone that implied something inappropriate was going on.

I shot him a threatening look, then startled as a shadow loomed over me. I turned to see Angelo standing behind me.

The guys instantly switched topics and lowered their voices.

"Angelo!" I called, realizing my brother had started to walk off the moment I'd spotted him. He stopped walking, but I had to stand from the chair to go to him.

"Are you doing okay?" I asked.

His expression gave nothing away as he nodded.

I kept staring at him, silently pressing him for more details. Luckily, my plan worked.

"This hasn't been my favorite week of the year, but I'll be fine. Shit happens, and we move on."

Ouch. That seemed like an oversimplification if there ever was one.

"Okay, well, I wanted to tell you in person that I'm sorry about how everything went down. And to thank you for, you know, saving my life. And Luca's."

Angelo nodded.

"If there's anything I could do for you..." I began, then stopped. What exactly could I do? I wasn't about to shoot someone for him.

Angelo dipped his head in acknowledgment of my words. "Thanks," was all he said before heading back into the house.

I sighed, then made my way to the bar for some water. I stayed outside for another hour or so, then trekked around to the front of the house to look for Luca. He wasn't there, so I headed inside to check out our room.

I stepped into the room right as Luca emerged from the shower, a crisp white towel secured below his waist. Droplets of moisture coated his chest and a trail of dark hair led down beneath the edge of the towel. A heaviness settled deep in my core as I drank in the sight of him.

The soft smile on his lips told me Luca's thoughts were nothing like mine. A pang of regret hit me at the missed opportunity of joining him in the shower, but I reassured myself that it didn't matter. My favorite part of marriage was that I could have Luca whenever I wanted. He was mine.

I stalked towards him and rose to my toes, kissing him softly at first, then with more determination. I hooked my fingers beneath the towel, ready to pry it loose, when Luca gripped my hand and stepped backwards.

"Hey!" he scolded. "What are you doing?"

I giggled. "I thought that was obvious, but if you want me to go first…" I lifted my sundress up and over my head, then reached behind my back and unclasped my bra.

Luca's eyes widened as my breasts tumbled free. His towel tented around his groin.

I beamed with pride.

"We are in your parents' house. Your brothers are right down the hall," he protested, his gaze still locked on my breasts.

"That never stopped you in the past," I reminded him.

"It did too, and besides, we were younger then. We are adults now. There are expectations." He squeezed his eyes shut. "I'm not touching you."

"Fine." I walked to the bed, pleased that the comforter had already been lowered in preparation for bedtime. I sprawled out in the middle of the bed, then ran my own hand across my breasts. My nipples had pebbled, whether from arousal or the cool air, I couldn't tell. Luca sucked in a sharp breath as I squeezed one breast before tracing my finger around the nipple.

"If you won't touch me, I'll just touch myself," I taunted. I flattened my palm to my belly and slid it lower, dipping inside my panties. I stroked along my slit, offering a soft moan for the sake of the performance.

Luca growled in response. "You play dirty," he said.

"Mmm hmm," I replied, closing my eyes for dramatic effect while keeping one hand on my breast and another inside my panties.

"I could just watch you, let you finish yourself," he threatened.

"True, but that doesn't usually satiate me quite the same, so I'd probably still come for more in a couple hours." It was a stupid bluff and we both knew it, but Luca launched himself over me without another word. The towel landed on the floor beside the bed, and Luca's tongue replaced the hand on my breast while his fingers worked my panties off my legs.

"Fuck, you actually made yourself wet," he cried.

I suppressed a laugh. "Looking at you made me wet, Luca," I admitted. "But I'm not entirely useless. I do know what I like."

Luca straddled me and gripped the wrist of the fingers I'd touched myself with. He sucked my pointer finger, cleaning all of my own juices from my skin. "No, you need me."

"Do I?" I teased.

He bent down again, nipping at my breasts, then alternating sharp, quick bites from his teeth with slow, languishing laps from his tongue. I moaned loudly, already forgetting where we were until his hand pressed firmly over my mouth. He kept indulging my breasts with attention and the tension in my belly ratcheted up. Luca could make me come like this, and he knew it.

My breaths were fast and ragged, and I bit at the hand covering my mouth until Luca yanked it away. I gulped for air, but right then he sucked harder on my right breast and I cried out with the pleasure.

Luca sat upright, leaving me panting and desperate for more. "You can't do that on your own, can you?" he asked.

I scowled, but pulled him closer. He kissed me hard, and our tongues thrashed together as if wrestling. Luca nudged my legs apart, then found my entrance. I wrapped my legs around his hips right as he thrust into me, filling me to the hilt.

"Oh my God!" I cried.

Luca's mouth clamped down tighter over mine as he withdrew his cock, only to pound into me, harder this time. The pleasure built quickly now, too quickly, given how high it already was from his expert treatment of my breasts. I felt myself reach the peak, certain I couldn't survive the exquisitely intense pleasure much longer.

Just as my orgasm ripped through me, Luca tugged a pillow over both of our heads, cocooning our mouths beneath its protection as I screamed his name. Luca thrust a few more times, then pulled out of me, rising to his knees, and coming all over my chest.

His eyes shut as his head fell backwards for a moment. Then he gazed down at me, smiling. "If you weren't so loud, we could do this more often here."

"Hmm. Well, seems like you enjoyed yourself," I said, dipping my finger into the sticky mess he'd made of my torso.

Luca groaned. "I didn't want to risk it getting all over the bed." He climbed off of me, grabbed a handful of tissues, and returned to wipe me clean. Then, he flushed the tissues and retrieved a damp washcloth, gently cleaning me more thoroughly.

"We're married, Luca. My parents must realize we have sex."

"Not necessarily," he replied. "If your dad knew I've touched you like that, he'd probably have killed me."

I laughed, then thought more of it. "Okay, well, someday, when you get me pregnant, even my dad will have to realize what that means."

Luca's eyes flared at the mention of me pregnant. Even though Luca claimed he wasn't ready for that, I still knew the idea of his baby growing inside me triggered Luca's possessive side like nothing else.

"Okay, but even then he doesn't need to know how much you like it when I touch you."

"Fine," I conceded. "Try it again and I'll be quieter this time. Promise. Practice makes perfect."

Luca chuckled and curled up beside me, rolling me until my back nestled against his chest. I relaxed against him for a moment, then spoke again.

"So…about that whole baby thing," I said, my voice quiet. "Now that life is calm, do you think we're ready?"

"Calm?" Luca's voice was a roar. "You almost died last week. Again. Your brother just got out of jail. Oh yeah, and you have remembered marrying me for only a matter of days. What part of that is calm?"

I sighed. Certainly not his tone, I thought. "Our lives are never going to be boring, so if that's what you're waiting for, we'll be waiting forever."

"I know," he said. "But I feel like I just got you back, and I'm not ready to share you yet."

I rolled to face him, kissed him softly, then crawled out of bed to brush my teeth and find my pjs.

CHAPTER 5

Luca

I woke early at the Conti's the next morning, unaccustomed to the din of a full house. I helped myself to some coffee then left to meet Alessio for breakfast before work. When I returned to the house, the crowd seemed slightly calmer than the previous day, but as I made my way toward the back to find Giada, I realized the group may have just shifted outdoors.

For an early fall day, the temperature was idyllic. The sun shone brightly above a cloudless blue sky, and I supposed, directly under the sunlight, that it could be a perfect pool day. My wife apparently thought as much, as she lounged on one of the poolside chairs, her black and gold bikini coordinating perfectly with her sunglasses and showcasing every one of her gorgeous curves.

Her sunglasses blocked my view of her eyes, and I couldn't tell if she was simply listening to music on her earbuds or actually sleeping. Her brother Matteo occupied the chair next to her, and her cousin Mia lay beside her on her stomach, clearly unconscious. Matteo glanced up from his reading as I approached and offered a half wave.

I smiled at Matteo, then leaned close to Giada. She didn't move or acknowledge me, so her eyes had to be closed. Feeling mischievous, I reached in the pool, then splashed my wife. The second the frigid droplets of water hit her warm skin, she shrieked and sat upright. She saw me, and her jaw dropped in shock.

"Oops," I said, grinning.

"That was mean," she said, dropping her earbuds on the lounge chair and rising to her feet.

"No. Mean would've been pushing you in," I replied, lifting my wife and quickly tossing her into the pool before she could dodge.

"Uh oh," Matteo trilled, clearly expecting his sister to murder me.

I'd carefully calculated my actions, though. I knew Giada planned to wash her hair later that evening, which meant she wouldn't be too upset over an impromptu swim. And if there was one thing that could distract me from the stress of my work day, it would be sparring with my wife at her feistiest.

"You are a monster," she said, kicking her feet to swim towards the steps.

I stared back at her, still grinning. "It's too bad I'm like twice your size, and you can't retaliate by pushing me in," I said.

"I wouldn't dream of trying to retaliate against my sweet husband," Giada said, slowly climbing out of the pool.

I should've been worried, but the sight of her stalking towards me, her tanned skin glistening as droplets of water cascaded down her torso, was mesmerizing. She looked radiant, almost like some hallucinatory vision that was too good to be true.

She reached me, rose to her toes, and kissed me on the mouth, wrapping her wet arms around my waist as she did. I felt the water soaking through my shirt, but I couldn't have cared less.

"You're lucky my memories are back, and I remember all the things you can do with your tongue later to repay me for that little stunt," she whispered into my ear.

I cleared my throat, trying my hardest to focus on work, or my papà, or anything at all that would stop my dick from rising to full attention in front of everyone staring at us. Right then, Adrian walked outside. And just like that, my problem was cured.

I resisted the urge to wrap a towel around Giada to hide her from her ex-boyfriend, but barely. An attractive woman with dark blonde hair walked beside Adrian, chatting comfortably with him. She looked somewhat familiar, but I didn't think I'd actually seen her before.

"Is that his girlfriend?" I whispered to Giada.

She glanced at Adrian. "Who? Annie?" Giada laughed. "That's his sister. She was at our wedding."

I gazed back at the pair and instantly picked up on the resemblance now. The siblings had the same bold, blue eyes and strong, straight noses. The woman was average height and build, but had feminine instead of the hardened muscle of her brother.

"Come on, I'll re-introduce you," Giada said.

"Do you want to grab your cover-up first?" I asked, knowing damn well my wife would have no issue prancing around half naked in front of the whole group.

"He's seen it all before," she said, her reminder wholly unnecessary. Giada sauntered up to the pair.

"Hi Adrian. Hi Annie. I would hug you, but I'm soaking wet since someone shoved me in the pool." Giada paused and turned to me. "Annie, I'm sure you remember Luca Marino. Luca, you remember Annie Patras."

"Nice to see you again," I said, politely offering my hand. I couldn't help but notice the quizzical expression on Adrian's face, like he couldn't quite understand how I'd taken on Giada and lived to tell the story. Or maybe he was confused as to why random patches of my clothes were similarly soaked.

"So, I don't think dinner will be until seven. If you want to borrow a suit, I have more. Or you're welcome to just hang out. Make yourself at home," Giada said to Annie.

Before the poor woman could reply though, Matteo stepped up. He had tossed on a shirt since Annie and Adrian had arrived, and seemed oddly eager.

"Hey, I think we met at the wedding," he said. "I'm Matteo, Giada's brother. The nice one," he added with a chuckle.

Annie nodded. "Hi again."

"Come on, it's not really good pool weather anymore. I'll give you a tour," Matteo offered.

Annie went with him without hesitation.

"Hmm. So all the Patras kids have questionable taste," I teased, eliciting a glare from both my wife and Adrian. I was about to excuse myself to head inside to change before dinner, but Adrian spoke up first.

"I need to talk to Angelo. Is he inside?"

"Is everything okay?" Giada asked.

Adrian nodded.

"He was in the second-floor den the last I saw him. He's turned it into his makeshift office," Giada said.

Adrian started inside without another word.

"Are you coming in now?" I asked my wife.

She turned and settled back onto her lounger. "No, now I need to dry." She patted the chair beside her, formerly occupied by Matteo. "So do you."

"You're not showering before dinner?"

"Naa. I'll do that right before bed. How was work?"

I considered the question. Since I'd missed some days lately, my schedule was more chaotic than I'd like. Alessio had covered more than his fair share though, and he kept me chipper when we were catching up on the rest of the crap, too. But my papà had been a pain lately.

"Fine," I finally answered. "I'm just annoyed with my papà. He brought on a few more new guys, and I don't think he's vetted them fully."

Giada wrinkled her nose. "Well, he's been doing this for a while, so maybe just trust he knows what he's doing and don't let it stress you out?"

I laughed at her ability to oversimplify it all. She was right, of course, but telling me not to worry about something had no impact on my likelihood of actually worrying about said thing.

"Yeah, you're right," I agreed. Then I pulled out my phone and texted Roberto. He was in Italy at the moment, which made him the perfect man for the job. "Want more intel on the new guys. Call w updates."

He replied with a thumbs-up emoji less than a minute later.

I shoved my phone back into my pocket and then turned back to my wife to ask about her day.

~

Giada

*D*inner went smoothly that evening, although the appearance of the Patras siblings had thrown me a bit. Adrian and Angelo seemed uncharacteristically chummy, I supposed ever since Adrian had secured Angelo's release from jail. And Matteo had latched on to Annie, which perplexed me even more. He'd met her, what, once before?

Earlier in the day, while lounging by the pool, I'd chatted with Matteo. I'd tried to scope out details on his love life, but he was evasive as always. In the past, I'd suspected Matteo had a crush on Gabby, and as much as my friend had always denied it, I knew she had some feelings about him, too. They'd never been close, but Matteo had always made a point to hang out with me more when Gabriella was also at the house. So, if anyone in my family could help me devise a plan to rebuild my relationship with her, it would be Matteo.

Still, if he was interested in Annie now, I didn't want to get in the way of that. I couldn't remember ever meeting a serious girlfriend of Matteo's, and he'd always enjoyed a reputation of being a player. Kind of like the male version of an heiress, Matteo had made a life out of doing very little work and a whole lot of partying. He was a good man though, and a great brother, and I knew his avoidance of work wasn't so much laziness as a disinterest in participating in our specific family business.

If he could find a woman who made him happy, that would be amazing, even if it was my ex's big sister. Maybe that would help shift the focus off of Angelo, too.

I'd spent a good chunk of my time in the sunshine thinking about Angelo. He'd never admit to being sad, but I knew he must be. He couldn't just get over the death of a girlfriend that easily, even if she was kind of awful. I'd never liked her or thought she'd be a good fit for him, but that wasn't the point. He was struggling, and he'd come to my help when I needed it, so now, I needed to repay him.

Unfortunately, I knew he'd never ask for help or admit anything was less than perfect. So, I needed to help him in a way that made him think he was helping me. After hearing the insensitive comments my aunts made to my mom—in front of Angelo —about how she'd have to wait forever for another wedding now, I knew step one had to be getting Angelo out of my parents' house. But he couldn't go back to the place he'd shared with Julia. He'd need someplace new. He also would need a distraction until he was ready to start dating again.

I had figured out a way to help him with both of those problems. Now I just had to get him to agree.

I cornered him the moment the aunts started to clear the table.

"Angelo? Can we talk for a minute?"

My brother's brows furrowed, but he nodded. I motioned towards the back and he followed. Luca had been mid-discussion with my father but froze, watching me with uncertainty in his eyes. I shook my head to urge him to stay put, but I knew he'd come after me as soon as he could extricate himself from my dad. So, I needed to get as far away as possible to ensure Angelo and I could talk in private.

"Let's walk," I said once we were on the back patio, my tone casual.

Angelo's frown deepened. "Giada, you don't have to thank me anymore. I don't want to talk about any of…that. I'm—"

I raised a hand. "I don't want to talk about that, either. I just feel super full from that meal and you know Mom's going to be offended if I refuse dessert and then if I look even the slightest bit bloated, all the aunts will assume I'm pregnant."

"Are you?" he asked, slowly starting on the path leading away from the house.

"No!" I snapped. "I have zero interest in a baby right now."

"That's too bad. Seems they all could use a distraction."

I knew exactly who he meant, and I didn't disagree. But I was not going to be the distraction. At least, not in that way. "Well, maybe Matteo can get someone knocked up. He never shoulders his share of negative family attention."

Angelo chuckled, and we picked up the pace. The family property was massive, extending far past the pool house around a garden and towards a small wooded area. As a child, I'd always hoped we could use the extra acreage for horses. Now, I appreciated the space to wander.

"I actually need a favor," I began.

"Is this a joke?"

"No! But it's not like a bad favor. I don't want to borrow money or anything."

Angelo instinctively reached for my elbow to stabilize me as I stumbled over a rock. "I'd probably rather give you money than

56

whatever you're about to ask for," he said, ignoring the meek "thanks" I'd muttered after he helped me.

"It's not even a favor really. I just have this idea. Can you at least listen to the whole thing before you say no?"

My brother didn't reply, so I forged ahead. "We both know I'm never going to be able to make a traditional nine-to-five job work, but I really like work. I mean, I love the design stuff. And I want to do more than what my firm lets me do, but I'm not exactly qualified to ever take over and they won't let me even handle my own client accounts with my crappy attendance record."

I paused, but Angelo said nothing.

"I had a client the other day who bought this older home and basically gutted the whole thing, like a full renovation. So we were designing it from scratch."

"Why not just buy a new place if you're going to tear down the whole thing?" he asked.

"Because they couldn't afford a new house in the neighborhood they wanted. Have you even looked at property values right now?"

Angelo glared, confirming my hunch that he'd been looking into moving.

"Besides, the bones were good so they didn't actually tear it down," I continued.

"What does this have to do with me?"

"Glad you asked. So, I would love to start flipping houses, and with my connections and knowledge of the design industry, I can do an amazing job on the interior of these houses."

Angelo raised a brow but didn't voice his disagreement.

"But what I need are some guys who could do the actual work. Like, construction guys."

Angelo opened his mouth to protest. I waved my hands at him like a crazy person.

"Before you say no, think about this. It's a completely legitimate business. It'll have a lot of back-and-forth cash flow too, in case you know anyone who needs that to bolster any other business matters."

"Giada…" his tone was filled with warning.

"I'm just saying. It's win-win." I paused. "Oh, and I forgot the best part. The first house we'll do is going to be your house."

"I don't have a house."

I tugged my phone from my pocket and navigated straight to the listing I'd saved. It was for a charming mid-century cottage halfway in between the two places Angelo most frequently worked— the docks and the main construction site. The house had a traditional, functional layout with three bedrooms and three and a half bathrooms, a quaint garden, and a worn white-picket fence surrounding the entire property.

From what I'd gathered in my research, an elderly couple had purchased the home as newlyweds, and their kids were now eager to sell since, apparently, the parents had both passed. The home had been lovingly cared for, but had received absolutely no updates for the past twenty-five years. The pictures online were garbage, making the place look like it had been overtaken by gangs when really it just needed some TLC and well-placed updates.

"This is hideous," Angelo said.

"Look at the location."

He shrugged. "Yeah, it's a good location. But I'm not looking to buy now."

"Why not? You can't tell me you want to stay here forever, and I'm guessing there's a reason you're not heading back to your place too."

Angelo sighed. "To flip houses, you don't just need a designer and contractors, you also need realtors."

I smiled and handed him Christian Morelli's business card. He was Italian, a family friend, and a realtor.

"He can meet with us tomorrow to look at the house. Just

think—no more aunts or mom pestering you all the time. You can get a fresh start and your sister will help you redesign the whole place so it is the house of your dreams. I'll even offer my services for free since you're my first client, but after this one goes smoothly, I'm thinking we can make this an official partnership."

Angelo's face crinkled into something resembling a mixture of disgust and confusion. "You want to be partners?"

I thrust my bottom lip into a dramatic pout. "Just give it some thought. You've got nothing to lose, and a whole new brilliant and profitable business venture to gain."

I finished my sales pitch right as Luca caught up to us.

"Everything okay?" he asked.

Angelo turned to me, then Luca. "Did you know about this?" he asked my husband.

Luca stared at me, not needing to fake his own bewilderment.

"I figured I'd wait till you agreed to fill in Luca."

Angelo flung his hands in the air and stomped back towards the house, but I sensed something under his exasperation. I was almost certain we'd be looking at the house the next day.

~

Adrian

I awoke the next morning in my own bed, and I knew before checking the time on my phone that it must be late. I felt too well-rested for it to be early. Not that it mattered. It was a Saturday, and my only plans until nightfall involved cleaning my house and hitting the gym. Once Melissa was off work, she and I planned to see a movie. I predicted we'd end up staying in and ordering takeout, but hopefully we'd at least have sex before falling asleep.

Somehow, I'd blinked and we'd turned into a boring old

married couple. Sadly, I wasn't sure I minded. Just because the relationship felt easy didn't make it a bad thing. Predictability was a perk when both people had busy work schedules like Melissa and me.

Still, something bothered me. Melissa had been off work the night before, too. She'd asked what we were doing, but I'd told her I had a work dinner and couldn't hang out. In reality, Marco had specified for me to bring a date to the dinner at his house.

His instruction was nothing more than a courtesy, of course. Marco didn't care if I was single; he just wanted to keep the dinner casual and make it feel more like a family affair and less like a work affair. But still, the fact that I didn't tell Melissa bothered me more than the fact that I hadn't invited her.

Inviting my sister had been a no-brainer. I didn't want Annie mixed up with the Contis anymore than I wanted Melissa involved, but Annie had already met them. And in their own misguided way, they'd helped her after she'd been attacked by a psycho. Angelo had assured me then that no matter what the future held, Annie would be protected. And if there was one thing the Conti men were good for, it was their word.

I rolled out of bed and dressed in my gym clothes, then let out the dog. Matteo texted while I waited for my coffee to brew.

"Good 2 see Annie last nite. Hope we weren't too overwhelming for her," he wrote.

I frowned at the message, trying to decipher some ulterior meaning. Matteo and I were friendly, but we weren't exactly friends. At least not the type to text random pleasantries.

"I think she had fun," I replied. "She doesn't have a lot of friends in the area still so it's good for her to get out."

I clicked send before realizing I probably overshared. Granted, it was the truth. Growing up, Annie had been an extrovert with a bubbly personality. She'd made friends instantly upon moving to the area, and I expected her to be infinitely more popular than me despite me having spent years in New England for law school. But after the attack, she'd become withdrawn and distrusting of strangers. Now, she preferred to stay in or spend time with people she knew well.

She still met with a therapist regularly, so I tried to stay out of it and not worry about her, but as with most things, that was easier said than done.

"She left her sunglasses at the house," Matteo wrote.

I started to reply that I'd pick them up sometime, but three little dots appeared, indicating he was typing more.

"She mentioned where she lived last night, and I'll be in her neighborhood later today. Can you send me her number so I can text her to make sure she'll be around then?"

I debated insisting on getting the sunglasses myself, then dismissed the idea. If my sister had told Matteo where she lived, she was obviously comfortable with him. And if he really wanted her number, he could track it down whether or not I sent it to him now. I clicked to share her contact information with him, then texted my sister a heads up.

Then, I wolfed my breakfast before heading to the gym.

CHAPTER 6

Giada

I loved spending a couple of days back home with my family, but it was definitely nice returning to my own apartment with Luca. Angelo had agreed to go look at the house with me the previous day, and that visit couldn't have gone better. The house was every bit as disheveled and awful on the surface as I'd predicted, but Angelo had thankfully looked past that all and shared my appreciation for the property's good bones.

This morning, Angelo texted that he was making an offer on the house. He refused to share any of the details of the offer with me, but I trusted he and Christian could handle that part on their own. And he promised to let me "consult" with him on the design plans. I wasn't sure exactly what his version of a consultation entailed, but I was giddy while I awaited the good news.

Luca seemed shocked that I'd even proposed such a partnership to my brother, but he didn't protest my insistence on working with Angelo. I'd mentioned to Luca before that I thought I'd enjoy redesigning houses for flips, but I got the impression he didn't take the idea too seriously. Not that I could blame him. I tended to come up with lots of brilliant ideas, but my follow-through was less than ideal.

I'd been droning on about different design ideas I had for Angelo's new place since we'd started prepping a chopped salad for dinner. We were both finishing the last bites when my phone rang.

I didn't recognize the number on my phone, so I let the call go through to voicemail. I'd nearly forgotten about the call by the time my phone interrupted us again with the bold "ping" alerting me to the message.

Luca winced. He hated voicemail in general, but felt strongly that if a message was required, it should be short. Of course, that rule didn't apply to his mother, who could leave him a recording of her entire life story without him complaining.

Luca constantly accepted calls during meals, so I wasn't about to spend the rest of the meal wondering who had called and left such a lengthy message. Probably, it was a telemarketer or physician's office, but I'd never know until I pressed play. I kept the message on speakerphone, figuring that was less rude.

The message started with silence, then a moment of heavy breathing. Luca's frown deepened just before a voice interrupted the silence.

"Giada? I…God I hope this is still your number. I, um…well, it's Gabby," she said. It was an unnecessary clarification, as I'd recognized her voice from the moment she said my name. "Gabriella Giordano? Um, I know I said I'd never talk to you again. Well, I said a lot of things, but…" She sighed, and I squeezed my eyes shut, praying the reason she was struggling so much with this call was that she wanted to reconnect.

"I got your letter," she continued. "And I wasn't going to call you, but… I need help. I don't know who else to ask. You said you have money, and I can pay you back. Someday. And it's…well, it's not for me. It's, my brother, and… He got in with some bad people and he owes them a lot of money, and they're going to kill him. If you could just…well, we need a loan…"

I gazed up at Luca, feeling my eyes fill with tears right as my best friend—former best friend—broke down into full-blown sobs. Luca's expression was tight, and nearly unreadable, but he'd set down his fork. That was something, at least.

"It's a lot of money, Giada. It's more than you have, I'm sure and… oh God. I don't know. If you meant what you said in your letter, please call me."

The call disconnected, and I drew my hand to my mouth, unable to even process what she'd just said. Luca stared at me for a moment, then rose to his feet, scooted my plate out of the way, and perched on the edge of the table in front of me, pulling me to him. I half-cried, half-hyperventilated against him, soaking in his familiar scent and the firm comfort of his chest until I was calm enough to think straight.

When Luca finally loosened his grip on me, he looked straight in my eyes. "What letter?"

It took me a moment to even realize what he was asking, but then it hit me. He still didn't know I'd even written it. "I wrote a letter to Gabby after my accident, when I was staying with Adrian. I didn't… like tell her anything. I just said I missed her, but I told her I'd always consider her a friend and that if she ever needed anything, I'd be there." I paused,. "We have to help her."

"Did Adrian see the letter?"

I frowned, annoyed by his focus on the wrong facts. "Yes. He sent it to her for me."

Luca scowled and pulled out his phone.

"Luca, enough with the letter. It doesn't matter!"

But he was already on the phone with Adrian. I rolled my eyes but pushed away from the table and made my way to our bedroom safe. There were a few places we kept cash, but that was the largest stash.

Luca caught up with me just as I reached the combination dial. "Adrian took a picture of it just in case. He's texting it to me."

"Of what?"

"Of your letter."

I blew out a sigh. "It doesn't matter about the letter. She's my friend, and I have to help her."

He gripped my hand firmly just as his phone dinged, alerting him to a text. "She hasn't been much of a friend to you lately."

I glared back at him.

"Okay, I'm not saying we won't help her," he clarified. "But we're not rushing into it blindly. I'd like to know what you told her before I jump into someone else's mess."

"I'm calling her back," I said.

"Giada, give me two minutes. Please." It wasn't his words so much as the way his eyes locked on mine, silently pleading, that convinced me.

I nodded, then leaned closer to read my own letter over his shoulder.

Dear Gabriella—

I've thought about writing you many times, but never followed through because I always assumed there would be a tomorrow, that sometime in the future, you and I would make up. But recently, I was in a car accident. It was bad. When I woke up in the hospital, I was alone and worse yet, I didn't even have my memories. The doctors say I've suffered a brain trauma, and I still have amnesia. I remember some things, like how much your friendship meant to me, but the entire last year is missing in my mind. I've missed you every day since our falling out, but it's worse now. The trauma of losing you is fresh in my mind again, all the wounds have reopened. I'm not naïve enough to think you'll ever forgive me, but I want you to know I am sorry. I'm sorry that you got hurt. I'm sorry that my personal life left you feeling scared and traumatized. And I'm so sorry that I've lost you over this. You deserve a happy, carefree life filled with laughter and love and friends who aren't so complicated. But if you ever miss me the way I miss you, please reach out. I'll always be here for you. And even if it isn't friendship you want from me, I hope you still know you can come to me. If you need a safe place to sleep, money, a cover story, an alibi, or even just someone to hold your hand, tell me. I will help you. I miss you so much and wish nothing but the best for you.

Love,
Giada

I finished reading before Luca. He was quiet as he read, but squeezed his eyes shut for a moment after. Then he turned to me.

"Oh Giada, I'm so sorry."

"It's not your fault." I remembered that fateful day well. I had been the one to suggest Gabby and I go fetch my stuff from

Luca's shipping crate. Luca had told us to wait for him and I didn't. Worse yet, Luca hadn't known we'd gone against his wishes. He sure didn't tell his guys to detain us and scare the crap out of both of us. None of it had been Luca's fault, but it also wasn't Gabriella's. I was the only one at fault.

But regardless, I didn't blame Gabby for cutting me out of her life after that traumatic night. What rational person would want a best friend who married into the mafia?

"It *is* my fault," he said. "You lost your best friend because of my lifestyle. I didn't…I mean, I knew you were close and that you missed her, but I didn't realize it hurt you this much."

I shrugged. "She's my best friend. And when I wrote this, all the pain of losing her was so raw. It's…better now. But I need to help her."

Luca nodded. "We will. I'll take care of it."

He didn't say anything else, but the look in his eyes made me think that maybe he was thinking the same thing as me. Maybe this was my chance to convince her to let me back in her life.

"I need to know how much money, who he owes, and when it's due," he said. "Call her and see if she and her brother will come over."

"Here? Tonight?"

"Yes."

I hesitated, then called on speaker phone. Gabriella answered right away, but took a moment to speak.

"Gabby, it's Giada," I said, glancing at Luca. "I got your message, and of course I'll help. We'll help."

She burst into tears but then thanked me. She started to ramble about the situation but Luca shook his head at me and motioned for me to wrap it up.

"Gabby, listen. We have money and Luca has lots of contacts. I promise we will do what we can to fix this, but not over the phone. Can you come to my house?"

There was silence.

"Bring your brother, and come over here as soon as you can so we can all talk about it."

"He'll be there? Luca?" she asked, her voice trembling.

I gritted my teeth, hating that my best friend was so terrified of my husband. "Gabby, he's the one who can help your brother, not me. I'll be here too, though, and I swear on the Holy Mother that you will be safe. Both of you. We just want to help."

She sniffled again. "It's not like he has any other choice."

I told her the address, and then we hung up.

~

Luca

Once Giada hung up with Gabriella, I called Thomas and had him on standby. Since he was the one supervising the morons that kidnapped my wife and her friend that fateful night, it only made sense that he be the one to help me resolve the situation. But I didn't want to scare off Gabby by having him come to the house for the meeting too, even though that would be more efficient.

Over an hour passed before the doorbell rang. Giada leapt from the couch and flew to the door in record time. I cringed to see her friend pull back when Giada so desperately wanted to hug her. I hung back, not wanting to intimidate anyone. I was determined not to ruin the chance to make up for the falling out I'd caused.

"Hi Carlo, how are you?" Giada said.

He didn't answer, so she showed them into the living room where I was waiting.

"Luca Marino," I said, offering my hand to Gabby's brother. "You must be Carlo."

Carlo's handshake was weak, but he looked strong. He looked like the type of guy who could handle himself in a bar fight. I recalled Giada saying he was a year or two younger than Gabby, and that he studied business in college. I wondered what had happened since graduation to make him dumb enough to get himself into this situation.

"Well, you and I could head into my study to talk in private if you want. No need to get the ladies involved more than they are," I said, gesturing towards the hallway.

"I'm already involved and I'm not leaving him alone with you," Gabriella said.

Giada flashed me an apologetic smile, but it was fine. I could handle people treating me like shit, so long as they didn't turn their wrath on her.

"Alright, have a seat. So if I'm going to help, I need a little more information," I began, fully cognizant of how weird it was to have this discussion in our living room. Gabby and Carlo shared a couch and Giada and I were across from each other, adjacent to them, on armchairs. We could be discussing book club from the looks of things.

"How are you going to help?" Carlo interrupted.

I kept my expression tight, not accustomed to back talk, especially from people who needed me. "I know people. I have connections."

"We just need money," he said.

"I doubt that, but…" I began.

Before I could continue, Gabby piped up. "They'll kill him if he doesn't pay."

"They won't. They get nothing if they kill him." I said, my voice still calm. "How much do you owe?"

Carlo cringed, his eyes darting briefly to his sister before focusing on the rug at his feet. "Twenty-four thousand."

Giada's eyes widened. That was more than I'd expected, too, but not unmanageable.

"Is that including interest?" I asked.

"I don't owe them interest. They're not a bank. They're just a bunch of thugs."

My jaw tightened. "How much do they say you owe them?"

He hesitated. "Thirty-six."

Jesus. I couldn't just hand over that much money without something in return. "Okay, well, unless you have some bargaining chip I'm unaware of, it's safe to assume that is the number you need to focus on."

Carlo scowled at me, but I kept going.

"Thugs," I paused, glaring pointedly as I used his term, "Like that don't really care what your original debt was if you didn't pay it back on time."

"I'm not paying them that much," he replied.

I rolled my eyes. "It sounds like you're not able to pay them anything. And if I'm paying them that much, I need to know who I'm paying and how you accrued this debt."

Carlo exchanged a glance with his sister before turning back to me. "You really have that kind of money?"

"I can get it."

"They don't take credit cards."

I stifled a laugh. "First, if I'm going to help you out, your sister is giving Giada a second chance." I turned to Gabby, who looked less surprised by this than Giada. "You go out to dinner with Giada tomorrow night. Once again next week. Listen to what she has to say and give her a chance. If you still don't want anything to do with her after next week, you don't have to ever see her again once Carlo's debt is paid off."

I paused, until Gabby agreed, avoiding all eye contact with Giada.

I turned back to her brother. "Start at the beginning."

Thankfully, he did. Apparently, he'd discovered he had a knack for poker in his last year of college. He'd come out ahead the majority of the time, so he kept joining bigger games. When he lost the big pot, he was playing against the wrong crowd. It wasn't a unique story by any means. That was what happened when you combined arrogance with greed and didn't exercise common sense.

"I'm sure he cheated," Carlo added.

"Doesn't really matter either way at this point. Do you have a last name for this Benny guy?"

Carlo shook his head.

"Is he Italian?"

"I think Mexican. Or maybe Puerto Rican."

I called Alessio, certain he'd know. He had an impeccable memory when it came to all of the major players on the northeast coast.

"Hey, you're on speakerphone here with some friends. We are looking for a guy named Benny. We think he's Latino. He runs some poker ring or something with card games."

"Benito Vasquez?" Alessio asked.

I turned to Carlo, but he simply shrugged.

"Maybe. Do you know anything else about him?"

"Uhh, hang on. I can get a picture."

"What's your number?" I asked Carlo. When he answered, I told Alessio to text the photo from his burner phone to that number. I didn't want to be involved at all.

"Yeah, that's him," Carlo said.

I motioned for Carlo's phone and deleted the text and image just as a precaution. Alessio switched to Italian then, telling me Benito had a reputation for being ruthless, and that he got his kicks out of stealing money from preppy rich kids and that he wouldn't stop until he'd taken all of their dad's money too.

"You need me in on this?" he asked, reverting to English.

"Nope. Thomas owes me for an earlier mess, so he's cleaning this up for our friend. Thank you."

I hung up and turned to Carlo. "Do you speak Italian?"

He shook his head sheepishly.

"We both speak a little," Gabby said, "But not enough to understand what that guy said."

I loosely translated what Alessio had said, but then explained. "What he means is that even if you pay him, there's nothing to stop him from coming after you again and again as long as he thinks there's any hope of getting money."

"Well, there isn't. We don't have any more. Even if we got our parents involved, they don't have this kind of cash."

"They have a house, retirement plans, cars," I began. "But that's not the point. The point is that as long as you pay him, he'll know you can."

"So, we don't pay him," Carlo concluded.

I cringed. "I wouldn't recommend that."

"You already said they won't kill him," Gabby reminded me.

"And I doubt they would, at least intentionally. But they sure could rough him up."

"They already did," she said. Her brother's cheeks flushed.

I looked at Carlo. "You seem to still have all your fingers, so trust me when I say whatever they've done to you so far doesn't even compare to what they could do. Have you ever had a tooth pulled?"

The poor kid looked nauseous.

"Luca!" Giada chastised me.

"Look, I think you need to have a realistic picture of what you're up against. You were cocky and greedy and stupid. You got involved in the wrong people and now look what you've done to your sister."

"I get it. I'm a fuckup. I already feel like shit. How is this helping?"

"I'm trying to explain to you that they're never going to leave you alone as long as they think you're solo in all of this. What'll make them back off is knowing that you're not worth the effort or risk to pursue more."

"Okay, so how do we do that?"

I took a deep breath, knowing none of them was going to like what I was about to say. "You come work for me."

I was right. Gabby and Giada both shouted "no" at the same time.

"I already have a day job," Carlo said.

I rolled my eyes. "Most of my business is at night. I've got clubs that need workers and I've got shipping crates that need someone to keep an eye on them overnight. You'll need to show up at least two or three times a week for Benny to believe you're really involved, and then he'll back off."

"Why would he back off just because I work for you?"

I frowned, wondering if Gabby truly hadn't told him. "Because even if you don't understand who I am, I assure you Benito does. And he knows that messing with one of my guys is the same as messing with me. And messing with me means you have hundreds of loyal men on multiple continents eager to hunt you down and make you pay."

Gabby's eyes widened, but Carlo seemed to get my point.

"But what about the money?"

"Either me or Thomas, one of my guys, will go with you the night after tomorrow. You'll pay Benito twenty-five grand and promise to return with another fifteen a week later."

"I don't owe him forty."

"You will by next week, and it's worth an extra four grand to avoid making him mad, anyway."

He wisely kept quiet, so I continued. "We will make sure Benny understands you are my family. We will see to it that Benny knows the consequences if anything happens to you or if he ever comes after you again."

I could tell Carlo had many more questions, but thankfully he still didn't interrupt.

"I don't imagine you're trained to do much for me, so we can talk in a couple of days, after you've made the first payment to

Benny. Then we can figure out how you can start to work off your debt.

Gabby was still shooting me daggers. "Why should we trust you?" she asked.

"Why should I give your brother forty thousand dollars and put myself or one of my best friends at risk?" I retorted.

She winced, but pressed further. "How is Carlo any better off owing you money than owing this other thug?"

"Look, trust me or don't. I'm good either way. I get nothing out of this deal. I have plenty of guys actually trained for their jobs willing to work for me, and I don't benefit from paying for other people's stupid gambling mistakes," I said. I caught Giada's expression out of the corner of my eye. She was frowning at me like a dog handler about to lose Westminster. I sighed, then decided to switch tactics.

"But it's also a better deal for Carlo because I'm offering him a way to pay off the debt. And I'm not charging him interest."

"What happens if he doesn't want to keep working for you?" Gabby asked.

"I suppose that's up to Benny. If Benny happens to notice you're no longer associating with us, there's nothing to stop him from going after you again."

"But you won't do anything to Carlo?" she asked.

I shook my head.

"Why not? Isn't that what you do? Chop off fingers and pull teeth when people don't do what you want?" Gabriella continued.

I blinked back surprise at her tone. Given that Gabby came to me desperate for help, her insistence that I was a monster perplexed me. Every part of me ached to tell her to fuck off and find the money for Carlo somewhere else. I didn't need to get mixed up in this shit, not if she was going to treat me like dirt anyway.

Giada stood and came to sit on the arm of my chair. She turned to her former friend. "Do you want Luca to help or not? If he's going to do you a favor, you could at least show a little gratitude."

Gabriella's expression remained stone cold, but her brother spoke.

"Yeah, ignore her. I'm the one in trouble, and I'm grateful," Carlo began. "She just wants to make sure I'm not digging myself into a bigger hole."

I nodded as though any of that was reasonable. "Carlo, regardless of whether you ever repay me a cent of the money I give you, I will not hurt you. Nor will any of the guys who work for me. And that's not because I want to do you any favors."

I paused and squeezed my wife's hand. "It's because Giada is everything to me. I would do anything for her, and she considers you family. So that makes you my family." I gazed at my wife, who smiled softly, then continued, addressing Carlo again. "So if you want to take my money and never see me again after you've paid off Benny, that's your prerogative. But the closer both of you appear to be to me, the safer you'll be from Benny."

Gabby had no response for that. I turned to Giada, who nodded. I couldn't read her expression well enough to tell if this is what she'd expected me to say or not. In truth, I was somewhat bluffing. Most likely, Benny wouldn't keep tabs on Carlo after he paid his debt. If Thomas said Carlo was with us, Benny would probably take his word and let it go. But I didn't know Benny so I couldn't be sure. And what I did know was that the longer I could keep Carlo under my thumb, the more chance there was for interaction between Giada and Gabby.

I didn't love forking over that kind of money to some punk kid, and I doubted anything Carlo could do would ever bring me that kind of value. But it was worth it if it brought Giada's best friend back into her life.

I wished I could get Carlo away from his sister for a moment so the girls could talk, but I didn't see that happening. So instead, I just lowered my voice, hoping Giada would take the hint.

"Thomas and I will be at my club the day after tomorrow, so if you come by at eight, you can talk with Thomas and work out the details, and then the two of you can go together," I said.

Giada turned to Gabby. "How are your parents?"

I heard Gabby mumble a response, but Carlo had begun talking. I kept him going for another five minutes while Giada and Gabby made small talk, and then our guests left.

Giada turned to me and exhaled a shaky breath. I roped my arms around her, pinning her arms to her side. As her breathing evened out, I loosened my grip until eventually, we were just hugging.

"Are you okay?" I asked her.

"Yeah. I can't believe Carlo got himself in so much trouble. He's so young."

"Well, he's got me looking out for him now, and Thomas."

"Are you really going to make him work for you?"

I breathed a laugh. "I can't imagine he's qualified for anything, but I'm hoping Thomas can find something for him. It would at least keep him out of trouble until he learns some street smarts."

"You didn't have to make Gabby hang out with me."

"Yes, I did. I'm not just handing over forty thousand dollars. That's more than a lot of people earn in a year. I don't know this kid, and it's no sweat off my back if they rip off his toenails and throw him in a river. What's in it for me is seeing you get back your best friend."

She sighed. "It won't work. She'll never forgive me."

I gazed down at her, brushing the hair off her forehead. "I think she will. You're pretty irresistible."

Giada groaned. "I need a drink. Want something?"

"Sure." I followed her into the kitchen.

"I really do feel terrible about Carlo. But I also feel a little hopeful. I mean, even if Gabriella still hates me, she spoke to me. That's at least progress, right?"

I nodded. "Absolutely."

"But it's horrible to be excited about the possibility of getting my friend back when it means her brother is in trouble."

I squeezed her shoulder. "It's not, and he'll be fine. I'll take care of him."

She stared at me for a long time and then smiled. After a moment, her expression changed again. "You haven't ever cut off someone's fingers, have you?"

"No, baby."

"That's a relief."

I laughed, but I was thankful she hadn't asked about the toenails.

CHAPTER 7

Giada

The next day, I sat at the conference table, surrounded by a mess of photos. To a casual onlooker, the collection probably appeared jumbled, but all I saw was organized chaos. A client had dropped off inspiration photos she'd torn from various magazines- some of them were home décor magazines, but others were actually showcasing builders focused on new construction.

After the initial client consultation, Audra had chuckled and called the client "old fashioned" for offering us paper photos since most of our clients had already curated their own complex inspiration boards on Pinterest. This client's more traditional method amused Audra in the way that would cause a southern lady to clutch her chest and coo "bless your heart," but I found it endearing. This was how my own passion for design had first sparked.

As a child, I loved collecting pretty pictures. My photos weren't of unicorns or rainbows, but well-designed living rooms and gorgeous dresses. I'd pasted my collections of torn-out magazine pages into one of two journals depending on if they were fashion-related or home design. As I'd aged, I obviously moved some of my design inspiration to the cloud, but I never stop tearing the prettiest pages from catalogs and magazines before dumping them into the recycling bin.

There was something about the ability to physically touch the designs that helped me better connect to the design idea. For this specific project, the scattered papers were particularly helpful. This client had just purchased an older home. The house was structurally sound, but dated, so she wanted a full renovation and redesign. The client wanted an updated interior with calming colors and clean lines—but also wanted to stay true to the home's late nineteenth-century roots. This was the client that had inspired me to propose the same type of arrangement to Angelo.

Audra had tasked me with compiling the magazine pictures into a digital inspiration board before our first in-depth meeting with the client. The project felt like a test of sorts, though I knew she'd simply take my ideas to the client and modify them as needed during the meeting. To me, the biggest challenge would be ensuring the rooms felt distinct, but unified. Flipping through the client's inspiration printouts, I'd already noted her love of the color blue. Specifically, a robin's egg blue. Since the client claimed she preferred creams and other neutral shades, adding blue to every room was definitely a bold move. But it was also a classy way to connect all of the rooms. The best part, in my opinion, was that she could easily update the design over time without completely ruining the overall look of the home.

I lost myself in the project for the better part of an hour. Piecing together all of the photos soothed me in a way few other activities could. I needed the distraction too, since tonight was my big dinner with Gabby. I could've spent all day panicking about the countless number of ways the dinner could go wrong, but instead, I focused all of my attention on the design.

I was just putting the finishing touches on the inspiration

board when my phone rang. I glanced at the caller ID, fully prepared to reject the call and message whoever it was that I'd get back to them on my way home from work.

I had not expected for Angelo to be the one trying to reach me. We'd spoken on my drive to work and he'd told me he would be busy all day and couldn't talk about house stuff until the following day. So if he was calling now, I knew there had to be a good reason.

"Angelo?" I said, pressing the phone to my ear. I half expected the caller to claim a different identity, but the voice that responded was unmistakably that of my oldest brother.

"Yeah, hey Giada, I was wondering—"

Angelo's words were cut off as a male voice wailed in the background. Angelo's voice was muffled as I pictured him covering the receiver to talk to someone else. Whatever was happening around Angelo, there was chaos for sure.

"Everything okay?" I asked after a minute.

"Uhh, yeah. Sorry. So, um, the other day you mentioned having a friend that was a doctor," Angelo said.

The pained moaning in the background was so distracting that I struggled to recall when I'd told my brother I was friends with a doctor. I didn't exactly have a lot of friends, so it seemed like I'd remember if one of them had that much education.

"Are you sure it was…" I began, but another groan cut off my train of thought. "Is someone hurt?"

Angelo's impatience was apparent from his sigh, "Yes, obviously. That's why I'm asking about a doctor. Rico got shot, and—"

"Rico got shot?" My voice was so loud that the receptionist peered over at me through the glass window of the conference room. I waved apologetically, grateful the door was shut at least.

Angelo started talking again, but I interrupted a second time. "Is he okay?"

"He will be if we can get a doctor. It's basically a glorified flesh-wound."

I heard cursing from Rico in the background that suggested he disagreed with my brother's assessment of his injury.

"You said one of your friends came over and fixed up Luca's arm when he got shot. Rico needs someone who won't worry about any official paperwork."

"Oh," I said, suddenly remembering. "You mean Adrian's girlfriend."

My brother was silent for a moment. "Adrian's girlfriend is the doctor who treated Luca," he finally said.

"Yeah. I think Luca paid her a ridiculous amount, but she does house calls and is great. Her name's Melissa. I have her number here if you don't have time to call Adrian, but he sounds like he's really in pain. Maybe he needs a real doctor."

"He's fine," Angelo snapped. "What's the number?"

I relayed the number and he disconnected without thanking me.

I'd lost my train of thought by that point, so I saved the file and began cleaning up the table. I should head home to get ready for my dinner with Gabby anyway.

~

Adrian

J pounded on the door so hard my fist hurt. I gazed up at the camera perched by the door, unable to stop glaring for even a moment. A few seconds later, a fuzzy voice came through the intercom attached to the doorbell.

"Geez, stop making so much noise. I'll let you in as soon as I'm dressed," Giada said.

I dropped my hand to my side and waited as patiently as I could muster.

As promised, the door swung open a minute later. A flustered-looking Giada motioned for me to enter. She wore a short, purple, striped sundress that made me think she was about to go out. But her hair was twisted on top of her head, and her face was bare, aside from the scowl she now aimed at me.

"Why were you trying to break down my door?" she asked.

"I needed to talk to you."

"Okay. Talk," she said. But then she glanced at her phone laying on the counter, and shook her head. "Actually, I need to do my hair. Come on. You can talk while I curl."

I blew out a sigh and followed Giada through her apartment and into her bedroom. My stomach clenched at the thought that this was where she slept with Luca, every fucking night. The room was gorgeous, clearly designed by her, but there were obvious signs of him, too.

"Come on, you can sit in here," she called from the bathroom.

I poked my head around the corner, relieved to see I'd be sitting not on the toilet, but on a small cushioned stool that appeared to be a spot to apply makeup. Giada began dividing her hair into sections and clipping it above her head. Once most of the hair was pinned up, she spritzed the rest with some fruity spray then began twisting small chunks of it around the barrel of a steaming wand.

Watching her move was both mesmerizing and infuriating. I wanted to stay mad, not to get distracted by how quickly she transformed her hair. I needed to focus on what she'd done to Melissa.

"Hot date tonight?" I challenged, certain any mention of Luca could open the door for me to bring up Melissa.

Giada wrinkled her nose. "Umm sorta? I mean, I'm meeting Gabby for dinner, so…" she stopped talking and chewed her lip. If she hadn't been so clearly nervous, I would've assumed she meant a different Gabby.

"Wait, your old friend Gabby?"

"Gabriella Giordano," she clarified.

"Wow. I thought she planned to never talk to you again."

"Yeah. Me too. But she needed a favor from Luca, and one of his conditions for helping her was that she give me a second chance, so here we are."

"You think she'll care if your hair is too straight?"

Giada turned to glare at me. "Obviously not, but girls notice things guys don't. I'd like her to see that I made an effort for her."

Giada's phone buzzed loudly, and she smiled as she checked the caller ID, then clicked to reject the call.

"So what did you need to talk about?" she asked.

Right. "Why did you get Melissa involved with Angelo?" I asked.

Giada released another section of her hair, finger combing it before taking the clip out from between her lips and placing it on the counter. "Uhh because Rico is a moron, and Angelo called and asked for her number."

"How did they even know Melissa was a doctor?"

"They already knew that. They met her at the hospital, remember?"

They hadn't, but that wasn't the point. "Giada, you told them my girlfriend was willing to do under-the-table medical treatments in shady circumstances."

"O—kaaaaay," she said. "I mean, that's the truth, right?"

I blew out a sigh. "It's bad enough that Luca tricked her into doing shit for him, but now you've dragged her into this mess with Angelo too?"

Giada shrugged. "I'm sorry. I didn't realize it was some big secret." She dropped the hot iron and rummaged through a drawer till she found a little pencil. I watched as she lined both of her eyes, then used some chunky stick to apply some rosy color along her cheekbone.

"Well, you should've asked me first," I said.

"Okay. I didn't think it was a big deal," she replied, in a tone that suggested she still didn't get it.

"It's a big deal for two reasons. First of all, I didn't want

Melissa mixed up with your family. It's bad enough she's gotten involved with Luca and the rest of the Marinos, but now you've dragged her into the Conti crap." I paused only to catch my breath and not long enough for her to interrupt. "Second, did you even think about how Angelo might react, learning I've known Melissa was willing to do shit like this all along and never told him? It's like you want me to end up like..." I stopped myself before saying Julia's name.

Giada turned to face me, and now, she looked pissed. "Really? That's the best analogy you can come up with?"

My stomach clenched, but I stayed strong. "You made it look like I was keeping secrets from your brother. The last thing I need is for him to think I've betrayed him."

"Oh, and that's on me?" she asked. "If you don't want him to think you're keeping shit from him, don't keep shit from him."

I opened my mouth to reply but heard a noise behind me. I jumped to my feet just in time to see Luca standing in the entry to the bathroom, hands on his hips.

Luca's gaze was on me, then shifted to his wife before returning to me.

~

Luca

I stared at my wife for a moment, unable to gather much from her expression. "Everything okay?" I asked.

Giada sighed, clearly irritated. I wasn't sure if her annoyance was directed at me or at Adrian, though. When I'd walked in, their voices were raised as if they'd been arguing. But, he was sitting in our bathroom with her while she got dressed. It wasn't exactly the scene I'd expected.

I crossed the room, took the curling iron from my wife's hand, then kissed her on the mouth.

"Hi," she murmured as I pulled back.

I turned to Adrian. He nodded a silent greeting to me, his calm demeanor telling me I hadn't interrupting anything inappropriate. Still, it bothered me that no one was explaining what they'd been discussing.

"Can I help you with something?" I asked Adrian.

He shook his head. "No. I was just asking your wife why she felt compelled to put her brother in touch with Melissa."

I considered his words, then it clicked. He was mad that his girlfriend was now on Angelo's radar. *Oh, the irony.*

"I think we can all agree that was inevitable," I said. "Unless you were planning on breaking up with her soon."

Adrian rolled his eyes.

"Honestly I'm surprised you hadn't already introduced the two of them."

"Yeah, Angelo was, too," Adrian said pointedly.

I offered him a tight smile. "Can I walk you to the door?"

"Good luck with Gabriella," he said to Giada.

"Thanks. And sorry about Melissa," she said, not sounding the least bit sorry.

I walked Adrian to the door, locking it behind him, then returned to the bathroom where my wife put the finishing touches on her makeup.

I cleared my throat as I leaned against the doorway. She met my gaze in the mirror, then returned to her mascara.

"I don't love coming home to find another man alone in my bedroom with my wife," I said. Then, I spotted her phone on the counter and lifted it. Instantly, the missed call from me appeared on the screen. "I also don't appreciate when you reject my calls."

"Sorry. Adrian was on some rant, and I figured it was better to just let him get it over with."

"I saw Adrian on the camera at our door. He looked pissed. I was worried about you."

Now she turned, walking to me and roping her arms around

my neck. "I'm sorry. I thought you were just telling me you were on your way and for me not to be late. It took me forever to get dressed though." She stepped back and twirled. "Do I look okay?"

"You look gorgeous. You ready?"

She inhaled slowly. "Yeah. Nervous, but ready."

"Just be yourself. She loved you once before. She'll love you again."

Giada snorted at that. "I just need a distraction."

I quirked a brow.

"Not that kind of distraction. I can't be late."

I flashed her my most dramatic pouty face, and she swatted my butt as a consolation prize.

"You didn't really worry Adrian was going to do something, did you?" Giada asked.

I shrugged. "I don't recall seeing him that angry before." As we walked to the car, I asked her what all Adrian had said. It was clear that Giada truly didn't understand why Adrian was annoyed.

"Giada, think about it," I began, pulling onto the main road. "If I could've sheltered you from my family, I would have. Really, if I could've kept you away from your own family, I would've done it. He's just being protective of her because he likes her."

"Well, I'm not sure what he thinks Angelo will do to her."

"Really?" I turned to her skeptically. "He doesn't have a great track record with the ladies. Women close to Angelo tend to get hurt."

"That was one woman, and she had it coming. I wish everyone could stop acting like that had anything to do with him. As long as Melissa doesn't try to kill me, I don't think she has anything to worry about with Angelo."

"Okay, but do you see why Adrian was annoyed that you told Angelo before he did?"

"Not really."

"I don't know how exactly it works with Angelo and his guys, but when someone works for me, I expect them to be honest with me. If they have some amazing resource, I want to know about it. I'd be pissed if one of my guys knew a great accountant, for example, but didn't tell me."

"I thought Adrian didn't work for Angelo."

"I'm sure he works for your family. I don't know the parameters of their relationship, but there's definitely something."

"I didn't mean to get Adrian in trouble. I was just trying to be helpful. Eddie needed someone, and Melissa seemed perfect for the job."

I agreed. "I don't think Adrian is in trouble. He's still riding high from busting Angelo out of jail, so nothing he does will matter for a while. But he might not realize that."

Giada nodded. "Yeah, I guess that makes sense." She flipped down her mirror and reapplied lipstick. "Wish me luck," she said as we neared the restaurant where she was meeting Gabby.

"You don't need luck. Anyone would be lucky to have you as a friend." I leaned over and pressed a kiss to her forehead. "Text when you're ready for me to pick you up, but if I'm busy, it'll be Lincoln."

"Oh goody," she joked. She blew me a kiss as I pulled to the curb, then climbed out of the car.

CHAPTER 8

Giada

Moisture coated my palms as I made my way into the restaurant where Gabby and I were meeting. I was a few minutes late and, as expected, Gabby was already there. I waved shyly, then made my way to the table.

"Sorry I'm late," I said in lieu of a greeting. "Some things never change, huh."

Gabby smiled tightly. "Hopefully that's true of your drink choice too. I ordered you a cosmopolitan.

"That's perfect," I replied. "Thank you." I settled into my seat then we both distracted ourselves staring at the menus for several minutes.

When the waitress returned with our cocktails, we ordered. Without our menus, Gabby and I were forced to stare at each other.

"So how are you?" I asked. "I mean, not just today, but like, how have you been the last year or so? Other than everything with Carlo."

Gabby shrugged shyly. "Good, I guess. I'm still at the same job, and it's going okay. I've had a lot of dates but no serious relation-ships. And honestly, Carlo has been doing well for the most part."

"That's good," I said. "I'm still working at the design firm. I love it. I still do a lot of shopping for décor for clients, but I also do a lot of work on the inspiration boards for the clients." I sipped my martini then told her about the project I worked on that afternoon." I would've finished it today, but Angelo called and distracted me," I said.

Gabby's eyes widened at the mention of my oldest brother. "How is Angelo doing? I, um, heard about his girlfriend."

I paused a beat, unsure of how she would've heard that. I supposed it would have been in the news, but the old Gabby never kept up with the news. "He's okay," I finally said. "He's taking some time off of dating and focusing more on work." I stopped myself before dwelling too long on the fact that some-thing at his work today had led to his best friend being shot. "He actually just bought a new house. It's a fixer-upper, so I'm going to be handling all the design aspects for him."

Gabby nodded, but her eyes conveyed her surprise at this revelation. She sipped her drink before speaking again. "Is married life everything you expected?"

Now I didn't have to work for my smile. "It's better. I really assumed things with Luca would get boring after a while, or at least that the attraction would die down a little, but that's defi-nitely not the case. Everything with him is just so much more than I ever dreamed."

Gabby quirked a brow, but nodded. "Well, that's good," she said, in a tone that made me assume she was thinking life with Luca better be good after I gave up my friend for him.

Our food came quickly, and we delved into small talk while we picked at our meals. We ordered a second round of drinks, both of us apparently realizing the conversation would flow more easily with alcohol.

"I really missed you," I admitted after a few more bites. "I hate how strained this feels too though. I miss how easy it used to be with the two of us, you know?"

Gabby nodded, but looked a tad reluctant to even admit that much.

"I have some friends at work, and I guess I'm friends with Adrian's new girlfriend, but it's just not the same. I don't think I can replace you so easily."

Now Gabriella smiled. "I missed you too."

"I thought about you a lot. Like when I'd get a manicure and they tried to sell me on those stupid, cliché designs or reverse French tips, I'd always think about what you would say."

"Me? You're the one who always insisted nails should be classic."

"Okay, but you appreciated the importance of traditional nail designs."

Gabby snort-laughed.

"Did you think about me at all over the last year and a half?"

My friend's expression softened. "Of course I did. You were always on my mind. I even had dreams about you." She rolled her eyes with that last part.

"But you never called or texted," I reminded her.

"You know I couldn't."

I didn't agree with her sentiment, but I also didn't want to dwell on the negatives. So, I kept quiet.

"I checked in on you after your accident," she said. "When you sent that letter, I thought maybe you were making it up to get me to come see you. I mean, with your husband's lifestyle, a car accident isn't the most likely way for you to go."

I debated telling her that the accident was actually related to his "lifestyle," as she put it, and decided I might as well be honest. She already thought the worst of him, so I might as well be completely open. "Luca was driving the car. He got shot, and it caused him to crash. But, fun fact, the shooter was aiming for me. Plot twist, huh!" I laughed maniacally.

Gabby's eyes widened, but she didn't comment on it.

"Wait, what do you mean checked on me? Like you came to the hospital?"

"No. I called Matteo. He said you were fine but the amnesia was real. He said Luca wouldn't let you see me anyway, not until you got your memories back."

"You stayed in touch with my brother but not me?"

"It's not like we talk often. I just happened to have his number still."

"My brother is no better than Luca. You know that, right? They're all in business together."

"Luca and your brothers?" Gabby frowned, like she wasn't completely surprised, but hadn't expected me to admit it.

I nodded. "Do you think they're terrible people, too?"

"They didn't almost get me killed."

"Neither did Luca. That was all my fault. If he'd known we were going to be there, he would have told someone, and they would've kept us safe. He works so hard to make sure I'm safe. He does the same for everyone who's important to me."

Gabby didn't have a response to that.

"Luca never had a choice. His father was the boss. He grew up in this world, and since he was a teenager, his only choice is to go along with it or be killed. Now he uses his power to help people like your brother." I paused. "And how are you okay with what Carlo did? He had a choice. He wasn't forced into this lifestyle. He chose to get involved with criminals and to gamble money that he knew he didn't have. It's his own damn fault he's in trouble now, and you have the gull to sit here and act like my husband is some monster when he's the one bailing Carlo out."

A tear squeezed out of the corner of Gabby's eye and instantly, guilt washed over me. As much as her abandonment had hurt me, I understood why she'd done it. And I didn't need to hurt her back.

"Carlo made a mistake. It was stupid, and he knows it. It's not a lifestyle for him."

"Does he go to a support group for the gambling addiction?

"He's not addicted," she said.

I rolled my eyes.

"He doesn't gamble anymore," she insisted.

I tipped the last sip of my martini into my mouth then gazed at my friend. "I truly hope you're right," I said. "He's a good man, and I don't want to see him dragged down by something silly like this. He's lucky to have you looking out for him."

Gabby mustered a smile. "Thanks."

I felt like our time was coming to an end, and I wanted to end on a good note. "Look, I know this was awkward. But if we hang out a few more times, it'll start to feel more like old times. And I really miss having a buddy for spa day."

Gabby smiled, then checked her watch. "I should head home," she said.

I nodded, surprised she'd stayed out this late. I sent a quick text to Luca to see if he was done working yet.

"Still not allowed to drive yourself?" Gabby asked, her tone less bitter than her words.

I didn't take the bait. "Few things are more miserable for me than dealing with traffic or trying to find parking in the city, so I try not to drive whenever possible." I paused, scanning Luca's quick response. He said he was almost done working and would meet me at home.

I set my phone down and gazed up at my friend. "Do you need a ride? Luca dropped me off but our friend Lincoln is coming to get me."

Gabriella shook her head. "No, I'm good. Is Lincoln, um, well, I mean, does he work for Luca?"

I considered that. "Yeah, I guess so, but not in the way you're thinking. Do you remember Alessio? Lincoln's his cousin.

Younger guy, still in school. He wanted a part-time job to pay for grad school or something."

She nodded stiffly and positioned her purse on her shoulder. "Look, I appreciate what you guys are doing for Carlo, and I'm sorry if the way things ended with us hurt you. I've always liked you, and it's not like we don't have fun together," Gabby began.

I smiled brightly, optimistic about her words.

"But you have to understand it's different for me. You're already involved in all of this and if anything happens to you, there's a whole hoard of men that will rush to your rescue. No one is looking out for me but me. So I can't get mixed up with it all again."

I gritted my teeth, but nodded. "I get what you're saying, but I'm not sure what you think could possibly go wrong if we're just hanging out. I'm not asking you to break into shipping crates at dark," I said, reminding her of the inherent stupidity of our activities the last time the evening went sour. "I just miss brunches and spa days with you."

Her expression softened, and I knew she missed those things too.

My phone buzzed, signaling Lincoln had arrived. "Just think about it, okay? La Bouche has a brand new Sunday menu if you're interested." I paused, rising to my feet. "And this time, thanks to Carlo, you're already mixed up in everything you're wanting to avoid."

Her eyes met mine, but she didn't reply to what I'd said. Instead, she thanked me for the dinner and wished me safe travels.

By the time I'd buckled myself into the passenger seat of Lincoln's car, I was feeling cautiously optimistic. A hopeful energy buzzed through me as I gazed out the window.

"Take me to the club," I said. "I'll ride home with Luca when he's done for the night."

Lincoln's hands tightened on the steering wheel. "Luca said I'd be taking you home."

"He's my home," I replied cheekily.

Lincoln didn't argue anymore, so I assumed we were heading back to the club. That would be a shorter drive, anyway. Hopefully, I could have a drink with Luca before we left. Maybe we could even dance.

"Aren't you supposed to sit in the back seat?" he asked.

"This isn't Uber. I'll sit where I want."

He shrugged. "Music?"

The radio was already playing softly, so I turned up the volume instead of answering. A moment later, I recognized the neighborhood. We were definitely heading to the club. I smiled, then reapplied my lipstick.

"How was your dinner?" he asked.

I wasn't sure how much he knew about why I'd been out, so I kept my response short. "Sorta awkward, but the food was good."

He didn't respond.

I peered around the car, frowning. "Isn't this Alessio's car?"

"Yeah. I drive a motorcycle. A Kawasaki Z400."

That piqued my interest. Lincoln pulled into the alley that led behind the club, rolling to a stop along the curb directly behind Luca's car. I climbed out and made my way towards the main parking lot on the side of the building. Before I reached the lot, I spotted a sleek green and black motorcycle parked on the sidewalk.

"This yours?" I asked, not bothering to turn to confirm he'd followed me.

"Yeah, but..." Lincoln sounded hesitant but stopped short of saying anything.

"May I?" I asked, reaching a hand towards it.

"You want to touch it?" he asked, his eyes darting side to side.

I nearly laughed at his innocence, then swung a leg over.

Luca

 was headed out when Lincoln texted to say that Giada had insisted he bring her to the club. I assumed that meant dinner went well.

"Your car is back," I said to Alessio. He followed me out the side door where we immediately spotted Lincoln and Giada. Lincoln stood on the sidewalk, visibly panicked. Giada was on his motorcycle.

"Che cazzo," Alessio mumbled, shaking his head. *What the fuck…* He started to take off in their direction, but I grabbed for his arm, fumbling it because I couldn't take my eyes off her.

Giada was straddling the large bike, her already short skirt hiked nearly to her ass, displaying her gorgeous toned thighs. The top half of her outfit had been perfectly decent was she was upright, but as she leaned forward to try to reach the handles, the flimsy material drooped lower and offered an excellent view down her cleavage. Her hair cascaded over her face and her long silver necklace shimmered between her gorgeous breasts.

I sucked in a deep breath.

"I'll handle it," Alessio offered.

"No, wait," I said. "That's…hot." I had specifically forbidden Lincoln from letting my wife on his bike, but at the time, I'd been thinking of her safety. At the moment, my thoughts were of an entirely different nature.

Alessio snickered under his breath. I peeled my eyes off Giada just long enough to glance at him and conclude that he was appreciating the sexy scene, too. Well, fine. Alessio could get away with that. Anyone else would be dead.

Lincoln seemed panicked that I'd follow through with my threats, but I didn't think he noticed yet that I was there.

"Fuck. I might have to get a bike," I said.

Alessio laughed harder, which caused Lincoln to look up. His face paled. He said something to Giada, but she clearly didn't share his sense of urgency. She gazed in my direction and the moment our eyes met, her eyebrow quirked. I could've sworn her eyes actually twinkled as she read my mind.

I approached slowly, not taking my eyes off her. Lincoln started apologizing and trying to explain, but I held up my hand to dismiss him, leaning over my wife instead.

"You are trouble," I told her.

Her eyes sparkled and her smile broadened. "It feels good," she said. "Like it just fits me."

"You look fucking hot," I whispered, letting my lip skim the edge of her ear as I spoke.

"Yeah I feel it. I could really get used to having something so big between my legs."

I burst into laughter against her cheek and then pressed a kiss to her forehead.

"Can I borrow your bike?" I asked Lincoln. "Like, just for an hour or two?"

Confusion washed over his face but he nodded.

"No," Alessio said, swatting his cousin. "Do not loan him this bike."

"Do you know how to drive it?" he asked.

"He doesn't want to drive it, dumbass," Alessio said. "Do not let him borrow it. He'll ruin it."

"I don't—" Lincoln began.

"You will never again want to sit on your bike after what he plans to do on it, Linc. I'm telling you, just say no."

Giada and I both giggled at Alessio's confidence in what we planned to do on the bike. Lincoln's expression changed slowly as he figured it out.

Giada turned to me. "They're all over Sicily," she reminded me.

I kissed her again. "You're right. We will get one there. I'm already making plans in my head."

"Long drives on the coast?" she teased.

"We'll see." I held my hand out to help her off, trying to distract myself from visions of those perfect thighs wrapped around my hips.

Lincoln began to mumble some sort of excuse, but I'd already pushed him out of my mind.

"Thanks for the ride, Linc," Giada trilled over her shoulder, copying Alessio's nickname for his cousin.

"I just need to grab my stuff then we can head out," I said, leading her back in the side entrance. "How was dinner?"

"Hard to say. Can we have a drink?"

"Here?"

She nodded.

"Okay, but no dancing," I said, fully cognizant of the fact that I couldn't say no to her. That fact became even more apparent when, less than an hour later, I stood on the corner of the dancefloor, holding Giada close to me as she swayed to the beat of the music. The press of her body against mine, the scent of her skin, and the pulse of the music thrumming through me was almost enough for me to enjoy the moment.

But it was hard to forget that my employees were all around. I couldn't fully relax in my own club the way I could somewhere else. So when the song ended, I led Giada off the dancefloor.

"We'll go to Italy at the end of the month," I promised. "We'll make love on a bike, and I'll take you dancing as much as you want."

Her eyes met mine. "I'm going to hold you to that, Mr. Marino."

"You better."

~

Adrian

*A*fter leaving Giada's, I had two whole hours to sweat about Melissa dealing with Angelo before she got off work. I'd told Angelo he should find a different doctor for Rico, but he seemed completely unconcerned with the possibility of his friend bleeding to death before Melissa finished her shift at the hospital.

Angelo had asked me to pick up Melissa and drive her straight to Rico's house, where they'd apparently stabilized the patient. I'd told him that she had her own car at work and wouldn't agree to leave it there, at which Angelo had chuckled.

"Why does it not surprise me that you can't control your current girl any more than your last one?" he'd asked.

I gritted my teeth, barely resisting the temptation to mention that I was equally unsurprised at the fact that he was still an asshole despite what happened to his last girlfriend. Giada swore he was different now, but I wasn't so sure.

I met Melissa at the main entrance to the hospital and, as I'd predicted, she insisted on driving herself. I settled for having her follow me in her own car. I'd never before been to Rico's apartment, but it was easy to find. I spotted Eddie in front, smoking a cigarette.

"Since when do you smoke?" I asked, scowling at him while I waited for Melissa to step out of her car.

"I don't, but this shit is stressful," he replied, turning his gaze to Melissa. "Dr. Adams, I presume?" he asked, his eyes roaming down her body. She'd removed the white coat, revealing fitted pants and a silky sleeveless top.

I glared at Eddie and was about a second away from growling that he should behave when Melissa smiled and extended her hand.

"Call me Melissa," she said. "Nice to meet you." Then she

wrinkled her nose. "Well, I mean, the circumstances aren't ideal, but it's always nice to meet a friend of Adrian's."

"A friend?" Eddie repeated, quirking a brow at me.

I scowled and he led the way. I wasn't sure what to expect or even how many guys would be inside, but I was surprised when we entered the dimly lit room and it was relatively quiet. The wailing I'd heard earlier was completely gone. Panic hit me as I realized we might have been too late. I'd never been too fond of Rico, but I also hadn't wanted him dead, especially not while waiting on Melissa and me to arrive.

Angelo rose from a chair near the couch and turned to face us. "Finally," he mumbled.

"Is he…" I stammered, unable to finish the sentence.

Angelo frowned, not understanding.

"Did he bleed out?" I asked.

"What? No," Angelo scowled at me before turning to Melissa. "I believe we've met briefly before, but I'm Angelo Conti."

Melissa nodded. "Yeah, you were in some sort of pissing match with Giada's husband at the hospital a while back," she said, clearly not the slightest bit fazed by the gravity of who she was talking to. "I assume this is the patient?" she asked, gesturing to the couch.

Rico was sprawled on his back on the leather couch, a few blood-soaked towels wedged under his arm and a makeshift tourniquet tied above the elbow. His eyes were open but glossy. Sweat clung to his floppy black hair, affixing it to his forehead.

"How long has he been like this?" Melissa asked, crouching by his side and checking his pulse on the wrist of his non-injured arm.

"Uhh, it was around three o'clock when Eddie shot him," Angelo began.

"Wait, Eddie shot him?" I turned from Eddie to Angelo.

Eddie looked nauseous and Angelo's jaw hardened into a line as he nodded.

I had so many follow-up questions, but Melissa interrupted.

"No, I mean his demeanor. His pulse is low, he's not alert, and his eyes are glossed over. Did you give him something? I can't tell if he's in shock, or—"

"Yes," Angelo replied calmly.

Melissa swiveled to him. "Yes, you gave him something? What and how much?"

Angelo turned to Eddie, who shrugged.

"I didn't measure. He just had a tiny hit of smack."

"Smack," Melissa repeated. "Heroin?"

Eddie nodded. I cringed, expecting Melissa to freak out. Instead, she calmly checked his pulse again, timing it with her phone.

"Has he done heroin before?" she asked.

"Probably? But not on the regular or anything," Eddie said.

"Maybe once or twice ever," Angelo said. "Rico's not usually into stuff like that."

"So why drug him now?" I asked.

"He was in a lot of pain. And he kept thrashing around when we were trying to get the bullet out."

"You took out the bullet?" Melissa asked, her eyes wide. She slipped her hands into latex gloves and began untying the bandages.

"It was near the surface," Angelo said. "We sanitized the scalpel first."

I prayed Melissa wouldn't ask why he had a scalpel on hand, and she didn't.

"I need more light," she said. "Also, for future reference, this is not how you do a tourniquet. If you truly want to stop blood flow, you'd need it much tighter."

"We didn't want him to lose his arm," Eddie said.

"Do you have the bullet?" Melissa asked.

"Yes," Angelo said, reaching for a bag on the counter. "It's intact so I wouldn't expect you to find any fragments inside."

Melissa glanced at it for only a moment before nodding. "That's good. I still need to clean out the wound though."

We all watched as she poured saline over his arm. Rico stiffened and groaned, but didn't really protest. After a minute, Melissa began poking at the wound with a giant pair of tweezers. Now, Rico thrashed to the side.

"Hold him," she said, annoyed.

Angelo nodded for Eddie to perform the task. He secured Rico's chest and arms, but left his feet free to kick. I moved over and pinned his legs to the couch.

"So how exactly did you shoot him?" I asked Eddie.

"I'd rather not get into details in mixed company," Eddie replied.

Angelo snorted. "They were screwing around. Bullet ricocheted off a tree and hit him. Ironically, it was Rico's own gun that Eddie used."

"That's not as uncommon as you'd think," Melissa chimed in without peering up from her work. "Owning a gun is the number one risk factor for getting shot. And lots of people are shot with their own gun. That's why those of us that see this crap like to encourage responsible gun ownership. Grown men should know better than to mess around with a loaded gun."

Her chiding tone made me uneasy, but Angelo nodded.

"I agree completely. I think Rico has probably learned his lesson, and I figured a fair punishment for Eddie would be letting Rico shoot him."

This apparently wasn't news to Eddie, but Melissa's head jerked up. "What? No. I'm not treating one bullet hole just so you idiots can go make another."

Angelo raised his brows then turned to me. "I see why you like her."

Melissa scowled.

"Not too many people are bold enough to call us idiots," Angelo explained.

"Well, there are other words for the behavior that caused this, but none of them are any more flattering," she said. She set down the tweezers and drenched a cotton ball with rubbing alcohol. "Hold him. This will burn."

Rico thrashed against us as she disinfected the wound.

When the area looked pristine, Melissa reached for fresh gauze, then paused to open her phone's camera. She focused the lens on the wound right as Angelo snatched the phone out of her hands.

"What are you doing?" he asked, his voice thick with annoyance.

"Taking a picture of the injury. It's easier to tell how it's healing and if an infection is developing if I have a reference of what it looked like at first. I'll have to check on him in a few days, and we can track progress with the photos." She held her hand out as if expecting Angelo to return her phone, but instead, he handed her his own phone, open to the camera. Melissa sighed but snapped the photos and then began bandaging the arm.

She pressed a palm to Rico's forehead and checked his pulse again. "Do you have any Narcan?"

Angelo nodded.

"You think he overdosed?" I asked, recognizing the drug name as the one used to revive people after an overdose.

"No," Melissa said. "And it's probably been too long since he took the drug to be very effective, but I'd just hate to have wasted an hour of my time cleaning a wound just to have him die from a drug overdose."

She rose to her feet and turned to Angelo. "You'll need to keep tabs on his heart rate for a few hours. It's okay if he sleeps, but make sure he's breathing, and call me if his pulse drops below thirty beats per minute."

Angelo nodded, then handed Melissa a roll of cash. She eyed it without counting, then shoved it in her pocket. "I should check on him in a few days."

"Sure, doc."

"And I'm serious, no more shooting. Find a different punishment for this moron," she said, gesturing to Eddie.

Eddie was visibly relieved. I started towards the door with Melissa, but Angelo stopped me.

"Thanks again, Doctor Adams. Eddie can walk you out. I need to chat with your boy toy for a minute," Angelo said.

I rolled my eyes but nodded for Melissa to leave. Then, I turned to Angelo, arms crossed. "You don't have to thank me again," I said.

Angelo snorted. "You know damn well what we need to chat about. Why didn't I know your girlfriend was open to under-the-table emergency medicine treatment?"

I shrugged. "I can't answer that for you. How would I know what you do or don't know?"

Angelo's gaze narrowed. "You never told me, Patras, and you know it."

"You never asked," I replied.

"That isn't how this relationship works."

I frowned. "Well, I didn't know that. I suppose now I do."

Angelo glared at me for another minute before relaxing. "Tell your girlfriend I said thanks." He turned and walked back to his friend.

CHAPTER 9

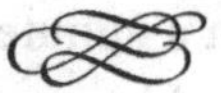

Luca

Carlo Giordano had arrived at my club at 7:55. I appreciated his punctuality and the sheepish way he'd asked the bouncer if there was a Thomas somewhere. I wondered if the kid had always lacked confidence or if that was new, thanks to his run-in with Benny.

Thomas had not been thrilled about me volunteering him to babysit a new guy just so Giada could rekindle a friendship that we'd all agreed was a bit high maintenance. But, to his credit, he agreed to do it anyway. He'd had a busy day, so he had just sauntered into my office to call Mr. Vasquez when Carlo arrived.

I sent him to bring Carlo back, and I made the call myself. Not surprisingly, the number I had for him called some minion who worked for him, but thankfully, my family name carried enough weight to get me transferred directly to Benito.

"Is this the famed Luca Marino?" he asked as he picked up the call.

"Yes, sir. Is this the famed Benito Vasquez?" I replied, stifling an eye roll.

"My friends call me Benny," he said.

Thomas poked his head around the door. I waved to Carlo then motioned for them to come in. Thomas directed Carlo to a chair then shut the door behind them.

"Well, I'd be honored to call you Benny, too, but let me get to the point first. I've been out of the office for a few days tending to a personal matter, and so it was just brought to my attention that one of my guys seems to have accrued quite the debt with you." I clicked the call over to speaker but motioned for Carlo to keep his mouth shut.

"Ahh, no. I think I'd know if that were the case."

"He's a new member of the team," I said. "Carlo Giordano? Seems he overestimated his card-playing prowess and worked up a balance."

There was a pause, and I assumed Benny was checking with one of his guys. I waited as patiently as possible.

"Ok, yeah. The kid owes me thirty-six thousand," he said. "Plus interest."

Carlo opened his mouth, but Thomas shut him up with a glare.

I chuckled amicably. "Well, the original debt was twenty-five, but I think it's up to thirty-six now with the interest. Carlo doesn't have a penny, but I feel bad that I hadn't kept closer tabs on him, so I'll make sure you get your money. My guy Thomas can swing by tonight with Carlo and get you twenty-five. We'll need a few days to cover the interest, but I'm thinking we could bring you another fifteen a week from today, and then we'd call it even. Is that amenable to you?"

I paused, but not long enough for him to answer. "And listen, I heard there may have been some… motivation, shall we say, from your guys, to try to get Carlo to pay up. I'm willing to overlook that because he is new to my team, so I understand you may not have known he was part of the Marino family. But going forward, obviously we'll need you to ensure your guys keep their hands to themselves and bring any concerns about Carlo or any other of my friends directly to me."

"Of course. I don't think anyone did anything to the kid," he mumbled.

"Well, yeah, you know how his type is. Can't keep them out of trouble," I said, still glaring at Carlo, who looked nauseous.

"And listen," I continued. "I can't believe how long we've both been in town and haven't managed to work together, but it seems like you and I should be friends. Don't you agree?"

"Uh, yeah. I think we have a lot in common."

"Absolutely. So, assuming those payoff terms are amenable to you, let me know what time I should have Thomas and Carlo swing by with the first payment."

Benny took his time answering. "Well, my concern is the interest."

"Understood, and that's why we've upped the number to forty instead of the original twenty-five. Unfortunately, I'm not willing to go higher than that, and like I said, Carlo has nothing. So you're welcome to take your chances with him, but obviously if anything bad happens to a member of the Marino family like Carlo, we'll have no choice but to respond appropriately."

Benny cleared his throat. "Sure, sure. So, I looked at my records and I think forty is just about right. We can work with that. I'll be here all evening, so they can drop off the cash whenever."

"Sounds good. And always good to chat with a new friend."

I disconnected the call before I had to endure any more bullshit.

Thomas yawned then rose from his chair. "We don't have twenty-five here. We'll have to stop and grab some from Giovanni on the way. Maybe around 11? What do you want me to do with him in the meantime?" He kicked the foot of Carlo's chair.

I considered the options. "He can stay here for now. I'd like to discuss his job prospects."

Thomas nodded and left the office, shutting the door behind him.

"What makes you think Benny will leave me alone after this?" Carlo asked.

I sighed, unaccustomed to people having so little confidence in me. "Because I'll kill him and his entire family if he doesn't." I shrugged as if it were no big deal. "My papà established a reputation for the Marino name, and I've done a decent job of upholding it. Trust me when I say people like Benito desire to be on my good side."

Carlo chewed the side of his lip.

"So, you've got a business degree and some sort of day job?"

Carlo nodded and told me about the work he did for some textbook company. Nothing about his job sounded even remotely useful to me.

"You work out though," I said, more as an observation than a question.

Carlo nodded again.

"Can you fight?"

His eyes widened.

I massaged my temples. "I'm not asking you to join some underground fight club. Just curious if you've tried boxing or anything. A lot of us go to this gym nearby. I'll get you the info, and you should join. I don't know you well enough to trust you with anything confidential, and I'm not sure what other skills you have that would be useful for me. I need night shift guards for my docks, but you'd need a concealed carry permit and a weapon for that, and those things take time." I paused. "Do you have a record?"

"Like a criminal record?"

I nodded and Carlo shook his head.

"Alright, well go ahead and start the permit process, and we'll get you hired on for that eventually. In the meantime, you can work security inside my other club. Sometimes the patrons get handsy with the dancers or the waitresses, and we don't like that. It's easy work, and you won't be on your own."

Carlo nodded. "How long will I have to work for you to pay off my debt?"

I chuckled at the notion that he'd actually pay it off. "Carlo, if you're working three nights a week for me doing some minimum wage job, it would take you years to pay off a forty thou debt. Frankly, I'm just considering this a gift, with the hopes that it helps my wife get back to her friend. If I were you though, I'd stick with it for at least a year. If you keep it up longer, I could hire you on as an official employee if you deserve it."

"I already have a job," he said.

"Yes, we've established that. But your job clearly doesn't satisfy whatever is in you that makes you want to go off gambling with thugs. Working for me should keep you out of trouble and teach you some life skills."

Carlo looked reluctant but nodded. I stood, stretching my shoulders before heading to the door.

"Let me introduce you to Marcus. He can start training you until Thomas is ready to take you to Benny."

"Okay." Carlo paused. "And thank you. My sister was really stressed about me getting myself killed."

"You're welcome."

～

Adrian

The night before, I'd invited Melissa to my place after we left Rico's, but she'd claimed she was tired. She was off the next day though, so I picked up dinner and met her once I left work. For some reason, I was annoyed before I even reached her door. I felt like I should be appreciative, that she'd handled the mess with Angelo so well. He'd called me today to say Rico was up and about and seemed back to normal, aside from his arm.

But even though Melissa had quite literally saved the day, my feelings were far from gratitude.

The second she answered the door, it was apparent Melissa felt the same. She flashed me a smile and offered her cheek for me to kiss, but her heart wasn't in it.

"How's your friend?" she asked, leading the way back to the kitchen where we spread the food out on the table.

"Rico is not my friend, but he's good. Angelo called to tell me."

She nodded. "Yeah, I'll probably go over tomorrow after work to check on him and change the bandages."

I winced. I had to be in court the next day, and I wasn't sure how early I'd get out. "I'm not sure I can go with you tomorrow. Can it wait another day?"

"Why do you need to go with me? I already know where he lives."

"Right, but I don't want you dealing with those guys alone."

Melissa rolled her eyes but said nothing.

"What does that mean?" I asked.

She dipped some food onto her plate then shrugged, clearly not planning on answering.

"Melissa, talk to me. I can tell you're thinking something."

She chewed a bite angrily, then raised her head to look at me. "Well, for starters, I think it's offensive that you seem to think I'm some poor defenseless kid that you have to protect. I'm an adult and can take care of myself. Also, I'm not sure what gave you the impression that you have any say over who I do or don't see."

"I'm not suggesting you can't take care of yourself. I just know what these guys are like, and—"

"Of course you do, Adrian," she interrupted. "You know what

they're like because you're one of them. Do you seriously not get that?"

"I am not one of them," I replied calmly.

"Look, I get that you're in denial, but let's face the facts. You do legal work for the mafia. Okay? You get that, right?"

Now it was my turn to roll my eyes. "A lot of attorneys do work for people accused of organized crime involvement. It's a legal minefield."

Melissa snorted. "You also do personal favors for these mobsters. You act like you're so high and mighty, but the truth of the matter is that you got involved because you needed the money." She paused. "You and I aren't that different, Adrian. We're both highly educated people who went into specialized fields because we wanted to help people and make a difference. But both of us realized school is fucking expensive and we can't just go through life playing by the rules if we want to pay our bills."

I said nothing. She wasn't wrong.

"The problem is that you are a hypocrite. You seem to think your involvement is okay, but that I'm just making bad decisions by doing the same thing," Melissa said.

"I'm only trying to protect you. If I'd known what I know now years ago, I wouldn't have gotten involved."

"Okay, that's fair. But I'm not going into it blind. I'm not naïve and that seems to be the problem for you. You want some gullible damsel-in-distress type. You don't want the woman who has seen firsthand the damage these guys can inflict and still makes house calls. I'm perfectly aware of the risks, and I accept that. I can live with it." She paused. "But you can't."

I shoved a bite of food into my mouth to buy time to reply, but I wasn't hungry. My appetite had gone and the food just hardened on my tongue. Melissa was right. I hated the fear and guilt and anxiety that came with her involvement with the Marinos. For her to be involved with the Contis now too amplified everything by a thousand. I could handle the stress of my own involvement, but throwing her into the mix made it unbearable.

On top of all that, I wasn't sure I'd ever stop resenting her for being okay with making me worry. If she were truly the woman for me, she'd consider my needs. My feelings would matter to her.

I tried to think of something else, some positive memory with Melissa. But I came up blank. Our relationship had been easy and relatively uneventful because we were the same fucking person. And I didn't want to end up with myself. I wasn't even sure I could see a future with Melissa.

"So you're saying you want to keep working for the Contis and Marinos?" I finally asked.

Melissa shrugged. "Not like full time. But yes, I plan to keep answering when they call. With those cash payments I can plan for the future of my dreams."

"Does that future involve me?"

Her jaw clenched. "I think that's up to you. Are you going to give me some sort of ultimatum?"

"No," I said. What would be the point, anyway? She'd made her thoughts clear. I pushed back from the table. "I'm sorry. I need some time to think."

Melissa followed me to the door, where we both paused. She gazed up at me like she expected me to say something else, but instead I just kissed her.

Something told me that might be the last time.

CHAPTER 10

Luca

Thanks to my papà's extended trip to Italy, I'd grown accustomed to being the only Marino on U.S. soil. I suspected there was a strong correlation between the length of his absences and my blood pressure, with the latter dropping a few points with each additional week of his residence in Italy.

As with all good things though, my papà's absence, too, came to an end. He summoned me to my own club the day after his flight, apparently deciding my new desk chair was the most comfortable place for him to work while he remained in town.

We ate sandwiches from the bar while we caught up, then he shut the door to discuss business updates. I went first, skimming over the past month quickly. As far as I was concerned, business had been good. Things had been calm on all fronts, aside from everything with Julia. But even that was now fully resolved.

My papà had been vague about his business dealings while he'd been back in Italy, but that hadn't roused any suspicion on my part. That's how the dynamic between us always went. He stuck his nose into every detail of my life—both personal and professional. But when it came to his own business dealings—he kept me on a scant need-to-know basis. For some reason, I was okay with that.

He droned on about some of his specific recent undertakings, and I started to zone out, wondering what Giada was up to and what she'd be wearing—or not wearing—when I came home. She'd been extra affectionate since her memories returned, and I was not complaining.

I snapped out of my daydream the moment my papà casually announced he'd brought on more new men.

"What?" I asked.

He shrugged casually, as if it wasn't a big deal. "We're expanding our business practices, Luca. I can't cover everything here and in Italy with a barebones team."

"You don't have to. You have me, and my guys. We're covering things here."

"Not everything," Papà insisted.

He wasn't wrong, but it was a mere technicality. A nuance, really. I could handle all of our business dealings in the tri-state area. The only reason papà and his guys were still involved was because my papà was a control freak who didn't trust me and prided himself on dipping his hand into everything bearing the family name.

"I thought you were going to start pulling back some. Mom thinks you're wrapping things up for retirement."

My papà snorted. "You know men like us don't retire."

"Sure, but you can at least slow down. Focus on the projects you actually enjoy. Spend more time traveling and relaxing. Give Mom some attention before she goes crazy."

"Too late," he joked.

I remained silent while my papà sipped his soda, then he gazed up at me again.

"That's why I brought on more men, so I can do less. We're on the same page, you and I."

As he gestured back and forth between us, I couldn't help but think we weren't just not on the same page; we weren't even reading the same book.

"They've already taken the oath, and they'll be here soon to meet you," he continued.

"What?" my voice came out like a roar, and I rose to my feet so quickly that my chair clattered backwards.

"Calm down, Luca," my papà said with an eye roll.

"Calm down? Do you hear yourself? You brought in new men, without telling me, without even letting me vet them."

"I'm telling you now. And you seem to forget how this works. When they swear loyalty to me, they swear it to you, too. My men are your men."

Now it was my turn to roll my eyes, but I was smart enough to turn my back before doing it. I may be pushing thirty but I didn't doubt my papà would still punish me for disrespect if I gave him reason.

I took a calming breath, then turned back to face him. "Fine. But you can't expect me to trust men I don't know. I don't want them involved in any of my business dealings. I don't want them knowing anything damning about me or my crew. Can we at least agree on that?"

My papà shook his head, but mumbled a placating "sure."

I sighed, then settled back into my chair.

"They're here now and want to meet you," he told me.

Of course they were. "Fine. Let's get this over with." I stood, opened the office door, then peered down the hallway. I saw no one, aside from Maximo and Daniele, my papà's personal guards.

My papà patted me on the shoulder. "Let's go have a drink with them. Keep this social." He led me down the hallway to the main area of the club. This early in the afternoon, the floor was nearly dead, but since we were technically open for business, at least I knew no business would be discussed.

"Keep an open mind," Papà said under his breath as we

approached two eager-looking men. They both appeared to be in their thirties, which made them old for new recruits. Usually, we vetted guys for years before letting them into the inner circle, but I supposed this new version of my papà couldn't be bothered with such traditions.

"So good to meet you," the taller of the two men said, extending a hand. "I'm Elio."

I shook his hand, appreciating that he at least had a firm shake. Then I turned to the next guy.

"Matt," he said with a broad smile like we were on a first date.

"Matt?" I repeated, certain my papà would have to have suffered a stroke before making a man with an American name.

"Mattia," Papà said, patting the guy on the back.

"Do you have last names?"

"Puglisi," Matt said, pointing to himself. Then he gestured at Elio. "And he's a Randazzo."

The way he said it made me wonder if I should recognize the name. Both were incredibly common Italian names, more so in Sicily. But I didn't notice any significance from either.

"Are you guys cousins or something? I asked, noting they both had dark brown, curly hair, broad noses, and brown eyes shaded by thick lids. Both men were bigger guys, tall and with a decent amount of muscle, but Mattia probably had an extra fifteen pounds of fat on Elio.

They both chuckled like I'd told a hilarious joke.

My papà nodded for us to sit at a table, then he made his way to the bar.

"No relation. We met on a job at a transport company a couple years back," Elio said.

"What company?" I asked. Elio offered a few more details, and I followed up with more questions. Elio did most of the speaking, but I noticed he never gave more info than I demanded. He was casual about it, but he was definitely holding something back.

My papà approached the table with Cassidy close on his heel

with a tray of drinks. She set the drinks in front of each of us, and I thanked her with a polite smile before turning to my papà.

"I need to make a call, so you three can get to know each other and I'll join you in a bit."

Relieved, I turned my attention back to the guys. Without papà around, I could interrogate in peace. I focused my questions on Mattia for a minute, then switched back to Elio. Between the two of them, Elio was the one who made my skin prickle with suspicion. I didn't have good feelings about him, and my instincts were usually right.

I didn't tell them much about myself, at least nothing one couldn't learn from a quick internet search, and then Alessio joined me to double up on them. I introduced him as my best friend from high school, but I didn't doubt both of them knew exactly who he was.

Alessio jumped in for a good half an hour, and then my papà returned from his mystery "phone call" and declared he was headed home for the day. I promised to stop by the next day to catch up with Mom. Then I left with Alessio.

"I don't trust him," I said the moment we were alone.

"Elio?" Alessio confirmed, reading my mind exactly.

I nodded.

"Me neither. His story was too rehearsed. I'll look into it."

"Thanks."

~

Adrian

The next two weeks were miserable, so when I got a call from the prosecutor's office asking me and Angelo to come by, I didn't expect anything good. I even tried to recruit my boss, Mr. Russo, to tag along or send another partner. I was that sure they were about to tell us they'd come up with some wonky charges for Angelo. Mr. Russo reminded me that the prosecutor wouldn't have been so informal about the request if they planned on charging Angelo, and he insisted I could handle it solo.

I was still shocked when the prosecutor said the words out loud. "We wanted to let you know that we have decided not to press charges for the death of Julia Carbone."

Angelo frowned and turned to me.

"Is that final? You won't change your minds?" I asked.

The man shrugged. "As you know, there is no statute of limitations for murder. However, the police have officially closed their investigation on this matter, so we don't anticipate any new evidence rolling in that undermines our decision. And without new, compelling evidence, we have nothing to base new charges on."

I suspected this was the sort of thing they'd bring up down the road in a trial if Angelo were ever accused of something else, but for now, this was as good of news as we could hope for.

Angelo sauntered out of the city building looking lighter for the first time in weeks. I, on the other hand, still felt like shit.

"Come on. I'll buy you a drink. Just the two of us," he offered.

Normally, nothing about that proposal would appeal to me, but at the moment, it didn't sound so bad. Apparently, I'd hit a low point in my life.

We walked to the nearest bar and, even though the place was mostly empty, we went to a table in the corner. Angelo draped his suit jacket over a chair then gazed at me. "What do you want?"

I considered my usual order in light of the time of day. "Get me an IPA," I said.

I checked my phone while Angelo sidled up to the bar to order. Not unsurprising, my only emails and texts pertained to work. I texted Mr. Russo the good news and said Angelo insisted on taking me to lunch, which I figured sounded better than admitting I was drinking in the middle of the workday, and he told me to take the rest of the day off and keep the Contis happy.

I sighed and set my phone face down on the table as Angelo returned.

"Thanks for securing my freedom," Angelo said cheekily, clanking his glass against mine before downing a large swig.

"Do you feel relieved now that it's finally over?" I asked.

Angelo appeared to consider the question. "Hard to say. I like to stay busy, so prison would've been torture. But some external punishment might have helped with my guilt complex."

The honesty of his response caught me off guard. I fidgeted with my beer instead of answering, positioning my glass over the small napkin.

"So, how about you? I assume your recent crankiness is because of what happened with Melissa. Honestly, I sort of expected you to be living it up."

"What?"

"She told me you dumped her. I figured you did it so you could go play the field but instead you've been all mopey."

"Well, I don't want to play the field just yet. I actually liked Melissa. A lot. I thought we'd end up together."

Angelo winced. "Yeah, I don't see how that would have worked."

"Why not?"

He shrugged. "You're both too focused on your work. And you're both know-it-alls and so stubborn. You're too similar to be together long-term."

I blew out a breath. His observations sounded similar to what Melissa had said, yet it was oddly more annoying coming from Angelo. "Well, that's not how I viewed it. And I didn't exactly dump her. It was mostly mutual."

"Not what she said."

"She told you what happened?"

He shook his head. "Not really. I figured you were pissed about her helping Rico. I'm not sure why, honestly, since she already does that shit for the Marinos. And after everything she did for my sister, she's already got lifetime protection from my family."

"She said I didn't trust her or treat her like an adult or something. She thought I was too protective."

Angelo nodded as if he agreed. "Be honest though, wouldn't you have preferred she need that? You strike me as the type that needs to be the hero. Like, you can't handle a true equal. You want a girl who needs you to save her."

I groaned and took a long swig of my ale. That definitely sounded like something Melissa had said. What were her exact words? That I'd wanted her to be a damsel in distress? *Ridiculous.*

We hadn't actually broken up that night. I'd gone home to think, then we'd talked the next day. We resolved nothing, and then the day after that, we met up for coffee and I told her I didn't think it would work. She'd agreed, and she wished me the best. It was a depressingly calm breakup given how long we'd been seeing each other.

I shook my head to clear my thoughts. "Everyone always tells me I'm too nice. Is that my problem? Is there some truth to that stupid saying, nice guys finish last?"

Angelo cracked a smile but shrugged. "I don't know. No one would ever accuse me of being too nice, yet here I am too."

He had a point, but our situations still struck me as different. I tried to explain. "It's just a pattern for me. Like, every time I get involved, I throw everything into the relationship, and then it all blows up in my face. I'm so ready for the rest of my life, and then I get chucked back to square one. I just have the worst luck when it comes to relationships."

I gazed up from my beer and noticed Angelo staring at me with a peculiar expression on his face. I realized how my words must have sounded, especially given what he'd just been through, and I paled. "Shit man, I'm sorry. I didn't—"

"No, no. Go on. Tell me how you are the least lucky in love," Angelo taunted.

I sighed, fully aware that I was the asshole for once. Angelo obviously had it worse. Except, well, I wasn't even sure he'd really loved Julia. She always struck me as more of a pet to him, a pretty thing he kept on his arm but which could be replaced at a moment's notice.

"I'm sorry," I finally repeated. "If I'm being honest, I have no clue how you're feeling. You never really share that sort of thing with me or, as far as I can tell, anyone. I don't know anything about your feelings for Julia or what you'd planned for the future."

"I would've married her," he said with nary a pause.

That admission wasn't surprising to me, but the way he said it seemed significant. Not that he wanted to marry her or couldn't wait to do so, but that he would have. Like, it was just something that he'd do next.

"The thing is," Angelo continued. "I'm picky when it comes to who I'll actually date. I mean, I'll sleep with anyone, but—"

The waitress's arrival at our table cut off Angelo mid-sentence. She blushed, clearly having heard his words, then stammered while asking if we wanted another round. Angelo told her we would and repeated our orders. She smiled shyly at him then scurried off.

I cringed, trying to understand why women had that reaction to him. Yeah, I could see that the guy was attractive in a boring, traditional sort of way, and I supposed he had that whole alpha-male thing rolling off him in waves. But could women really not see past the cocky exterior?

"Well, anyway," Angelo continued. "Sex is one thing, but I don't date just anyone. It's hard in my line of work to make any relationship feasible, so I have to find someone that won't ask too many questions and will stay out of it."

"And Julia fit that bill?"

"I thought so, but apparently not."

The waitress returned with our drinks, beaming so brightly at

Angelo that she sloshed mine over the side as she set it down. I wiped up the spill with the napkin while Angelo flashed her that pervy grin of his and said, "Thank you sweetheart."

As she walked away, Angelo gazed at the napkin beneath his drink. "Bethany," he read aloud, smiling at the phone number. He gazed at the waitress, still watching from across the room, then winked and wedged the napkin into his pocket.

"Gag," I said.

He chuckled. "I used to be jealous of my sister."

"Because you secretly love Luca?" I teased.

"No, because they can just be with each other without all the secrets. She's already in this world, and as naïve and oblivious as she was, he doesn't have to constantly worry about dragging her down. But for me? Anyone I get involved with is at risk, just because of me and who I am."

Angelo paused and we both sipped our drinks. "I can't get too attached to anyone because my lifestyle might put them in jeopardy, and then I'll feel even shittier."

I sighed. "Sorry man. I get what you're saying, but I don't have an answer for you." I gazed over at the waitress, still eyeing us. "You could probably bang the waitress in the bathroom if you need a pick-me-up though."

Angelo considered this suggestion for far too long for my comfort.

"I should get back to the office. Russo told me I could take the rest of the day off, but I need to finish up a few things. Thank you for the drinks, and congrats on your freedom," I said.

Angelo nodded, and I left the bar.

CHAPTER 11

Luca

Marco summoned us back to the house for yet another celebration the next week. This time, we were toasting to the official dismissal of all charges against Angelo. Marco had invited all of my guys too, which seemed odd. Giovanni and Roberto were busy, but Thomas and Alessio came, with Alessio's cousin Linc in tow.

"Do you have a minute to talk shop?" Alessio asked, handing me another glass of whiskey.

"For you? Always," I said. "But not here." I'd had enough alcohol to feel happy and pleasantly buzzed. All of my nerves that had been on fire as I'd walked into enemy territory hours before now had relaxed. But I still wasn't about to discuss confidential matters pertaining to my business in a room filled with employees of a man who still hated me about fifty percent of the time. Sure, Angelo and I could work together when we needed to, but at the end of the day, there wasn't a doubt in my mind that he'd sell me down the river if he thought he'd get away with it.

"Actually, I think this is the perfect venue for this conversation," Alessio said. He turned, caught Lorenzo's eye, and nodded.

I watched as Lorenzo whispered something to the guy beside him then approached us.

He smiled warmly at me, and I returned the gesture. It was odd how far we'd come, Lorenzo and me. Five years ago, I would've killed him if I had the chance, but now, I didn't mind him so much. Maybe it was that I was married now, or that he seemed genuinely interested in his own girlfriend, or perhaps I'd just matured. Whatever it was, I actually trusted the man. And that was huge.

"I heard Gabby reached out," he said, casting a glance to the table where Giada and her aunt sat gushing over the cake.

"Yeah," I said. "I hope they can patch things up." And I meant it. Giada needed more friends, but they needed to be women I could trust, or at least control via their husbands or boyfriends. I was not eager to experience another Gabriella-type incident, but now that her brother was entrenched in my work, maybe things would be different.

"How is everything going with your girlfriend? Does Marco like her?" I asked him.

Lorenzo winced. "She's good, but they haven't really met."

"Oh," I said, filing that detail away for later.

"So...can we talk business now?" Alessio asked, raising his eyebrows.

I frowned, which prompted Lorenzo to chuckle.

"Luca, Enzo, and I both wanted to discuss something with you, and we thought you'd absorb it better coming from both of us."

"Absorb?" I clenched my abs, reaching for my drink so at least I'd have something to occupy my hands.

Alessio brushed off the question. "We all want Giada to stay safe and for you to not be distracted by worries about her safety. And we both agree with you that she shouldn't be driving herself all the time. Maybe on occasion or for short trips, sure. But given your position and your business and her family's business, it makes sense for her to have someone with her keeping an eye on her most of the time."

I tipped my drink back into my mouth, letting the smooth liquid roll over my tongue. Maybe I was already a tad drunk, because nothing Alessio was saying made any sense. Giada had always been in a precarious position because of me and her father. She'd be the perfect target for my enemies or Marco's.

"Is there some new threat against Giada? Something specific?" I asked, trying to understand.

"No, but…"

"She still calls me for a ride sometimes," Lorenzo butted in. "And Marco doesn't generally mind, but it's still…"

"Not appropriate," Alessio finished for him.

I swirled the ice around in my glass, nodding. I was well aware that my wife's preferred driver was technically loyal to her father, not me. He was also on her father's payroll, not mine. Neither fact was an issue per se, as her father thankfully valued her safety nearly as much as I did. But it was a tad nontraditional.

"And it doesn't make sense for me to drive her," Alessio continued.

I agreed with that. While I trusted Alessio with my wife more than anyone else, he had more important things to do as my second in command. "There's Thomas or Giovanni, or even Roberto," I reminded him. I cringed a little saying Roberto aloud. He was the newest addition to my innermost circle, and my trust was not quite fully developed with him yet. I'd let him transport my money, my personal weapons, even my mother. But my Giada…that was a different question.

"Luca, you know they're too busy for that. They have better things to do with their time, and you need to let them do the jobs you brought them on to do. And look at you. You don't even trust them fully." Alessio turned to Lorenzo. "Did you see that face he made?"

Lorenzo nodded.

"It doesn't matter anyway. Giada is picky. She won't ride with just anyone. Not Roberto. Maybe not even Thomas or Giovanni."

"We thought of a better person," Alessio said.

I raised an eyebrow, growing impatient.

"Someone very similar to me, who you can count on just the same," Alessio continued, clearly not picking up on my growing annoyance.

"And I asked Giada about it, and she confirmed she'd be fine with him driving her," Lorenzo chimed in.

"Who?" I said dryly. I knew even before Alessio spoke that I'd reject the name, based solely off of his brief wince.

"Linc!"

"No," I replied. I tossed the last swig of my drink into my throat and swiveled away. "End of discussion. I'm going to go dance with my wife now."

Alessio jumped in front of me. "No, we're not done talking. You're a smart man, and you don't put off things like this, so I don't know why you're being so weird about this. If not Linc, you need to pick someone else."

"Luca, think about it," Lorenzo chimed in. "He's smart, educated, and loyal. He knows the area, and he's a good kid. And the fact that Giada is comfortable with him goes a long way."

It did, really, but that wasn't enough. "He doesn't even have a car."

Alessio rolled his eyes, not even deigning to acknowledge that concern. "You know Lincoln is loyal, Luca, and he wants to do more. We both know I'm the reason you're not letting him get more involved, and this is a good way around that."

"You are forgetting a significant fact," I retorted through gritted teeth. "You say I can trust him, but he's not even..." I cut myself off and scowled at Lorenzo. He surely knew that Lincoln wasn't yet a made man, so to speak, but I wasn't about to confirm that fact in front of someone who didn't work for me.

"You can fix that real fast, Luca. Or not. He's not going to have confidential information, just your wife."

I shook my head. "There's no 'just' when it comes to Giada. She's everything."

"Luca, I know. I'm not saying he's ready now. We will train him. I will. And then, we'll test him."

"Test him? How?"

Now it was Lorenzo who spoke up. "He doesn't know me. Tell me when you think he's ready, and then we'll set him up."

I blew out a sigh. I couldn't believe they'd been discussing this behind my back long enough to develop some sort of complete scheme. I didn't have time to think of another problem with their plan before I felt a warm hand press against the small of my back.

I turned to Giada, swallowing my annoyance with Alessio and Lorenzo and attempting to force a smile back onto my face.

"You look tense," she said to me before turning to Lorenzo and Alessio. "Stop stressing him out. This is a party."

Giada dragged me off to the dance floor before I could say another word.

~

Giada

The day after the party, I met Angelo at his new house to show him the samples I'd selected for his kitchen. He'd chosen a darker hardwood floor to run throughout the entire house, including the kitchen. So, his only decisions for today were countertops, cabinets, and backsplash...which, as he was currently discovering, was actually kind of a lot.

Angelo squeezed his eyes shut, almost as if pained. "Can't you just decide?"

"No. I narrowed everything down already. The whole fun in remodeling is to pick what you want in your house."

"Those counters all look the same."

I rolled my eyes. They looked nothing alike. They weren't even all the same material. I'd brought him two quartz options, one marble, and four granite.

Angelo blew a breath out of his nose. His teeth were gritted and something about the way he seemed to be concentrating on breathing reminded me of a woman in labor.

"Are you okay?" I asked.

He grimaced again. "Just a little heartburn."

I watched as my brother retrieved a handful of tablets from his pocket and tossed them into his mouth. "Maybe you should see a doctor," I suggested.

He ignored my tip. "What's the difference between the counters again?"

I explained, for the third time, the variations in durability and maintenance.

"Granite," Angelo said between gritted teeth.

"Great," I said, keeping my tone cheerful. Progress was good.

"And I hate the white cabinets."

I plastered a smile on my face even though his words crushed my soul just a little. "Okay, well, these darker cabinets coordinate well with the floors, but you don't want the room to be too dark."

"I like dark."

"What about putting these cabinets up top and using the light gray cabinets for the bottom? Or keeping the uppers all open with glass shelves and doors."

"Veto." Angelo said.

He sunk onto a folding chair we'd set up, rubbing his hand over his chest.

I gazed at all the samples. "Okay, so we'll do these dark cabinets for both uppers and lowers," I began, waiting a moment till he glanced up. "Then combine it with this subway tile backsplash, and these counters. Do you like that?" I held up the options together. The counters were a pale creamy beige with specs of black and the backsplash was off-white, so the final look would be balanced and warm, not dark.

Angelo stared at the options, then nodded. "Yeah. That's good."

"Perfect. I'll get these ordered, and then next week we'll need to finalize the options for the bathroom."

"What do I have to pick for there?"

"Well, you don't want hardwood in the bathroom, so we'll need a tile flooring, and then a tile surround for the shower. And cabinets and counters for the vanity." I stopped talking before mentioning that we'd also need mirrors, light fixtures, faucets, towel rods, and pretty much everything else.

Angelo already looked a bit pale. I didn't want to push him over the edge when this was all supposed to be fun. Although, maybe he really wasn't feeling well.

"How long has the heartburn been bothering you?" I asked. I was no expert, but it didn't seem like the sort of thing that should be this uncomfortable. Or last so long.

He shrugged. "Couple weeks now. Maybe longer."

"And it's always this bad?"

"No," he admitted. He rubbed his chest again and I pulled out my phone, googling the symptoms.

A moment later, I gasped. "I'm calling the paramedics. You're clearly having a heart attack."

"No!" Angelo barked. "I swear to God Giada if you call 911…" He lunged for my phone but groaned and clutched his midsection in pain.

Thinking fast, I dialed Melissa instead. By some miracle, she answered.

"It's Giada," I said. "I'm with Angelo and I think he's having a heart attack."

"Call 911," she replied without hesitation.

I stared pointedly at my brother.

"It's heartburn!" he shouted back.

"He's refusing," I said. "Can you convince him to go to the hospital?" I handed the phone to my brother, who answered a few yes or no questions and then disconnected.

"She's coming over," he said.

I texted her the address, then turned back to my brother.

"I don't think you should have called her," he said.

"I'd rather you go to the hospital."

"No, I mean, she's not with Adrian anymore."

"She's not? They broke up?"

"Yeah. He said it was mutual. She said he dumped her."

"Oh." I hadn't known that. The news shouldn't have bothered me, but for some reason, it did. "Do you think they'll get back together?"

Angelo shrugged. "Probably not."

"Are they both…okay?"

My brother grunted again and hunched over.

I sighed. "Mom will kill me if I let you keel over in the kitchen. Why are you being so stubborn? Can we just go to the hospital?"

"No." His words came out like a squeak. "If I die, I die. Mom will get over it. No one else will care."

I winced. Maybe this was just Angelo's usual blasé attitude, but maybe it wasn't. His life had been total shit lately. I wasn't accustomed to feeling sorry for him, but he also hadn't ever before been much of a sympathetic character.

"I'd care," I finally said.

"You hate me."

"Oh come on. We're siblings. We're supposed to hate each other until we grow up, and then we're besties till death." I cringed at my own words. "And that death shouldn't be for a while."

A knock at the door saved him from needing to reply. I

dashed over to let Melissa in, waiting until she focused all of her attention on my brother before staring at her. She didn't look devastated over the breakup, but then again I wasn't sure how off she could look. Surely doctors couldn't just let themselves go to shit like the rest of us when they were sad.

Melissa had already listened to Angelo's heart by the time I snapped out of my own thoughts.

"Do you have high blood pressure?"

"Of course I do. You know what my life is like."

Melissa cocked her head to the side, seemingly considering this tidbit. After a moment, she sighed. "You really should own a blood pressure cuff if you know you have high blood pressure."

"If it's my time to go, fine."

She rolled her eyes. "Sure, except blood pressure won't necessarily kill you. Maybe you'll have a stroke that'll leave you unable to walk. Or feed yourself. Or unable to talk. Would you enjoy that?"

My brother grunted in response.

"Show me where it hurts," she said.

Angelo cringed and waved his hand around his entire midsection. Melissa knelt beside him and began pressing on seemingly random sections of his abdomen. When she pushed down right above his belly button, Angelo roared.

"So, guessing it's a bit tender there?" she asked.

He nodded, scowling.

"How long have you had this pain?"

"It comes and goes. Like I told my sister, it's just heartburn."

"How's your appetite been?"

"Not great. Not sure if you realize this, but my life has been shit lately."

Melissa rose to her feet and turned to me. "I don't think it's a heart attack, but if it were me, I'd still go to the hospital to find out." She swiveled to Angelo. "If I had to guess, I'd say you have an ulcer. Stress, drinking too much alcohol, poor diet, lack of sleep, and too many pain meds can exacerbate it. It could be caused by something like bacteria though, so you should go to the doctor. Your pain won't get better until it's treated."

"How will they treat it?" Angelo asked.

"Well, first they'd probably run some bloodwork and do an endoscopy to confirm the diagnosis, then they'd give you meds depending on what caused the ulcer."

"Can't you just give me the meds?"

"No. I'm not a GI doc. I can drive you to the ER, or I can help you get an appointment for an endoscopy though."

"Let's just do the ER. Can't they do the test there?" I asked.

Melissa's lips parted, but Angelo spoke first. "No ER. Make an appointment for tomorrow."

"I'm not sure if anyone can see you tomorrow, but—" Melissa began. She stopped abruptly when she saw the death glare my brother shot her.

Angelo finally blinked, then tossed another handful of antacids into his mouth.

"He's had like ten of those just since we called you," I said.

My brother's glare shifted to me.

"Can you get him home to rest? He'll feel better laying down. I'll try to find someone to get him in tomorrow," Melissa said.

I started to thank her, when a noise at the door caused all of us to jerk to attention. A moment later, Mom fluttered around the corner. She scowled at the unfinished room, chucked her purse on a ladder, then rushed to her oldest son.

"You called Mom?" Angelo asked, his eyes dripping with accusation.

I shrugged. I wasn't about to let him die on my watch. And it had been a text, not a call.

I nodded for Melissa to follow me to the door while Mom fussed over Angelo.

"Thanks so much for coming over. He's so stubborn. I wasn't sure who else to call."

Melissa smiled. "It's fine. Today is my day off and I had nothing else to do, so…"

"I, um, heard about you and Adrian," I said, hoping it wasn't bad for me to comment on it.

"He told you?" she asked.

"Yes. Well, no. I mean, Angelo told me, not Adrian."

"Oh." Melissa seemed relieved by this answer.

"Any chance you'll get back together?"

She cringed, but I wasn't sure if it was because of the question or the fact that I was asking it. "We're not really compatible," she finally said.

"If you want me to talk to him, I could. Adrian is a really good guy, so—"

"He is," she agreed. "But we're looking for different things. It sucks, but I think this is best in the long run."

I stared at her a moment longer, wishing I could explain it all to her, make her understand that still I felt awful about how I'd treated Adrian. At least when he was happily coupled with Melissa, my guilt was absolved. But now? I had nothing to make me feel better about the knowledge that Adrian was all alone.

I didn't say anything though, because it wasn't her job to make me feel better. And she was right. Ending a relationship was the best option if it wasn't right.

"Well, I'm here if you need to talk to anyone," I finally said.

"Thanks," she mumbled, letting herself out.

I returned to the kitchen in time to see my mom helping Angelo to his feet.

"It isn't your sister's job to take care of you, you know?" she was saying. "If you were married by now—"

"Mom!" I snapped.

Angelo's eyes flitted to me, his expression grateful.

"It's been a matter of weeks. He doesn't need to move on yet if he's not ready. He certainly doesn't need to get married."

"He'll never be ready if we follow his timetable," she said

before turning back to my brother. "Men like you need a partner you can trust. You're not going to be less stressed out if you keep living this way and treating all your feelings with alcohol and parties. You need stability."

"Are you good to drive yourself home Angelo, or do you want me to drive your car?" I interrupted.

"I can drive," he said. He did look a bit better, actually. His color was back to normal, and he was standing unassisted. Probably the best thing I could do for him now would be to get Mom off his case.

"Mom can you drop me off at home?"

She hesitated, glancing at Angelo again before agreeing.

~

Luca

Giada was home late that night, thanks to some medical issue with Angelo. The timing worked well though since I'd had a busy day. Alessio and I had split up to tackle all of the drama that had arisen, so we weren't able to touch base until that night. We'd ordered food and met up at my place to discuss everything.

"I've looked into Elio and Mattia. So far, they're clean. But it's weird," Alessio said, spearing a noodle on his fork. Somehow, he'd gotten me hooked on this new ramen restaurant. He'd brought over enough food for an army tonight, and even grabbed a few meat versions for Giada and me.

"Weird how?" I asked, suppressing a moan as I chewed a bite. I could see all of the different ingredients separate in the bowl, yet somehow all the flavors melded perfectly.

"It's like they're too clean. They have history, but it feels too neat to be real."

"So you're thinking they're undercover agents?"

Alessio wrinkled his nose. "Honestly, no. I think that would feel sloppier. This almost seems like some sort of infiltration by a rival."

"A rival," I repeated. "Well, who hates my papà?" I asked.

We both chuckled. Everyone hated my papà.

"I know I need to come up with more before we talk to him again, but let's just keep our distance in the meantime."

I nodded, shoving another oversized bite into my mouth.

"How's it going with Gabby?"

I chewed and wiped my mouth on a paper napkin before answering. "She and Giada went to brunch and got their nails done, so I think that's a good sign. Giada said the conversation is still a bit stilted, but they're making progress. And she's been so busy trying to fix Angelo's entire life by remodeling his house that I think she's being less pushy with Gabby than she otherwise would."

"Well, that's good, right? I mean, you're comfortable with her spending so much time with Angelo?"

I considered the question for a full minute before answering. "I am, actually. Not just because he saved her, but he seems to be a different person. Like, he no longer feels threatened by her, or us, anymore."

"Giada told me she thinks he's depressed."

I shrugged. That wasn't surprising, given his life circumstances.

"And Carlo?" Alessio asked.

"We got his debt paid off, and so far he's showed up for work and done what I've asked. We haven't given him a lot of responsibility yet, but he might actually prove useful someday. I think he's more cut out for this work than his sister would like to admit."

"You aren't worried about his shitty judgment?"

"He's a crappy card player, that's all. Maybe a tad too cocky for his own good, but this whole experience knocked him down a few pegs. I'll keep watching him for a few weeks, but I think his head's on straight now."

Alessio nodded and reached for another carton of food.

"Anything else I'm out of the loop on?" I asked, seeing on my phone that Giada had just entered the building.

My friend considered the question before shaking his head. "No, I think that's all. Oh, I set up a meeting for you with Jerrod Kelso next week. Thought you could see about getting some of his shipping contracts."

I hesitated. The name sounded familiar, but I was so exhausted at the moment that I couldn't recall why I'd wanted to get in business with the guy.

Alessio read my expression and chuckled. "I'll catch you up before the meeting. You've got a few days still."

"Thanks," I mumbled, turning my attention to the door just as my beautiful wife walked in.

CHAPTER 12

Giada

The next week was a blur. Determined not to dwell on any possible subtext behind Adrian and Melissa's breakup, I'd thrown myself into the design project for Angelo. He needed the distraction just as much as I did, frankly. It turned out he did have a stomach ulcer. According to my mom, he'd been a total baby about the test to diagnose the ulcer, but as far as I could tell, Angelo was at least attempting to follow the treatment plan.

In my efforts to distract my brother from his discomfort, I'd persuaded him to finalize the decisions on all major aspects of the project. All counters, flooring, cabinets, and fixtures had been ordered. Angelo was hiring his usual construction guys for the install, and I was unclear on how much of the décor he'd let me play a part in. I hoped he'd at least let me guide him towards the best window treatments, paint colors, and area rugs, if not select all the accents.

In the meantime, I'd decided on a special project for Angelo. The idea had come to me only a few days prior, when I overheard my mom reminding Angelo that the doctor said he should sit down and relax to eat his meals rather than wolfing junk on the go. I'd been wanting to arrange some extra touch for the house, something to surprise him with, and now I had the perfect idea. I found a local woodworker and commissioned him to make a custom dining table for Angelo's new house. Hopefully, the new dining table would be the centerpiece for the new home, and could usher in a new, happier era for my brother.

The craftsman's workshop was way across town, and his first available appointment was on the one day that Lincoln was not available to drive me. I'd debated asking Enzo, but Luca had only recently made a big deal out of how I was supposed to stop hitting him up for favors. I didn't want to wait another week to check out the guy's work, and I definitely didn't want to try to make any decisions through a video chat, so that's how I wound up driving myself across town on a Friday morning.

I'd made it to the workshop with no problems, but finding my way back home was proving harder.

I squinted at my GPS, fairly certain the map directed me to drive in a circle. I clicked, switching to the alternate route, but that path was largely red—a massive chunk of traffic. I groaned, wishing I'd just waited for Lincoln's next day off. As much as I loved my freedom, I hated navigating congested city streets. At least if someone were driving me, I could scroll Instagram while they dealt with the traffic.

I slammed on my brakes at the next intersection, deciding last minute that a ticket for running the red light probably wouldn't improve my morning. While stopped, I zoomed in on the route highlighted by my GPS. There appeared to be another alternate route. It wasn't the most direct path home, but it claimed to be the fastest. And as long as GPS read the directions aloud to me, it shouldn't matter if I had thirty turns or two. I could keep up.

I veered right at the next opportunity, feeling freer by the second as I steered away from all the congestion. I followed the navigation, cutting across several blocks, then turned down a narrow back street. I glanced around for posted signs, hoping to confirm I was headed in the right direction down what had to be a one-way alley, but saw none. I also saw no oncoming traffic though, so it seemed fine.

Actually, I saw no cars at all, except for one beat-up gray sedan behind me. If that car weren't there, I would've backed up and found a route that avoided the alley. But if someone else were following me, I figured, I must be headed in the correct direction at least.

My instincts said the safest way to navigate the narrow alley would be slowly, but a wave of claustrophobia washed over me. I pressed the gas harder, accelerating towards an opening ahead. There wasn't a stop sign, so I merely slowed as I approached the equally narrow drive intersecting with the alley.

In a flash, a dinged-up blue car rounded the corner, pulling out right in front of me. I sucked in a sharp breath and slammed on my brakes. I narrowly missed their bumper, then honked to signal my annoyance. Drivers these days were so distracted that it was downright reckless.

Instead of waving an apology or just driving off though, the driver of the blue car suddenly gunned it—in reverse.

I closed my eyes and braced for impact right as the car slammed into my front bumper. My Audi bounced back, then forwards. I opened my eyes, relieved that I'd barely felt anything. The moron ahead hadn't hit me too hard, after all. Most likely, my car wouldn't even be too banged up. The beautiful metallic blue paint job would probably need significant touchups though.

A little light flashed above the center console and a robot voice said, "collision detected. Notifying emergency contact." I cringed, shifting the car into park long enough to tap out, "no accident, I'm fine," to Luca. I sent the text then gazed up. The man from the blue car had swung open his door and was climbing out.

My gut told me he was not the type of guy I'd like to chat with along this hidden alley. He clutched some papers in his hand, probably proof of insurance or something, but based on how he'd been driving, he was probably drunk. Maybe even high.

I considered just rolling my window down, telling him I was fine, and just dealing with the damage on my own. Luca had more than enough money to repair my car. On the other hand, it wasn't like I could leave until this moron moved his car, anyway since he was blocking the whole damn alley.

Besides, we weren't alone.

The guy in the car behind us was still there, and had witnessed everything.

If I wanted Luca to trust me to keep driving myself, I probably should do the adult thing and follow proper post-collision protocol.

I lowered my window right as the other driver reached my car.

"Sorry about that. Totally my fault there," he mumbled, lifting his hand.

I nodded with gritted teeth.

"We should exchange information. Your bumper looks bad." He thrust the papers through the opening in my window.

I opened my mouth to tell him I'd get my own insurance from the glove compartment when I saw what was in his hand beneath the papers. It was a large black gun.

Shit.

My eyes darted to the rearview mirror, checking if the witness was still watching us, praying he was calling the cops. But the driver's seat was empty.

"Get out of the car," the man said.

I hesitated, debating how likely he was to shoot me.

His hand moved and I jumped, but he only pushed the button to unlock the doors. I turned towards my glove box, praying I'd left my own gun there.

Instead, I saw the man from the car behind me opening my passenger door. He climbed in beside me, pressing a dirty knife to the edge of my throat.

"These earrings look expensive. You've got three seconds to get out of the car before I take them and the ear."

Shaking, I stepped out of the car. I clutched my phone tightly but left my purse on the seat.

"There's cash in my purse. Take it, take the car," I stammered, trying to back away from the guy with a gun.

He laughed maniacally, revealing a mouthful of crooked, cracked teeth and rancid breath. "Aww honey, we'll take your pretty car, but I think we might have some fun with you too."

A click sounded as my trunk swung open. The gunman yanked my phone from my hand then nudged me towards the trunk.

My stomach dropped like I'd just been flipped upside down on a rollercoaster. But before I could panic more, something smashed into the back of my head, and everything went dark.

~

Luca

I shook hands with Mr. Kelso right as my phone vibrated against my thigh.

"Good to meet you," I said. "Can I get you a drink?"

He smiled warmly before answering. "Only if you'll join me. I never drink alone."

I chuckled like there was any hint of that being the truth, then motioned for the closest waitress. She scurried over, the tassels of her bikini top swaying with her steps.

"Marcelli, could you bring us three..." I paused, glancing at Mr. Kelso for direction.

"Shall we do tequila?" the man suggested.

I smiled as if it weren't a ridiculous suggestion. Who the fuck drank straight tequila at three o'clock in the afternoon?

"Make it the Don Julio," I said.

The girl beamed and scampered off.

"Not a fan of Patron?" Mr. Kelso asked.

"I don't mind it, but the Don Julio is smoother and more flavorful in my opinion."

This tidbit seemed to impress my new friend. I motioned for him to sit, then Alessio and I followed suit. I slide my phone out of my pocket, frowning at the recent text from Giada.

All she'd said was, "no accident, I'm fine." Zero context or elaboration. My pulse kicked up at even the possibility that she'd be in an accident. I quickly scrolled up to confirm she'd sent nothing earlier to clarify the message.

"What's going on? Are you ok?" I tapped out, licking my lips.

I angled my phone to Alessio, letting him read the message. I locked eyes with my friend, hoping he correctly interpreted my perturbed expression. Thankfully, he stood, reaching for his own phone. Just knowing he was calling her already offered a little relief.

"Scusi," I apologized to my guest, quickly translating. "Sorry. I, uh, weird text from my wife. Something about an accident. My associate is trying to reach her to make sure everything is okay."

Mr. Kelso frowned. "No problem. Uh, if you need to reschedule though, I'm afraid my calendar is packed the rest of this visit, but you could come see me on the West coast anytime."

"No, let's chat now. I'm sure she's fine. Probably some design mishap. She's been helping her brother remodel a house he bought, so this likely has something to do with that."

Mr. Kelso feigned interest, and Marcelli arrived with our drinks. We clinked glasses, then each sipped the golden-amber liquid. As we began talking, I cast a glance at Alessio every few minutes. And each time, he was still staring nervously at his phone instead of talking or offering me a reassuring thumbs up. I felt my blood pressure creep higher and higher.

~

Giada

I awoke with the worst hangover of my life. The pounding of my head seemed to ricochet through my entire body, shaking me with each painful thrum. I peeled my eyes open and tried to orient myself.

I sucked in a breath as it all rushed back to me. I clenched my hands over my mouth, unsure if I was trying not to vomit or scream. The trunk was suffocating, and my pulse raced at the thought that I might soon run out of oxygen. I appreciated the fact that my hands were free, at least, and I began searching for some sort of release button. I was positive I'd read somewhere that all trunks contained a button to open from the inside, so I just had to find the latch.

Well, find it…and figure out when to use it. I didn't want to fling myself out onto the highway. Although, I also didn't want to escape in some dark alley where they could just chase me down or shoot me.

Maybe I needed a weapon too.

I swore silently, wishing they hadn't taken my phone. *God*, or that I hadn't texted Luca I was okay. If I'd just said nothing at all, he would've gotten the alert from the car about the accident and immediately gone to me. He could've tracked my phone and saved me before I'd even woken up to this nightmare.

I swept my arms around the space, searching for anything I could use as an object. I found nothing. Stupid Luca and his OCD cleanliness. If I'd had it my way, my trunk would be filled with useful crap I could repurpose.

My heart clutched at the thought of Luca. *God*, he would be devastated if anything happened to me. I wasn't even sure he'd recover this time. We'd been through so much lately, too much really, especially just for me to…

No.

I cut off my train of thought and forced myself to refocus. I whispered the words of the Lord's Prayer, reveling in the familiarity of each syllable without letting myself dwell on the meaning. And then, I scooted to the back of the trunk to feel around for the release latch. My hand grazed something that felt distinctly like a handle, but before I could open it, the car swerved abruptly then slammed to a halt.

My body careened towards the main compartment of the car, then rolled back where I'd started, smashing into the back of the trunk with a jolt. Thankfully, my arm was still raised above my face, blocking my head from severe injury. Still, the impact stunned me, and I gazed around the darkened space for a long moment, disoriented.

I snapped back to the present as I heard shouts outside the car. I needed to act now. Maybe the guys were distracted by something and I could sneak away unnoticed. Or maybe they'd reached our final destination and this was my final chance to escape. Either way, I had to act now.

I gripped the latch again, drew in a deep breath, then braced myself as I clutched the handle with all my might.

"Thank you," I whispered as the trunk opened with a quiet click. My prayers had been answered, at least in small part. I held the lid of the trunk, my fingers cramping with the effort to keep it from swinging wide open as I shifted. I used the sliver of light to search for any possible weapon but quickly confirmed my earlier suspicions that the trunk was, in fact, empty aside from me.

Using my free hand, I slipped off my shoe and clutched it tightly as I raised the lid a little higher. I would shimmy out of the trunk, holding the shoe as a weapon, then sprint like hell away from the car. I didn't think the plan was ideal, but it was good enough. It had to be.

I winced as sunlight pierced my eyes, blinking quickly to orient myself. I swung a leg over the edge of the trunk, gripping my shoe tightly.

"Giada!" cried a familiar voice.

Relief hit me like a freight train as I tumbled out of the trunk.

A muffled gunshot rang out, and I tried to stand so I could see what was happening.

"Stay down Giada!" the voice called. It was definitely Lorenzo. I'd recognize his bossy tone anywhere.

I peered around the tire in time to see him approach a man lying on the street. I watched as Enzo kicked a gun several feet away from the man, then stomped on the man's wrist repeatedly before bringing his boot on the side of the man's scull.

Nausea churned in my belly as Lorenzo squatted, pressing his own gun to the side of the man's forehead. I ducked back behind the tire, covering my eyes while waiting for another gunshot.

A moment later, arms wrapped around me. Enzo lifted me off the pavement, squeezing me close to his chest.

"Grazie a dio," he murmured, burying his face in my hair. He pulled back then, eying me with laser focus. "Are you okay? Did they touch you? Hurt you in any way?"

"I don't know. They knocked me out," I stammered, reaching my hand up to the back of my skull.

"Okay, any pain other than your head?"

I shook my head, causing the tears I didn't know I was shedding to ricochet onto his shirt.

"Shh, it's okay Giada. I've got you," he said.

I gazed past him towards the man stretched out on the pavement, then I jerked back.

"There were two!" I shrieked, certain the other guy was about to jump out at us.

Enzo tightened his grip on me. "I know. I got them. You're

safe." He peered around us, then added, "And backup should be here any second now."

He'd barely finished speaking when a black SUV barreled across the empty parking lot towards us. I stiffened, but Lorenzo whispered, "It's Eddie."

Three guys flew out of the SUV the second it stopped, and all three had guns drawn.

"I think they were carjackers," Enzo said. He paused and gazed around. "I don't see any cameras."

"Me neither," Eddie agreed.

I peered around too, though less interested in cameras than in figuring out where I was. We appeared to be at some sort of budget storage facility. There didn't appear to be anyone else nearby.

"I need to get Giada to a doctor. They hit her head," Enzo said, his jaw tightening around the words. "Can you guys clean this up and move her car? It should still be drivable."

Eddie nodded quickly, concern filling his eyes. "Tony, take the car to the warehouse. Rico and I will get rid of these guys and double check for cameras." He paused. "Does Marco know?"

Enzo blew out a breath. "We'll call Luca first, then I'll update Marco." He lifted me again and carried me towards his car. The front corner by the driver's side bore a massive dent, but otherwise it looked drivable.

"Hang on!" Rico called. He scurried after us carrying my purse and phone, pausing to scoop up the shoe I'd dropped.

Enzo positioned me in the passenger seat, clipping my belt around me, then set my other shoe and purse on the floor. He started to hand me my phone, then swore. I blinked, realizing it wasn't turning on.

"They took the chip out so we couldn't track you," he explained. "You can use mine to call Luca."

He shut my door then climbed behind the wheel. He peeled out of the lot, focusing his eyes squarely on the road.

"How did you find me without my phone?" I asked, my teeth starting to chatter.

"Your car has a tracker," he replied, gazing at me. "I was finishing up a late lunch when I got an alert that the car had been in an accident. When I checked the location, it didn't seem like someplace you'd be on purpose. And then the speed you were going, I knew something had to be wrong if you were going that fast."

I shivered. "I thought the alert would go to Luca. Shouldn't he be my emergency contact?"

"I guess no one thought to change it. Honestly, I forgot your car even had that setting. We dismantle all that GPS and tracking shit in all the other cars."

I opened my mouth to say something else, but my teeth were chattering too hard. I was so cold, and I couldn't stop shaking.

"You've got to call Luca, let him know you're alright and..." Enzo abruptly stopped talking when he turned to me. "Giada?"

"They were taking me someplace so they could..." I couldn't catch my breath enough to finish the sentence. I heard myself breathing, hard and fast, but still felt like I was suffocating. "They said they were going to..." Again I stopped. No matter how much I inhaled, I wasn't getting enough breath.

"Giada," Enzo cautioned. He swore under his breath, then took a sharp right turn.

The car jerked to a stop, and Lorenzo killed the engine before flying out of the car. He opened my door, unbuckled my belt, and pulled me to him.

"You're okay now, Giada. I've got you," he said, his voice quiet.

For a moment, I thought he was shaking me for some reason, but then I realized I was shivering so hard that I was moving us both. "So c-c-cold," I stammered.

"I know, Princess. You're in shock. You need to relax, think happy thoughts. We're like, a half hour out from the hospital."

I tried to think happy thoughts, but all that came to me was visions of that awful man with his terrible teeth and hideous breath. "They hit my car," I said. "We were in some alley, and one of them was in front and the other behind me and I—"

"Hey!" Enzo interrupted. "It's okay. You can tell me later. You're safe now. I need you to look at me."

I peered up, honing in on his dark brown eyes.

"Okay good, now tell me two things you see, right now."

"Eyes," I said.

"Yes. What color are my eyes?"

"Brown."

"Good. One more thing," he urged.

My gaze dropped to his shirt, where the black residue of my mascara had smeared across his chest. "Stain," I said, teeth still chattering. "Non-waterproof mascara."

Enzo chuckled at my specificity then pulled me closer. His hand rubbed up and down along my back. "Good, Giada. See? You're right here with me. You're totally fine. Okay?" He paused. "Now I want you to tell me two things you hear right now."

At first, there was only the clatter of my teeth, but after a moment, I heard distant traffic noises, birds, and the rapid thunk-thunk-thunk of Enzo's heart. I told him all three, feeling my shaking slow as I spoke.

"Yes," he encouraged. "You're a pro at this. Now we are moving on to smell. Give me two things you can smell."

I inhaled slowly. With my face pressed against Enzo's shirt, the first scents I noticed were his after shave, deodorant, and a hint of sweat. But a beat later, there was a hint of cilantro. "You ate Mexican for lunch," I said, my voice coming out accusatory.

Enzo's chuckle reverberated against my cheek, but he moved on to my next sense. "Alright, last one. Tell me two things you can touch, right now."

Lorenzo had wrapped his arms so tightly around me by this point that I couldn't shiver if I tried. I also couldn't move my hands. He waited for my answer, then encouraged me. "Come on Giada, you can do this."

"I can't," I said. "I can't move my arms."

Enzo loosened his grip and reached for one of my hands. He pressed my palm against my cheek.

"Stubble," I said.

"I shaved this morning," he replied, dropping my hand.

I had stopped shaking, my teeth had stopped chattering, and I felt almost okay. "What sorcery is this?" I asked.

"It's a grounding exercise. Pulls you out of panic attacks. Helpful with shock victims."

"That's a handy trick."

"I know lots of handy things," he replied.

I rest my cheek against his chest, letting his warmth fully permeate my soul. Lorenzo was right. In his arms, I felt safe, like I was cocooned in a bubble, immune to any harm. But I couldn't stay like that forever.

"You can let go now," I said.

Enzo didn't move. After a minute, he chuckled, but didn't loosen his grip. "No, I can't. I need another minute." He paused. "You scared me, Princess. I wasn't sure if they'd left you somewhere, or if they had you with them, and I didn't know if they'd hurt you."

I didn't have a response to that, but a moment later he gradually loosened his grip.

"We should call Luca, let him know you're okay, and then he can meet us at the hospital," he said.

"I don't want to go to a hospital."

"Giada, if they hit you hard enough to knock you out, you need to be checked out by a doctor. You could have a concussion or something."

"Melissa can check. Dr. Adams," I said.

"She can't run any tests if you're not at a hospital." Enzo positioned me in my seat, buckled my belt, then climbed into the driver's seat again. "It's not up for discussion," he said.

He started the car and offered me the phone. "Do you want to call Luca or should I?"

I wanted to be with Luca so badly, but I couldn't talk to him like this. Telling him what happened would only make me freak out again. "I can't," I mumbled. "Can you just call Alessio?"

Enzo stared at me for a moment, then dialed. He clutched the phone to his ear, as if he realized I couldn't handle hearing anyone else's panic. He was quiet for a moment, then spoke.

"Is Luca with you?" he asked, pausing. "No, listen. I am here with Giada. She is fine. She had a little knock on the head, so I'm taking her to St. Mary's. We'll be there in about thirty or forty minutes. Can Luca meet us there?"

I gazed expectantly at him as he spoke. I couldn't hear what Alessio was saying, and he maybe wasn't even speaking English, but I could gather the gist of it from his tone.

"Alessio, she's right here with me, so I'm not going to go into details. She's...shaken up."

Alessio's words grew even more agitated with that. I motioned for Enzo to give me the phone. Instead, he clicked it to speaker. Alessio was in the middle of some rant in Italian, but I interrupted.

"Alessio, it's me. I'm okay. Enzo's making me go to the hospital. Can you please just have Luca meet me there?"

"He's going to want to talk to you."

"He can talk to her all he wants at St. Mary's," Lorenzo cut in. "We'll see you soon.." He started to hang up, then added, "Oh, and Giada's phone is out of commission, so use this number if you need to reach her before then."

Enzo hung up, then reached for my hand. He squeezed it firmly, then left his hand resting on my thigh just above my knee. I squeezed my eyes shut, trying to figure out how to stop myself from replaying the horrors of the day for the rest of the ride.

"Name that song or I-spy?" Enzo asked, interrupting my thoughts.

"Uhh what?"

He turned to me and grinned. "After all those years you spent tormenting me with your dumb little car games, did you really think I'd forget how to play? Come on. First to guess wins, and no cheating by looking at the display. Best out of five," he said, switching on the radio.

And somehow, despite the odds, I was smiling. Because for years, Enzo had driven me back and forth to boarding school and then to college. During all those long car rides, I'd tire of scrolling through my phone after a while and would pressure him into games. At the time, I'd had no clue about his mafia ties, and looking back, it made me even happier to know I'd forced a budding gangster to engage in a fierce game of guess-the-song.

CHAPTER 13

Luca

I was so anxious I could barely see straight by the time we reached the hospital. Alessio dropped me off at the entrance of the emergency room so I could get to her faster, but now that I was alone, the fear was near crippling. This felt like before, when I'd arrived to the hospital after the accident only to find my wife in a coma, then suffering from amnesia. I was dreading whatever I'd find when I reached her.

Except, as the nurse led me towards Bed 4, where she said I'd find my wife, I heard laughter. Giada's laughter, mixed with a man's.

Relief flooded me, followed quickly by a tight pang of jealousy when the nurse tugged open the curtain. Giada sat upright in a hospital bed. Also on the bed, facing her, was Lorenzo. Her hand was clasped tightly within his, and she was smiling brightly.

Giada's eyes widened as she saw me. "Luca!" she exclaimed, almost like a sigh.

I stepped closer, eying Lorenzo. Only then did he seem to realize he was still holding my wife's hand.

He pulled back quickly, rising from the bed. "Thumb wars," he said, as if that explained anything. He cleared his throat. "I'll be in the waiting room."

For a moment, I wasn't sure what to do. If Giada wanted him and not me...

"Luca," Giada breathed my name, then burst into sobs. I climbed into the bed beside her, pulling her onto my lap as she fell apart. She was still crying when Alessio reached the room.

His expression was full of concern when his eyes met mine, but I didn't know what to tell him. I had no fucking clue what had happened. So I just shrugged and shook my head.

I wasn't sure how long I held her, or how long she'd cried, when a nurse popped in. She was a different nurse than who had shown me to her room, but I'm guessing this nurse had been in the room before, since she looked surprised to see me and not Enzo.

"Hi," she said hesitantly.

Giada's head popped up. She wiped her eyes with her hand and peered out at the young woman.

"They're ready for us in CT," the nurse said. She rolled a wheelchair close to the bed.

I untangled myself from my wife, then scooted off the bed. "I'm Luca Marino," I said. "Giada's husband. What's the CT for? Is everything okay?"

The nurse gazed uncertainly from Giada to me, then back again. "The gentleman who brought her in said she had a bump on the head and was unconscious for a little while. We want to rule out any brain bleed or concussion."

"Brain bleed?" my pulse skyrocketed.

"I just want to go home," Giada mumbled.

"Once we confirm you're okay," I said, walking around the bed and helping her into the wheelchair.

I backed up while the nurse rotated the wheelchair towards the door, then began to walk with them.

"Sorry, sir, no visitors or family allowed in CT. You can wait here and we'll bring her right back."

I slumped onto the bed, physically pained by the separation. But I wasn't about to let another second pass when she could have bleeding in her fucking brain. I sat there, terrified, for a full minute, before texting Alessio.

"They took her to CT. What happened? Did Enzo tell you?"

A moment later, Alessio and Enzo both appeared.

"Go outside and talk," Alessio urged. "I'll text the second she's back."

I considered that, then left with Lorenzo. We walked to a bench at the far end of some stupid decorative garden near the parking garage. "What the fuck happened?" I spit the second we sat.

He raised his hands defensively. "I got an automatic notification from her car that she was in an accident. I must still be the emergency contact."

My stomach clenched. "She texted me about an accident. She said she was fine. We tried calling then, but—"

Enzo shushed me with his hand. "It wasn't a real accident. Sounds like it was a carjacking. Two guys in different cars. She was too upset to give me any details, so I don't know what exactly happened, but—"

"What the hell do you know?" I clenched my fists, barely containing my fast-growing fury.

"When I got the alert, I checked the tracking on her car, and it didn't seem right. She wasn't too far from that Larraby warehouse, but in a rough neighborhood. And then the car took off, fast. I watched the tracking, and it was coming towards me, so I called Angelo and Eddie and I took off towards the car."

"You couldn't have called me?"

The man winced. "I'm sorry Luca, but I didn't want to delay any more. I had a bad feeling and just wanted to get to the car."

I gritted my teeth, but motioned for him to continue.

"I spotted her car around 21st and Malden streets and told the guys. I could see that Giada wasn't driving. It was two guys. I…" Enzo paused, making a face. "I called Eddie and told him to head back to the address where the accident occurred in case Giada was still there, but I stuck with the car. They went towards an old storage facility. There was no one else around, and they'd slowed down, so I rammed the car and got them to stop."

"Where was Giada?"

He ignored my question. "I shot the driver in the arm. The other guy got out and tried to run, so I took him out. I wanted to find out where Giada was before I…" His voice trailed off rather than admit he was trying to kill the guys.

He took a breath, then said. "They had knocked her out and thrown her in the trunk. She got out on her own."

I flew to my feet. I couldn't sit down while listening to such infuriating information.

"The driver had a gun, so I returned to him. I kicked it out of the way then took care of him. He and his accomplice, they're both gone. Eddy, Rico, and Tony moved Giada's car and cleaned up the scene. No cameras, no trace of anything." He paused. "We told the ER that she fell off a ladder doing some home reno and knocked herself out."

I scowled. A thousand thoughts fluttered through my head. None of them were good.

"She was really upset, Luca. She was shaking and seemed really out of it. I just got her here as fast as I could, but she hasn't really talked about it any."

"Did she look okay? Could you see any other injuries?" I asked.

"No other injuries I could see."

I hesitated before asking the next question. I didn't want to ask it, but I had to know. "Did they…touch her?"

Lorenzo's expression conveyed that he understood exactly what I was asking.

"She said nothing else hurt. I didn't see any other injuries, and after the nurses had her change into a gown, I took her clothes."

"You were in the room when she changed?" I asked.

"No. I stepped out, then came back," he said, sounding annoyed by my interruptions. "But I looked at her clothes, and I didn't see any rips or blood or…other substances."

I inhaled slowly through my nose, closing my eyes and holding my breath for a count of three before exhaling. Part of me felt oddly possessive of Giada now, like he'd somehow violated her by inspecting her panties for signs of an even more vile attack, but the bigger part of me felt only relief.

"We got her purse back and her phone, but they'd removed the card so it doesn't work now," Enzo said after a lengthy silence.

"She's okay," I said.

"Yeah," he agreed. "I think she's good. Just shaken up. I think they told her what they were going to do to her once they got to their storage unit and…"

"Jesus!" I said. I paced a few feet away, letting loose a string of expletives in my native tongue.

After a moment, Enzo stood and followed me. "They didn't do it, Luca. She's okay. They didn't get a chance to—"

I swiveled to face him, this man that, at one time in the not-so-distant past, I'd hated so intensely that I nearly beat him to death.

But now, I didn't hate him. Now, I hugged him.

I felt Enzo stiffen at my embrace, but I didn't care. Had he been a minute later, had he called me instead of going after her, had he delayed in any way whatsoever, those monsters could have hurt Giada.

I released Lorenzo before things got too weird.

"She's safe because of you," I told him. "I owe you…my life. I owe you everything."

"I was just doing my job," he said calmly.

I rolled my eyes.

"And I did it for her, not you," he added.

A text from Alessio came through. "Back," was all it said.

"They're back," I told him, motioning for him to come along. Ten minutes ago, I was annoyed that this man had stuck around. But now, I wasn't sure I'd ever want him to leave her side.

Alessio and Lorenzo stayed in the waiting room while I rejoined Giada in her room. She still seemed fragile, in that tacky green and tan hospital gown, but a stoic expression now replaced her distraught one from earlier.

"How are you doing?" I asked, hesitating at the head of her bed, unsure where she'd want me to sit.

"I'm fine. My head doesn't even hurt anymore. They said a doctor will review the scans and come talk to us shortly."

I nodded. "Do you need anything? Water? A snack?"

She shook her head.

I reached for her hand and squeezed. She returned the gesture, then bit her lip.

"I'm so sorry, Luca. I know you had a big meeting today, and I had no business driving out there alone. I was just so impatient and stubborn and—"

"Giada, no!" I interrupted. "I don't care about my meeting. It was over anyway, but that's not what matters to me." I perched on the edge of her bed and waited until she shifted, making room for me to scoot behind her. I folded her back against my torso, wrapping my arms around her stomach as if I thought she'd try to escape.

"You did nothing wrong. None of this was your fault. I'm just glad you're okay. We're all just glad you're okay."

"Did Enzo tell you what happened?"

"Yes. He told me what he knows. If you want to fill in the rest later, that's fine, but if not, that's okay too." I tightened my hold on her. "It doesn't matter what happened. It's over now. And I'm not letting you out of my sight again."

She inhaled a ragged breath, then settled her head against my chest. Less than a half hour passed before a doctor came in. He said Giada's scans were clear, and after a quick repeat exam, he cleared her to head home. I was supposed to monitor her for signs of a concussion and we had to follow up with her regular doctor in a few days, but that was fine with me. I wasn't kidding when I said I wasn't letting her out of my sight again.

Giada had complained a lot about the younger, more possessive version of me. But the more we survived together, the more I realized the wisdom of my earlier ways. If I could lock Giada in a tower to keep her safe, I would. Because I wasn't about to let anything happen to her again.

~

Giada

As promised, Luca didn't leave my side for the next three days. If it weren't for his dad being in town and demanding he actually handle some tasks himself, Luca probably wouldn't have left the apartment for the rest of our lives. On day four, he personally drove me to the new house to work with Angelo. To my surprise, he let my brother drive me home at the end of the day. On the fifth day, Luca insisted I accompany him to work.

If I hadn't felt like a kid tagging along on a take-your-daughter-to-work day, I might have enjoyed the change of pace. The club was filled with lots of familiar faces and interesting action, but all the guys eyed me like I was in trouble for something. The only redeeming parts of the day ended up being the long lunch Luca treated me to and the quickie that followed in his private office.

The next day, I convinced Luca to let me go to work. Lincoln would drive me—and wait outside the office the entire day. I felt surprisingly good being back to my normal routine, but I really only had a few hours of work to do at the office. On the way home, Lincoln and I stopped at the florist, and then he drove me to Enzo's apartment.

I hadn't expected Lincoln to agree when I'd mentioned the detour, and I didn't dare ask if he'd run the plan by Luca or not. I hadn't yet been to Enzo's place. He'd only moved in with his girlfriend Sara a couple of weeks earlier.

"I shouldn't be too long," I told Lincoln, heading up to the door. I smoothed my hair before knocking, oddly nervous about seeing Enzo again after the other day.

I heard footsteps approaching the door, followed by a delay. Finally, the lock clicked and the door swung open. I was face to face with a tanned, muscular torso. My nerves started to get the better of me as my eyes slowly scrolled up to meet Lorenzo's face. He looked tired, confused, and worried.

"Giada! How did you get here?" he asked, tugging me by the arm into his girlfriend's apartment. Enzo peered behind me, then shut and locked the door.

His shirtlessness had caught me so off guard, that it took me a moment to remember. "Linc," I finally said. "Alessio's cousin, Lincoln."

Enzo rolled his eyes. "Yeah, I know who he is. "Why are you carrying flowers?"

"Why are you half naked?" I asked. Then, realizing he might interpret my words as an accusation, I clarified. "I mean, were you asleep? Or am I interrupting…something else?" I strained to listen for sounds of Sara, but music was playing quietly from the bedroom, masking all other noises.

Instead of answering, Enzo turned around and walked towards his bedroom. I followed him further into the apartment, but paused by the living room. When he returned, he was wearing a tee shirt.

"Is Sara here?" I asked.

He shook his head.

I sighed with relief, but then Enzo's expression changed, leading me to think he noticed my relief and might have gotten the wrong idea.

"I don't...I mean, I wasn't complaining about your..." I gestured to his torso. "You look good shirtless. Just as fit as I remember. Maybe more."

He quirked a brow. "Giada, it's been a long week. If you're about to do something that's going to get me beat up, maybe—"

"I'm not!" I interrupted. I thrust the flowers towards him. "Geez. I just wanted to say thank you."

Enzo eyed the flowers like they might bite him. "Are these for Sara?"

"No, they're for you." I started into his kitchen, making myself at home. "Do you have a vase?"

"Uhh."

I blew out a sigh and began opening cabinets which may logically house a vase or two. I lucked out on my second try, so I filled it with water then arranged the flowers. Enzo watched me curiously, but without speaking. As I dropped the cellophane wrapping for the bouquet into his trash, he stood.

"Do you want a drink?" he offered, opening his refrigerator.

"Yes. Please."

"Like soda, water, coffee, wine?"

I was always in the mood for coffee, but I spotted a white wine next to the condiments in his fridge and decided that would best suit the conversation. "Wine, as long as you're drinking too," I said.

He grabbed the bottle, yanked the cork out with his teeth, then retrieved two stemless glasses from a cabinet. "I'm not working today, and you're being weird, so I think I might need this drink."

I sipped my wine the second he handed me the glass, relishing the slight sting as the cool, crisp liquid trickled down my throat. Enzo led me to the couch and motioned for me to sit. Then he grabbed a sock and some other stray items off the chair adjacent to the couch and plopped down there.

"Still won't sit by me, huh?" I teased.

"You were about to explain why you brought me flowers," he said, ignoring my question.

I followed his gaze to the bouquet, which coordinated perfectly with the décor even though I'd never actually been inside this apartment before. "The flowers were a thank you present. I know it's a bit…non-traditional for a girl to give a man flowers, but I wasn't sure what else would be appropriate. There isn't really a proper protocol for expressing gratitude in this situation."

Enzo stiffened, and his eyebrows furrowed. "This situation being…?"

"We both know what you did for me, Lorenzo."

He stared back at me, his dark eyes focused on me so intently, his expression unreadable. After a moment, he blew out a breath, then reached for his wine. I did the same, watching him for any hint of emotion as we both sipped.

"You don't have to thank me," he finally said. "I'm glad your stupid car notified me. I'm glad I was nearby and that I got there before…" Enzo gazed out the window, waiting until he turned back to me to say more. "I was just doing my job."

"But you weren't. I mean, I'm not your responsibility anymore." I paused. "And Luca said you dented your car pretty badly."

Enzo drained his entire glass of wine while pondering my words, then stood to retrieve the bottle. He carried it back and set it on the coffee table, refilling his own glass, then offering me the tiny remaining amount. I shook my head, still having most of my first glass.

"You didn't have to bring me flowers," he finally said.

"I wanted to. I'm going to come up with a better present. Whiskey maybe."

"Whiskey?" he repeated, a bemused expression in his eyes.

"Oh, shut up. I just mean I'll figure out something more appropriate. I realize what you did deserves way more than a twelve-dollar bouquet of roses."

"Your husband and father and brothers already thanked me."

"They did?" I wasn't sure why that surprised me, but I'd never gotten the impression Angelo was big on gratitude.

He nodded. "None of them gave me flowers though," he added, a mischievous gleam in his eyes.

I flipped him my middle finger.

"Your dad gave me a promotion. And your husband gave me a present too, although he might take his back if you tell him I was 'half naked' when you showed up."

"What did Luca give you?" I asked. Luca was an amazing gift-giver, at least with me. He always found the exact right thing for every occasion.

Enzo stood and walked away, and at first, I thought he was going to get another bottle of wine, but then he tossed a set of car key fob to me. I peered at it, confused, then noticed Alfa Romeo etched on the metallic fob.

I felt my jaw drop. "Luca got you a car?"

Enzo chucked at my reaction, then nodded.

I dropped his keys onto the coffee table. "Wow. I see why you're not so impressed with the flowers."

He breathed a laugh. "The flowers are nice, Giada."

"Why didn't he tell me?" I wondered aloud.

"I think there's a lot Luca doesn't tell you," Enzo replied.

I gazed up at him, his words stinging in a way he perhaps hadn't intended. Enzo knew that was a sensitive subject. And he also realized there wasn't exactly an easy solution. But still, even though I'd come over to thank him, he was reminding me of the exact problem I'd always face in my marriage. I felt my eyes well up with tears and tried to hold it back. I desperately fumbled for any happy thought to distract me, but instead the only visions that flashed through my mind were of that stupid trunk they'd shoved me in and the rancid stench of that monster's breath.

"Shit, Giada, I'm sorry," Enzo said. "I didn't mean to upset you."

He swore again under his breath, this time in Italian, then he scooted over to the couch beside me, pulling me into his arms. Everything about his embrace was warm and comforting and familiar. Enzo even smelled the same as I remembered.

"Luca loves you so much, Giada. You know that. Everyone knows that. You are everything to him, and he'd tell you everything if he could."

I sniffled and tried to reign in my emotions. "It's fine, Enzo. I know. I'm just...I don't know. The last week has been an emotional rollercoaster and I feel like the tiniest things set me off. It's not your fault."

"You've been through a lot," he agreed.

He was right, obviously, but I didn't want to think about that. "I just wanted to thank you. It wasn't just your job. And I know you..." I paused, trying to think of the right words. "I mean, I know what you did, with the guys."

Enzo snorted. "After what they did, I had no choice."

I shrugged. "You could've waited and made Luca deal with them. And I know enough about how this world works to know that Luca wouldn't have done it quickly like you did. He would've made them suffer. And then I would've spent the rest of my life panicking about his soul and he would've had all this guilt, and now—"

"Now I'm the only one who'll burn in hell?" Enzo interrupted.

"No! That's not what I meant."

He cracked a smile, letting me know he wasn't completely serious. "I know, princess, I know. I was joking." He paused for a few more swallows of wine. "They were bad men, Giada. The world is a better place without them. I won't sit here and act like I do that sort of thing all the time or like I don't have any feelings about what I did. But if my soul is damned for all of eternity, it's surely not because of this."

I tried to swallow the lump in my throat, but my mouth had run painfully dry. I reached for my wine. "You're a good person, Enzo. That's what matters. And you did what you did not just to save my life but to save my marriage. You did what you did to make sure my life was easier, less stressful, happier. And you did it all with barely a moment to consider your options. That's incredible."

I could've sworn Enzo actually blushed at the praise, but he didn't say anything.

"I don't deserve a friend like you," I added.

At that, Enzo leaned forward to catch my attention. "That isn't true and you know it. I wouldn't do crazy shit like that for just anyone. I do it for you because you do deserve it. And I hope the occasion never arises, but you'd do the same for me if our positions were reversed."

I frowned. "You want me to execute a crazy rescue mission the next time you're kidnapped?

He grinned. "Well, maybe just have my back in general. So how are you doing?"

I shrugged. "My head is fine. No headaches or anything."

"I meant, like mentally."

"Oh." I peered around the room, noticing the space didn't really reflect Enzo's personality. Sara must have decorated. "Well, I can't sleep very well, but otherwise I guess I'm okay. Sadly, it's not the first time something scary like this has happened, so I know it'll just take some time and then I'll be back to normal."

"It's okay if you're not back to normal," Lorenzo said, frowning. "Nobody expects you to just bounce back from that. You're allowed to be a little traumatized."

"All of the men in my life deal with scary situations every day.

I can't complain to you and Luca when you guys are constantly facing down bad guys."

Enzo smirked. "We only face down the bad guys on even days. On odd days, we are the bad guys."

I rolled my eyes. "Not funny, and you know what I mean. Luca carries guns with him everywhere he goes. He must always feel how I do now."

"How do you feel now?"

"Like the entire world is out to get me," I admitted. "I feel like any minute someone could come at me."

"I think Luca carries guns so he doesn't feel that way."

"So you think I should carry a gun?"

"Don't you already?" He paused, but not long enough for me to answer. "I think you should learn how to use it. Practice more, anyway. And take some self-defense classes. Not because you'll ever need to use it, but because it'll build your confidence. You won't feel so scared anymore."

I shook my head. "Honestly, I don't ever want to be alone again. Even for a minute."

The crease between Enzo's brows thickened. "Have you told Luca that?"

"No, because he's already rearranged our whole lives to get me security twenty four-seven, and I'm not sure it's helping. It makes me feel crazy, and it's too much work for him. I can't do that to him."

Enzo stared at me as if he were debating telling me more, but decided against it.

"The past couple of days, I keep thinking about how I grew up. I mean, in the big house. I was never alone. The house was always busy and loud, and I never once felt unsafe."

"You were a kid. It's different. All of us feel safe until we grow up and realize all the shit going on in the world."

I shook my head. "I think it was the house. The big extended family part."

"So you gonna ask Sal and Camilla to move in with you?" Enzo's eyes twinkled with mischief as he spoke.

I chucked a floral accent pillow at him. "I'd sooner die. But I wouldn't mind Alessio."

Enzo blew out a sigh. "Tell Luca."

I nodded, more to acknowledge his statement and not to agree that I'd do what he said. "I'm guessing you didn't decorate this place," I said, jumping subjects abruptly.

He grinned and looked around. "What was your first clue?" he teased. Enzo stared around the room as if noticing it for the first time. "Speaking of your family home, well, I mean, is it weird that I feel more at home there than I do here?"

"I'm sure Sara would let you change up some things. I know a great decorator if you're interested."

"I don't think it's the stuff. It's just more a feeling, like this is her space. I'm just not sure I belong."

"You want to move her into the pool house instead?" I teased. Although, I suspected my dad wouldn't mind.

"No way. I just don't know if our lifestyles…mesh, if that makes sense."

I nodded. I'd felt that way a lot when I was with Adrian towards the end. Of course, now it seemed like Adrian had fully incorporated himself into the lifestyle, maybe even more than I had, but that was a moot point. "Do you tell her anything about your work?"

He shrugged. "I told her you crashed your car the other day, and I helped out."

"And she thought a luxury car was a normal reward for that?"

"She's not dumb. It's only a matter of time before she pieces it all together, and I'll never forgive myself if she ends up like…"

He stopped short of saying the name we were both thinking. Julia.

"It's not the same," I told him.

"I know. But Sara's a good person. She doesn't deserve to get caught up in my shit."

"Well, like I already said, you're a good person, too. And we all have shit our partners get to deal with. Don't sell yourself short."

He shrugged, and we both fell silent.

"I should get out of your hair," I said, rising to my feet.

Enzo stood slowly, stretching. "Thanks again for the flowers."

I rolled my eyes. "Thanks for saving my life. I wish words could express how grateful I am, how much it means to me that you'd do that for me."

His expression softened. "I'd do anything for you, Giada."

I was definitely the one to instigate the hug, but Lorenzo was a willing participant. As I rest my head on his chest and wrapped my arms around his waist, Enzo roped his arms around my back, holding me close. I relished the sensation of complete security, listened to the consistent beating of his pulse, and mimicked his slow, steady breathing with my own.

I could've stayed that way forever, cocooned in a familiar embrace. But instead, there was a sudden thunk behind me. I jumped back, already in full panic mode, but Enzo didn't completely release me.

"Hey, you're okay," he said, drooping his eyes to meet mine. Then, he let go of me.

I turned slowly, coming face to face with Sara. She stood just inside the doorway, a large shopping bag at her feet. Judging from her expression, she'd completely misinterpreted the situation. I watched as her eyes drifted from the empty wine bottle and glasses then back to Enzo and me. I stepped back, realizing we were still in quite the compromising position.

I half expected Sara to yell or cry or maybe even leave, but Enzo was the picture of calm. He walked over to her, pressed a kiss to her forehead, then picked up the tote bag she'd dropped. He carried it into the kitchen and began unpacking the items as if he were completely oblivious to the assumptions she had to be making.

"Giada brought us some flowers," he said lamely, folding the bag and shoving it under the sink after emptying it.

Sara turned back to me, still glaring.

"Lorenzo, um, did a favor for my husband and me," I explained, feeling my cheeks burn with mortification at my own awkwardness.

"Giada," Enzo spoke my name softly, but I recognized the chiding tone and stopped talking.

"It's fine," he added. He turned back to Sara. "Giada didn't realize Luca had already given me the car."

"You said that was from your boss," Sara replied.

"I said it was a gift for a job I did at work. Giada's father and husband work together sometimes. There's a lot of overlap between their businesses," Enzo explained.

Sara eyed me again before turning back to her boyfriend. "You guys drank an entire bottle of wine."

"Sorry, I'll buy you guys a new one," I offered, fully aware that wasn't her concern. "I had a rough week. I just—"

"Giada," Enzo cut in.

But I kept talking. After he'd done so much for me, I couldn't go and screw up his relationship. "Enzo's a friend. That's all. He was just comforting me and nothing happened."

"Giada!" Enzo's tone was sharper this time.

"I should go," I mumbled.

He nodded his approval. "I'll walk you out," he said.

I widened my eyes, trying to signal to him that he shouldn't walk me out if he wanted Sara to believe everything was innocent.

"Giada, you could've died last week and you just finished telling me you never want to be alone again. So I'm not letting you wander off into a parking lot." His voice was firm, almost harsh, and I gasped at the mention of my near-death experience.

Enzo turned to Sara. "I'll be right back," he promised. He slipped his bare feet into tennis shoes then opened the door for me.

We walked wordlessly down the hall, then both of us stared straight ahead while we waited for the elevator. I could see a fuzzy version of his reflection in the metallic door of the elevator and realized how stupid we were both being. I turned to face him.

"She thinks she walked in on something," I said.

"Don't worry about it."

"Enzo, she thinks you're cheating on her."

The elevator announced its arrival with a DING and we both stepped on. Enzo pushed the button for ground level, then shoved his hands into his pockets. "I'll tell her I'm not. It's fine, Giada. Sara's not…dramatic. And if I tell her to trust me, she will."

"Must be nice," I mumbled.

He ignored the comment. "And honestly, I'd rather she think I slept with you than know the truth. I don't want her involved in my work. At all."

I nodded. It made zero sense to me, but Enzo had mentioned before that he never wanted her to learn the truth about my family. I needed to respect his feelings.

"Okay," I mumbled. "But if you want me to talk to her—"

"I don't."

"From now on, I won't drop by unannounced. I'll only come over when she's home," I promised.

"I'd rather you only come by when she's not home, Giada."

"What? If she got to know me, we could be friends. I'm a like-able person and Sara must be pretty great if you love her."

"Yes, but I don't want you to be friends. You represent everything I want to keep her away from."

I understood enough of what he was saying to not be

offended, and as much as I wanted to persuade him otherwise, we were out of time. So instead, all I said was, "You won't be able to hide us from her forever," and then the elevator jerked to a stop and the doors parted.

We walked through the lobby and Lincoln rolled down his window, waving cheerfully as though he hadn't been half asleep before we approached.

"Thank you again," I said to Enzo. "And sorry about Sara."

"You're welcome, and it's fine," he said. "Take care, okay?"

I offered a lame nod, and Enzo pulled me in for another hug, this one short and much less incriminating. I expected him to walk back to his apartment and fix things with his girlfriend then, but instead, he turned to Lincoln.

"Look, I know you're Alessio's cousin and all, but Luca will still kill you if anything happens to his wife on your watch," he said.

"I didn't—" Lincoln began.

Enzo stepped closer and cut him off. "If you stop somewhere, you check out your surroundings, then open her door."

"I did!"

"Then you walk her to wherever she's going."

"She told me not to."

"You don't work for her. You work for Luca. And he wants you to walk her to the damn door. Understood?"

Lincoln nodded.

"Also, you might double check with Luca before taking his wife to the apartment of another man," he added.

"Lorenzo!" I snapped. "I can go where I want."

Enzo smirked at me before turning back to my driver. "Look man, I get it. She can be intimidating, but take it from someone who's been on Luca's bad side before. He's scarier. And when it comes to his princess, there's nothing he won't do to keep her safe."

Enzo stepped back, shut my door, then tapped the roof of the car as if to dismiss us. I relaxed back against my seat, and as Lincoln turned the car towards the street, I gazed up to the building. Sara stood by the open window of their apartment, watching us.

CHAPTER 14

Luca

I felt like I was caught in a weird time warp. Giada and I were married now, but she was back to spending almost all of her time back home. The crazy part was that it was actually working.

I'd spent the first week after the carjacking trying to keep an eye on her myself at all times, but that didn't work for either of us. My papà was in one of his usual funks about some local projects, and I didn't trust his new guys enough to let them handle any of my part of the work. So realistically, I couldn't be with Giada at all times. But selfishly, I'd also discovered that there was a bit of truth to that whole absence makes the heart grow fonder adage. Well, or at least it made the sex hotter.

Anyway, Lincoln picked her up each morning and drove her to the Conti house. She chatted design crap with Angelo, bundled up and lounged by the pool with Gabriella, or caught up on work projects in the sunroom. As an added perk, her mom was teaching her to cook.

Yeah.

Giada. Was. Learning. To. Cook.

Oh, and perhaps the strangest part of all, Giada and Gabby were taking a self-defense class. Okay, maybe that on its own wasn't too crazy, but the fact that their instructor was none other than Lorenzo Alfonsi sure seemed nuts to me. I didn't doubt the guy was qualified. He had military-grade sharpshooter skills, UFC-level street-fighting skills, and could wield a knife like a Samurai.

But up until recently, I'd done everything in my power to keep the guy away from my wife, and now I was willingly pushing her into his arms. Literally.

I appreciated the skills she was learning, even though I firmly believed she'd never need to use them as I would never again let her get in harm's way. Giada was comfortable with Enzo and she trusted him. More importantly, I trusted that he was teaching her the best way he could—because he cared about her safety too.

I'd watched a few minutes of some of their lessons. I would've loved to observe more, but my presence made Giada self-conscience. The moment she sensed my eyes on her, Giada shrugged away from Enzo's touch like he had the cooties. Gabriella, on the other hand, clearly relished all contact from Lorenzo.

I waited until we were pulling out of the driveway to mention it to Giada. Of course, the moment we were alone, she began to regale me with the details of her day. I smiled, loving her enthusiasm about it all. As mundane as any of it was, I would never grow tired of hearing her melodic voice recount it all.

When she finally came up for air, I squeezed her hand and smiled.

"Sorry," she said, lifting our joined hands to my upper thigh. "I missed you. That's why I'm so chatty."

"I like hearing about your day," I said, moving my hand back to the steering wheel.

"I'm boring."

"You're fascinating." I gazed at her as we pulled up to a red light. Her fingers inched up my thigh, making my already-fitted pants even tighter at the groin. I sucked in a breath, then remembered what I'd wanted to ask her. "You and Gabby seem to be getting along great. Are things back to normal with you?"

"Umm, maybe? I mean, not quite. We're definitely getting there. Working with Enzo is helping a lot."

"Yeah?"

"Mmm hmm. Like, well the obvious benefits, but also I think it gives her and I something else we can bond over, where there's no pressure."

"No pressure?"

Giada nodded and pulled back her hand abruptly. My body instantly craved her touch again, but my driving probably improved without the distraction.

"Yeah, since the point of us working with Enzo is to learn self-defense skills, there's no pressure for us to rekindle our friendship. When we go to dinner or the spa together, we're both painfully aware that the entire point of the outing is to bond and it just makes everything awkward."

"That makes sense. So Gabby is comfortable with Enzo?"

"Definitely."

She hadn't hesitated with her answer, but the innocence of her tone didn't fully tell me what I really wanted to know. So I pushed further. "Do you think there's maybe something more there?"

"Like what?"

"Do you think Gabriella is interested in Lorenzo?"

Giada's lips parted in a slight gasp as she considered the possibility. "Oh my gosh. I hadn't even thought about that because Enzo has Sara, but now that you mention it, yeah. I have noticed her being extra flirty. And she's started wearing an actual bra the last few times instead of her sports bra."

I frowned, not completely sure how that was connected, but I decided not to press it. "Do you think Enzo shares her feelings?"

"No way. He's with Sara. And he's definitely not the type of guy to cheat."

I opened my mouth to say something else, then stopped. Giada was probably right about Enzo, but then again, he seemed very hesitant to let Sara have anything to do with the Conti family. If he were to get involved with a woman like Gabriella, that could make his life a lot easier.

It could make my life a lot easier too.

When we got home, Giada busied herself with styling her hair and changing clothes. We had roughly an hour before we were meeting a few of the guys—plus a few of their ladies—for dinner. Giovanni had arranged it all, and we were meeting at the best Italian restaurant in town. His wife Lauren was coming, plus Thomas and his girlfriend Ana, and Alessio and Roberto were both coming solo.

Because of the way Giovanni had insisted we all attend the dinner, I'd known something was up. It wasn't anyone's birthday, and he sure as shit hadn't found a new job or made plans to relocate. So there was only one thing they could be planning to share as their big news. Still, the guy made us wait until after we ordered primo plati and the main course before making the big announcement.

The second he gazed at his wife and said they had some news to share, I turned my stare to Giada. I wanted to know exactly how she'd react when she heard. Usually, I could predict how she'd respond to something, but with this, I had no idea.

"We're expecting a baby!" Lauren announced, adding an ear-piercing shriek at the end of her statement.

Giada's mouth twitched before curving into a wide smile and her fingers tightened their grip on my hand.

To anyone else watching, Giada probably looked happy for

her friends. Excited, maybe even. But I knew the truth. My wife was jealous.

We celebrated the happy couple, discussed all the things I wasn't ready to learn about, from the importance of selecting the right obgyn to the insane market for maternity clothes. Then, thanks to pregnancy fatigue, we were all able to head home at a reasonable hour. Giada was quiet on the drive back to our apartment.

"Do you think they'll make good parents?" I asked her.

"Yeah. They seem really excited. I think anyone who loves their baby can be a good parent."

"They haven't been together that long though," I said, baiting her.

"They've been married longer than us."

"Sure, but they've only known each other a handful of years. I've loved you for a decade and a half."

Giada turned to me biting her bottom lip. "Well, if romantic words could get someone pregnant, we would totally have won the race."

"So there was a race," I confirmed.

She rolled her eyes. "You want me to admit I'm jealous?"

"Si."

Giada giggled. "Fine. I totally am. The idea of sharing something as huge as parenthood with you sounds so intimate and I can't wait to do it. And all the baby-associated planning and shopping and decorating would be amazing."

I pulled into my parking space and killed the engine. "But?" I prompted.

"But I still have nightmares and am nowhere near mentally ready to take on new anxieties. And you're already insanely over-protective of me. Can you imagine how over-the-top you'll be if I'm carrying your second-favorite person inside of me?"

My gaze dropped to her stomach and my chest tightened at the mere thought of her pregnant with my child. Maybe I was the one who was jealous. I swallowed back the longing and raised my eyes to hers. "Who says I'll like you more than I'll like our kid?"

Giada stuck her tongue out, so I scooped her into my arms and hoisted her over my shoulders. I carried her into the apartment like a caveman, not setting her down until we'd reached our bed.

We may not be ready to make a baby yet, but that wouldn't stop us from practicing.

I carefully undressed my wife, kissing every inch of her body as I uncovered it. Then she stared unabashedly as I worked the buckle on my pants and untucked my shirt.

"I swear you get slower at undressing the more you do it," she observed, still making no effort to help.

I bit back a grin and shucked the pants, then straddled her ribcage so she could help with the buttons. "Do you want me to hurry up?" I was fully prepared to rip the damn shirt if needed.

She considered my words and her tongue darted out to lick her upper lip in a way that made my cock twitch. "I want a lot of things right now," she admitted.

I grinned back at this incredible woman, currently pinned beneath me. Even at the end of a long day, Giada was gorgeous. The way her eyes twinkled up at me gave me hope for the future. And those full lips of hers, well, those gave me an entirely different genre of thoughts, but equally good.

"Well, you're in luck, because I plan to spend the rest of my life giving you every single thing you want," I replied. "So how about you start with telling me what you want right now."

She stretched beneath me and purred like a kitten. "I think I'd like to start with your tongue," she said, as if ordering off a menu.

"And where would you like it?" I asked.

Giada moaned instead of answering, but I knew exactly what she wanted. I circled the tip of my tongue around one of her pert nipples, then the other, and then I lifted her, shifting us both.

"Sit on my face, baby."

For once, my wife did as she was told.

~

Giada

*L*uca and I slept in late Saturday morning, both of us exhausted from an exhilarating night of doing all the things that don't make babies. Well, and maybe one round of the activity that does, but since I was still on birth control, it didn't matter anyway.

Luca went to the gym, and I busied myself tidying the apartment and then making omelets while he was gone. The eggs turned out oddly lumpy and brown, but Luca ate them without complaint. *Poor guy.* He was probably about to give up hope that my mom's cooking lessons would ever kick in.

"What do you want to do this afternoon?" he asked, stretching out on top of me on the couch, smushing the magazine I'd been holding.

"Don't you have work stuff?"

"I'm spending the day with you," he replied, not exactly answering the question.

I stroked my fingers through the soft, silky strands of his hair. "Well, there's a home show going on this week that I wouldn't mind checking out. And that new Vietnamese restaurant just opened in the same area so that would be perfect for an early dinner. Oh, and then mass, of course."

"Of course," he repeated.

There was a lengthy silence while I waited for him to protest each of these items. Instead, he just asked what he should wear to a home show.

I couldn't actually believe my luck, getting to spend the entire day with my favorite person, doing exactly what I wanted. Luca ended up enjoying the home show almost as much as me, though, and it was very interesting seeing all of the design ideas that he was drawn to. As we wandered around the massive convention hall though, I couldn't help but think about an idea that had been floating around in my brain since the carjacking.

I hadn't yet mentioned my idea to Luca because I worried he'd agree to anything I asked for, even if it wasn't what he wanted. But deep down, I suspected he'd be thrilled with the idea. There was another person who would be affected though, and my conscience told me I should talk with him first, though.

As we were finishing dinner, Luca glanced at his phone and mumbled an Italian curse under his breath.

"Sorry, amore, just…my papà."

"Do you need to call him?" I asked.

Luca's phone buzzed again, and he grimaced while reading the message.

I reached for his free hand and squeezed it. "Babe, it's fine. I can go to mass alone if you need to handle some work."

He peered up at me, visibly torn. I tried to offer him a reassuring smile. I loved when Luca attended mass with me. Sitting close to him, holding his hand, smelling his delicious aftershave, and sneaking glances at his handsome face always improved any experience. But I also sort of figured being in church couldn't hurt his chances of salvation, in the long-run.

Still, I was perfectly comfortable attending the service alone, and I had no concerns about my safety inside the house of God.

Luca tapped out a quick text, handed the waiter the check portfolio, then smiled up at me. A moment later, his phone notified him of another text.

"Alessio will join you for mass. I should make it back before the end of the service, but if not, he can walk you home."

"I'm fine to go alone," I said, not because I didn't want Alessio there, but because I knew he didn't love church. I understood why he didn't feel comfortable there, and I respected his decision, even though his issues were more with the interpretations of organized religion and not with God himself.

"He's meeting us there," Luca said. He rose to his feet and reached for my hand. I stood, surprisingly full, then followed him to the door.

He kissed me gingerly as we reached the church, then greeted a well-dressed Alessio with a simple handshake and a "grazie."

Alessio followed me to a row near the middle of the sanctuary, further back than I'd normally sit but as close as I figured he'd be comfortable. The homily was boring compared to the usual ones from Father Michael, and my mind wandered back to my earlier thoughts. All day, this plan had been front and center in my thoughts, and now, I was in church, unable to focus on anything but this possible future. And I was sitting next to the very man I needed to discuss it all with.

If that wasn't a sign from God, I didn't know what was.

I didn't dawdle leaving the sanctuary after the service, greeting only a fraction of the people I usually would. Luca hadn't returned yet, so Alessio and I started towards the apartment. The night air was crisp and cool, but as I tugged my peacoat tighter, it felt only refreshing.

"Can I ask you something?" I began.

"Oh, you're asking permission first now?" he teased.

"Would you ever consider moving?"

"Before retiring in West Palm Beach?"

"No, I mean like to a new house."

Alessio shrugged, his eyes trained on the sidewalk now. "Sure. I have zero attachment to my current place. I'm not really interested in home ownership if that's what you mean, though. Too much of a commitment and too much square footage."

I considered that, then asked another clarifying question. "But you'd never be interested in living with someone else, would you?"

"I'm too old for roommates unless we're fucking," he said. "Excuse my language."

"So you'd never live with Luca?"

"Well, I'm not about to start screwing around with him, so—"

"I'm being serious, Alessio. What if we had a bigger house, like, something like what I grew up in?"

He turned to me as we neared a crosswalk. "Luca does not have that kind of money. Not yet, anyway."

"Okay, not quite that big, but a house, at least. With plenty of space, and ideally a pool."

"I don't understand. Are you guys moving? Luca hasn't said anything."

"I haven't told Luca."

"You haven't told him that he's moving?" Confusion filled Alessio's face.

I waited till we crossed the street to answer. "No, I mean, haven't told him that I'm scared literally all the time, and I don't ever want to be alone again."

Alessio stopped abruptly, reaching for my arm to pull me back to him after I kept walking. He stared at me for a long moment, then said, "Giada."

I dabbed my free hand under my eye, determined not to screw up my makeup. "Look, it's fine. I will get back to normal eventually, but I just thought, well I thought I'd feel safer if it wasn't just me and Luca."

"It's never just you and Luca. You know that any one of our guys would do anything for you."

"Right, if they happen to be with me whenever it happens. Last time, no one was."

Alessio pulled me in for a hug, catching me completely off guard. He'd just never been an affectionate guy, and now here he was, literally embracing me.

He moved his hands to grip my biceps when he pulled back. "Have you talked to Luca about any of this?"

I shook my head. "No, because if I say something to Luca, he'll tell you to move in and you'll do it because you never say no to him, and he never says no to me."

Alessio chuckled. "Luca says no to you all the time. You just don't listen."

I supposed he wasn't wrong.

"I can move in tonight," he said. "You don't need to get a bigger place on my account."

I appreciated the offer, but that wasn't the point. "I want the bigger place. I want to start building a family, and not the biological kind. I want someplace where you could live long-term with your…partner, and any kids you have."

Alessio grimaced. "Okay, I was on board with this until that kid stuff. I'm not having kids. I'll be the fun uncle, but that's my limit."

I laughed, and Alessio released my arms. Just then, I spotted Luca a few feet away, striding towards us.

"Am I interrupting something?" he asked.

Alessio caught my eye, then faced my husband. "You'll have to ask your wife. You okay to get her home?"

"Of course," Luca replied. He turned to me, his eyes filled with concern. "Everything okay?"

I nodded. Maybe it wasn't yet, but it would be.

Luca pressed a kiss to my forehead, his lips lingering long enough to calm me. "Let's get home," he whispered. "Then we'll talk."

CHAPTER 15

PART TWO

EIGHT MONTHS LATER

Luca

I shifted nervously, careful to support the newborn's head while trying to smile for the millionth damn photo. Aldo fidgeted in his swaddle and peered up at me with big brown eyes. I was grateful he wasn't wailing at the moment, but I was still more than ready to pass him back to his mother.

I was far from an expert on babies, but Aldo seemed better than most. He cried a lot, ate nonstop, and had zero sense of night and day, but he was so adorable that it took little effort for all of us to overlook his shortcomings. Even the sound of his wailing was a little cute, to be honest. It could've been the size though. He was just so darn tiny. All the ladies kept saying how big he was, but he felt lighter than Giada's purse and he looked like a miniature version of an old man.

"Okay, Giada, get in there for one," the photographer directed.

I relaxed with relief, ready to pass the baby to her, until the photographer specified that I should keep holding him. I swung my free arm around my wife. Aldo's gaze focused on her, not that I blamed him. She was definitely a better sight than me.

"You're a natural," Giada said to me, tickling Aldo's toe in between shots.

"I feel like I'm holding a live grenade," I replied through clenched teeth.

"Well, I mean, just don't drop him, and we'll all be fine," she replied, pressing a kiss to my cheek before abandoning me to go chat with the ladies.

"Okay, I'm done," I said. "Giovanni, take your kid."

My friend chuckled but dutifully collected his baby, walking him back towards Lauren.

"This padrino job is no joke, huh," Alessio teased, patting me on the back.

I blew out a sigh. No one had been surprised when Giovanni and Lauren had chosen me as their baby's godfather, but in light of our business arrangement, we all appreciated the irony of the job title.

The kid had slept through the entire christening that morning, then cried without pause for a solid two hours while we all brunched. Lauren said he'd spent the entire night nursing, so she was exhausted.

Giovanni returned to us after depositing Aldo with his wife.

"How's this whole parenting gig going?" I asked.

Giovanni shook his head. "I don't know. It's all a blur. I thought it would be getting better now that he's a month old, but it's not. I can't remember the last time I was this tired. I understand now why people use sleep deprivation as a form of torture. I'm a mess."

Thomas winced. "Thanks for the heads up. Remind me not to tag along on your next job. You'll probably fall asleep and shoot off my foot."

"Remind me not to get anyone pregnant," Alessio said. "That kid is cute and all, but no way."

"Something tells me you don't need to worry about that in your current relationship," Giovanni said.

Alessio grinned then turned back to where the ladies were standing with Aldo. "Thank God. But you might," he said, swatting my arm.

I turned to follow his gaze and saw Giada holding the baby. He was fussing, his face all wrinkled up like an angry alien, but she was smiling and cooing at him like she'd never seen something so adorable.

"Cavolo," I mumbled. Literally, it translated to "cabbage," which didn't make a whole lot of sense in English, but now I was surrounded by Italians. They knew it was a mild swear word.

All three of them laughed, but I meant it. This was not good news. Giada and I were happy. Everything was going perfect for us at the moment. I had zero complaints about our relationship, and neither did Giada. At least, until now she hadn't. Anyone could decipher the look on her face at the moment. She was in love. With a baby.

After a moment, Giada must have sensed me staring, as she met my gaze and grinned. I shook my head, keeping my expression serious so she'd know what I meant. Not surprisingly, she nodded in response then blew me a kiss.

"Well, we all know what Giada's getting for Christmas," Thomas joked.

"Not a chance," I replied. "Giovanni, go get your kid. Please?"

He laughed, but didn't move.

"Hey, Giada mentioned that she's never seen The Godfather. I was thinking maybe we'd have a little movie marathon," Alessio said, grinning widely.

We all chuckled at that, even though I didn't doubt he meant it. He and Giada were good friends now, and with the move coming up in a couple of weeks, I knew they'd only get closer. I was good with that.

The past few months had been busy. No, busy was an understatement.

My papà had returned to Italy, leaving me in charge of our U.S. operations, and Giada had sold me on her plan of a big, family manor like what she'd grown up on.

Initially, I'd had my doubts. Yeah, I'd been lonely growing up. I would've killed for a sibling. But now? I generally preferred my privacy with Giada. We were long past the honeymoon stage of our marriage, but we still liked to make love anywhere and everywhere. And often. I didn't need an audience hampering that.

But I could handle Alessio. He was discrete and he'd stay out of our way. And his presence would make Giada feel safer, so that overrode any of my other concerns. So, I'd given Giada the acceptable geographic zone where we could live, since Alessio and I couldn't be too far from our work, then she'd set out looking for properties.

The type of property Giada described to me would probably run close to fifteen million dollars, which we didn't have, but she assured me we just needed room to grow. She looked for empty lots or fixer uppers. She'd focused her search on older homes with a lot of land and we both prepared to wait years for the right place. By some miracle, an old farmhouse went up for sale at some auction less than a week after I agreed to the plan.

The structure itself was one stiff breeze away from being condemned, but it sat on ten acres and a small pond less than twenty minutes from the club. We bought it with cash, used our own guys to demo the entire property. For the past seven months, we'd been building our dreamhouse from scratch. For now, we'd opted to build the main house and pool, but Giada had grand plans to add on at least two separate cottages or carriage houses in the future so Alessio—and whoever else—could live on property without actually being inside the main house.

With Angelo's connections in the building permits and

inspections departments, as well as his construction guys, the whole thing was just about done. Giada had handled all of the design aspects. Now that we neared the end of the project, I'd barely seen her the last few weeks as she focused all her time and attention on furnishing the place.

The house itself was smaller than her childhood home, but still massive, with plenty of square footage for any children she wanted, and all of the security measures I needed. We'd have room for entertaining and more than enough space for Alessio to live with us as long as he wanted, too. We were scheduled to move in three weeks, and Giada had scheduled a housewarming party for two weeks after that.

I wasn't entirely sure I understood what the rush was, but I also knew better than to disagree with Giada. Besides, I didn't love the chaos of the move. I'd be happier once we were fully settled into the new place.

Giada sidled up to me just then and rest her head on my shoulder. She'd apparently returned the baby to his parents, but I could still detect a hint of Aldo's baby powder mixed in with Giada's usual vanilla and jasmine scent.

"Welp, its official. He's the cutest baby ever. Our kids will never be that cute."

I shook my head. Okay, maybe I could disagree with my wife sometimes.

~

Giada

*L*uca claimed he needed to work after we got home from the christening. Personally, I thought he just wanted some space from me because he was worried I'd force him to impregnate me instantly.

Honestly, I wasn't completely opposed to the idea.

In my defense, Aldo was adorable. Like, off-the-charts cute. I didn't realize babies were so tiny. Or that they smelled so good. Or that their little legs scrunched up towards their tummies when you first lifted them.

But since I had the night free, I met up with Gabby instead. She and I were finally back to where we used to be friendship-wise. We didn't discuss her brother's involvement with my husband's business too often, but according to Luca, Carlo was doing well. He was dutifully working to pay off his debt and was showing potential for becoming more involved down the road.

Over the past nine months, Gabby and I had been training with Enzo. He'd taught us everything from basic self-defense maneuvers to shooting skills. I'd probably never be comfortable fighting—or even holding a gun in my hand—but at least now I theoretically knew how to do both. Plus the classes had built up my confidence and Gabby's, all while giving us a safe space to rebuild our shattered friendship.

For the last several months, I'd suspected Gabby had a crush on Enzo. She hadn't admitted it until about a month ago. She still hadn't told him, even though his relationship with Sara had fizzled out long before that.

Now they were just two single, attractive people not making the first move.

"I don't know what you're waiting for," I said, carrying our shots across the bar. Gabby carried a beer, which she dutifully deposited at Lincoln's table, adjacent to ours. We couldn't indulge in girl talk with the man at our table, but I felt bad making him sit in the car all night while Gabby and I had fun. He nodded his head in appreciation then returned to his phone.

"I'm waiting for him to ask me out. Or at least to show any sign he's interested," Gabby replied.

She had a point. She'd been flirting shamelessly with Enzo for ages now and he'd treated her no differently than he did me. Although, she'd flirted before he was single, so maybe he thought that was just how she behaved. And Luca maintained Enzo was flirty with me, so maybe that was another part of the problem. I didn't know. What I did know was that it would be awesome if two of my good friends could fall madly in love.

"What if he thinks he's too good for me?" she asked.

"Why would he think that?"

Gabby made a face, like it was obvious.

"You are absolutely deserving of a man like Enzo, and he does not think he's too good for you. Now let's toast to hot guys."

We did, then we both winced as the shots went down.

"So how is everything going with the house?" Gabby asked.

"Great! We're doing a final walkthrough a week from Wednesday, and then the movers come the following Monday. We'll stay at my parents for like a week so that I can get everything organized before we move in, but then it should be good to go."

"And you're sure you'll have enough time to get settled before the big party?"

I ignored the skepticism written all over my friend's face. "Yep. Zero concerns. It'll be perfect."

Gabby didn't look convinced. "Okay but what's the rush?"

"Luca's parents are coming to town for two weeks. I'm worried they'll insist on staying longer if we don't have the party while they're here."

"Oh. Well, that makes sense," she agreed.

A waitress arrived with another round of shots and tall glasses of water. She nodded to Lincoln's table. "From the guy over there."

I smiled and raised my glass to him in appreciation, even though I knew I'd be the one footing the bill. Well, or my husband would anyway.

"We'll need some long island iced teas too," Gabby told the waitress.

I quirked a brow and she merely shrugged. "We have a driver anyway," she explained.

"Good point." And if Luca and I decided to try for a baby soon, this might be my last night of debauchery for a while.

"So how's Angelo? Still enjoying his new house?"

"How could he not? It's perfectly designed." I replied. "He's still a mess though. Mom and Dad are talking about fixing him up with the kid of one of Dad's friends."

"Yikes."

"Yeah. But speaking of a fix up," I began, my eyes flitting to Lincoln's table, where two cute girls stood. They looked barely old enough to drink, but seemed fascinated by my driver. "What if you go out with Lincoln? He's cute. And then if that doesn't work out, maybe it'll at least get Enzo's attention."

Gabby snorted. "I think those girls are closer to his age than I am."

She might have been right, and I made a mental note to ask him his age later. "Age is just a number, babe. And come on, he's cute, right?"

"He is cute. But Enzo is hot. There's a difference."

She wasn't wrong.

CHAPTER 16

Luca

Giada and I were just finishing the final walkthrough at the new house when my papà called. I released my wife's hand, gesturing that I'd just be a moment. I answered the call in Italian, explaining where I was and asking if I could call him back in a bit.

"You need an alibi today," he said, not acknowledging anything I'd said. "Alessio and the others too."

"When?" I asked, my throat already feeling dry.

"I can give you an hour to get prepared, then hope to have the all-clear by evening. Let's plan to meet at Roselli's at six. I'll fill you in then."

"What about Giada? Or the Contis?"

"No, they're fine."

My papà disconnected before I could ask for more details. I took a moment to clear my expression before turning back to my wife, but she already knew something was wrong. Her brows furrowed as she gazed up at me.

"Tesoro, I'm sorry," I murmured. "My papà is having some

troubles. Nothing dangerous but Alessio and I have to go. I won't be back until evening." I thought about it, then added. "Linc too, actually."

Thankfully, Angelo was there for the walkthrough, since his guys had done most of the construction. I met his eye. "I need to head out and I'm taking Giada's driver with me. Can you drop her at our apartment?"

He nodded, then turned back to Eddie.

"You sure this is nothing dangerous?" Giada asked, lowering her voice.

"Positive. My papà just has terrible timing. I'm so sorry. Call me if you need anything." I pulled her in for a long, lingering kiss, ending it only when I remembered her brother was mere steps away.

Then, I called Alessio and arranged for all the guys to meet me at Rize. We spent the entire day at the club, dividing our time evenly between working and socializing, but staying well within view of the cameras and inside the public areas of the club at all times. I checked in with my papà periodically, but he refused to give me any details over the phone.

When it came time to meet my papà for dinner, I brought Alessio, leaving the rest of the guys at the club. My papà looked so jovial when he greeted us that I almost thought I'd misunderstood his earlier call.

"So good to see my son," he said, clapping me on the back before walking to a table in the front of the restaurant—right within view of the security camera. This table was about as far from our usual table as we could have gone. Our usual table, in the back corner, had become our usual precisely because of the privacy it offered. Apparently, we still needed that alibi.

Alessio and I followed my papà's cue and acted normally, despite the growing frustration over the flux in our plans for the day. A waiter brought wine, then took our orders. Once he'd collected all of the menus, my papà leaned in to speak.

"You're facing the cameras, so be careful when you talk, but they don't have sound," he began. "I'm about to get some unfortunate news that one of my close associates was found deceased today."

My fingers clenched into a fist under the table. Obviously, I'd known my papà had orchestrated some horrific crime today that justified the need for such a wide-sweeping alibi. However, it had not occurred to me that he'd taken out one of his own men. That detail was surprising. That was…huge.

"I received information that an undercover agent had infiltrated our organization. We're doing damage control, but I don't think anyone else has been implicated."

Alessio and I exchanged a glance. We'd had our suspicions about Elio Randazzo, but Papà had dismissed them. It was hard to feel vindicated or even a little good about being right when the man was now dead though.

Our meals arrived and my papà dove into his like he was on death row. I supposed he wanted to eat as much as he could before the phone call came in, informing him of the news, but it was still disturbing. My own appetite had withered even though I barely knew Elio, let alone had a role in killing him. Apparently, my papà's conscience operated on a different scale.

Finally, my papà's phone rang. He appeared bored as he wiped his mouth and reached for the phone. He excused himself from the table then walked a few feet away, positioning himself in direct view of the camera. I stole a few glances as he spoke, noting the dramatic looks of shock he flashed for the camera as he allegedly learned for the first time of his dear employee's untimely demise.

Alessio texted Thomas the code to let everyone head home, while I chugged the rest of my wine.

"He deserves an Oscar," I mumbled, covering my mouth with my hand while I spoke.

Alessio snorted.

We acted nonchalant when my papà returned to the table, prepared to play our part as the surprised recipients of bad news.

"I'm so sorry, boys, but I have to go," he said, clutching his chest dramatically. "I just received some…terrible news."

"Is everything okay?" I asked, furrowing my brows.

Papà reached for his water glass, sipping for what felt like an eternity. "No, actually. I just learned that one of my employees, Mattia Puglisi, died from a fentanyl overdose today." He shook his head dramatically. "I didn't even know he had a drug problem."

I was prepared to offer generic words of comfort, but then I realized what my papà had said. The discrepancy must have hit Alessio as well.

"Wait, Mattia is dead?" he asked.

My papà's frown tightened nearly to a glare. "Yes. It's so tragic. His friend Elio Randazzo found the body. Apparently, he's a mess too. I don't blame him, the poor fella. They were close. They both came to work for me at the same time."

I rose to my feet. "I'm so sorry. He seemed like a nice guy the brief times we met. I, um, well, let me know if there's anything we can do. We'll take care of the bill."

My papà nodded, offered me a quick hug, then shuffled out of the restaurant. Alessio and I asked for the bill.

"Wow," he said as the waiter boxed up our uneaten food. "I did not expect to hear that news."

"Yeah. He didn't seem like he had a drug problem," I said truthfully.

"No, I agree," Alessio said. "And he was so young."

"I wonder if he had a family."

Alessio shrugged.

We of course knew the answer to this and other questions about the guy's life, thanks to our in-depth stalking, but it made for good fodder for the alibi if needed.

I drove Alessio back to the club, where he'd left his car. We were quiet most of the drive.

"How confident are you that he got the right guy?" Alessio asked as I turned into the lot.

"I trust your intel over his," I replied, my voice sounding confident and clear despite the roiling of my stomach at the implication of my words. If we were right, not only did that mean that someone was still mixed up in our business that shouldn't be. No, if we were right, that also meant my papà ordered the murder of an innocent man.

"So what do we do?" Alessio asked.

I sighed and dragged a hand through my hair. "I don't know. I'll give it a few days and then talk to my papà. He's not an impulsive man so he must have had some evidence that Matt was up to no good."

"I'm less concerned about him having killed an innocent man than him leaving a dangerous one alive," Alessio said.

"Me too," I said. Both issues troubled me, but one matter was certainly more pressing than the other.

～

Giada

"*Y*ou don't have to go," Luca repeated for maybe the tenth time as the SUV pulled onto the street.

I squeezed his hand. "I'm not making you go to your friend's funeral alone."

"He wasn't my friend. I barely knew the guy."

I turned to Luca, tracing my thumb along his freshly-shaven jawline. He smelled like aftershave and looked like heaven in his tailored black suit. We had just left church and were headed to the cemetery for a funeral, so I probably shouldn't be drooling over my sexy husband, but it had been weeks since I'd seen him all dressed up.

"How come you don't wear suit jackets as often anymore?" I asked, now stroking just beneath his lapel.

Luca bit back a grin. "Probably because I forgot how irresistible you find me in them."

Alessio cleared his throat from the front passenger seat. "None of us have forgotten how she feels about you in a suit. Neither of you are subtle. Or discrete. And some of us can't bring a date to this sort of event, so—"

"Yeah, yeah, yeah," Luca cut him off. "Behave, Giada," he said to me, winking in a way that just made me want to grope him more.

"What was Alessio like as a kid, Linc?" I asked. He was driving us all, but so far had remained quiet.

"Umm, kinda the same as now," he said. We all laughed at that.

I settled against the seat and turned to Luca again. He was staring out the window now, a calm expression on his face. He'd said before that this funeral wasn't a big deal, but he'd been stressed ever since he'd learned of the death. He'd also told me that the official cause of death was accidental overdose but that this "accident" occurred shortly after his dad suspected the guy of being a cop.

All of that was top secret of course, but I appreciated Luca trusting me enough to share. It helped me decide how to best comfort him when I knew why he was so stressed. Although, sometimes, I didn't understand how he could function at all with the amount of shit he had to deal with.

In the front seat, Alessio and Linc began discussing some baseball game.

"Hey," I whispered, stroking the back of Luca's hand to get his attention. "You're not responsible for the things your dad does. You know that, right?"

Luca turned to me, his expression solemn. "Yes, amore."

"His actions are on his soul, not yours. You are a good son and a good person."

Luca squeezed my hand and then raised it to his lips. He lingered, with his mouth against my skin, sending tingles up my arm.

"When are you due for your next shot?" he asked, slowly lowering our hands to his lap.

It took me a minute to realize the only shot I took was my birth control, and that my appointment was in two weeks. Crappy timing because of the move and the housewarming, but birth control was definitely one of those things that had to be timed precisely to be effective.

"Two weeks."

"What happens if you…don't…go?" he asked, drawing the words out.

I hesitated. "Then it stops working."

Luca peered out the window again for a solid minute, leaving me in a confused panic. Just as I was about to shake him and ask what he was thinking, he turned back to me.

"How would you feel about cancelling the appointment?" he asked.

I cast a glance to the front seat, but they still weren't paying any attention to us. "If I don't get the shot, I could get pregnant. Like, any time we…"

Luca nodded. "I understand."

My heart thudded in my chest. "So you're saying you think we're ready to try?"

Luca's sheepish grin melted my heart. God that man was adorable when he smiled.

"Giada, I don't think anyone is ever ready for parenthood, but I can't imagine anyone would be a better mother than you, and I really can't wait to see you in action," he finally said. "Life is short. I don't want to get bogged down in the bad. I want to make all the good memories with you."

I licked my lips, trying to reign in my pulse. I would've killed to be alone with Luca now, so I could climb on his lap and trail kisses all over his body.

"If you're ready," he added, destroying the last ounce of my self-control.

I launched my upper body onto Luca, clutching his face in my hands and kissing him like we were alone. I felt Luca's smile widen against my lips as he kissed me back.

Alessio swore from the front seat, but I didn't even care. The car jerked to a stop a moment later and Luca casually unbuckled both of our belts and smoothed my hair back in place.

"I love you," he whispered. "Amore."

Lincoln opened the car door, rolled his eyes dramatically, then turned to his cousin. "Are you sure you want to move in with them?"

Luca and I both laughed, then walked hand and hand towards the gravesite.

CHAPTER 17

Luca

The following week was a blur. Between the funeral, my continued suspicions about Elio being the rat, and the actual move, I barely had time to breathe, let alone to talk with my wife about what I'd brought up before the funeral. Further complicating factors was Giada's insistence that we stay at her parents throughout the move.

I appreciated her desire to avoid the chaos of staying in a house that wasn't fully put together, but sleeping under her father's roof hardly made my life feel any more settled. I could not wait to actually live in our new home.

When Giada called me that afternoon and told me everything at the house was finally perfect, I nearly jumped for joy. She insisted on presenting the house to Alessio and I like we were contestants on one of those home design reality TV shows. We'd both seen the house many times by that point, but Giada had added some accents since our last visit—a few rugs, some decorative vases, curtains, and paintings.

Alessio and I followed her from room to room, oohing and

aahing at appropriate intervals, and then the tour finished at the back yard. The sod had been installed less than a week prior, so the yard didn't quite look idyllic yet, but I was optimistic it would improve before the big housewarming party Giada had planned.

"So, now we can all sleep here tonight."

I grinned, thrilled at the prospect. Alessio cleared his throat.

"Actually, I'm gonna let you two have some privacy until the party. I've got a couple weeks left on my lease, so I'll join you after the housewarming," he said.

This wasn't news to me, and I didn't expect Giada to take issue with it either, but she frowned.

"It's your house too," Giada said, pouting dramatically.

Technically, it wasn't, in terms of the actual deed and property tax records, but I knew what she meant.

"I appreciate that, Princess, and I'm so excited to come live here. I just want you guys to get settled on your own first." He offered her a quick side hug, but she turned to me, still pouty.

"Is this your doing?" she asked.

I lifted my hands defensively. "No! This was Alessio's decision."

She blew out a sigh. "If it's really just a couple weeks, fine. But, I mean, if you recall, the whole point of this big house was so that you could be here. I wanted to be surrounded by more people so I'd feel safer, not to just be alone in an even bigger, scarier space."

My stomach tightened and Alessio winced.

"I swear it's just until the party G, but if you want me to go get my stuff now, I will," he said.

Giada eyed him as if trying to determine if he were telling the truth. After a moment, she relented. "Okay. I suppose it will be nice to have a couple of weeks to settle in with this guy." She tilted her head towards me.

Alessio took off before she could change her mind, leaving me and my wife standing outside our brand-new dream home.

"Come here," I said, gesturing for her to follow me. We walked along the stepping stones around to the front door. I unlocked the door, propped it open with my foot, then grinned.

"Welcome home, amore," I said, scooping Giada into my arms and carrying her over the threshold of the house.

She shrieked dramatically and I paused in the foyer, trying to decide which room we should christen first. Grinning, I lowered her to the grand staircase. She eyed me suspiciously as I sat beside her, but when I patted my lap, she didn't hesitate to straddle me.

"So," I began. "We have a lot of rooms to make love in before Alessio officially moves in and cramps my style. But I also feel like we left a discussion hanging."

Giada raised a brow.

"I meant what I said about the baby. I'm ready if you are."

She smiled. "I thought you said no one is ever really ready."

I shrugged. *Touché*. "Well, there's no one I'd rather be completely unprepared with than you. So, are we doing this?"

Giada locked eyes with me as she unbuttoned the top of her floral dress. Then she inched backwards so she could unzip my fly. I wrapped one hand around her back to hold her in place while letting the other drift to her exposed breast. Giada worked at my pants until she'd freed my cock.

"Good thing I'm not wearing any panties," she whispered, licking her hand and then smearing the moisture over my growing length.

I groaned at the intense sensation. "Umm what was your plan if Alessio stayed?"

"There are a lot of rooms in this house, Luca." She shifted her hips, positioning me right at her entrance. "And before you get all excited, my birth control won't wear off for at least another week so there's zero chance of this being anything but practice."

"I am good with practice," I said, lowering my head so my teeth could graze her nipples as she seated herself fully on my length.

. . .

Adrian

*I*f I had to define my personal hell, it might involve an afternoon soiree celebrating the new home of the woman I once thought I'd marry and my nemesis, along with my more recent ex-girlfriend and a bunch of criminals who still made me nervous. And yet, here I was, all dressed up on a Sunday afternoon climbing out of Angelo's Escalade with a fucking juicer wrapped in silver tissue paper wedged under my arm.

I hadn't been surprised at all by the invite, and had even appreciated Giada's casual text letting me know that Melissa had rsvp'd yes to the event, in case that influenced my attendance one way or the other. I'd replied that it didn't matter, though it absolutely did. Then, I claimed I had tentative plans with my sister that afternoon anyway. Giada probably knew both statements were lies, but that woman was classy enough to let it go.

Her oldest brother, on the other hand, was not. He'd informed me I'd be riding with him and Eddie, even after I told him I had plans. Angelo didn't appear to even consider that I still felt awkward around his sister. Rather, he assumed Melissa was my only demon that day. But his conflicting advice of "show her you don't care" and "be the bigger man" still did little to soothe my nerves, especially since I didn't have my own car and was essentially trapped at the damn party until whenever Angelo decided he was ready to leave.

The exterior of the home reminded me a bit of the Conti house, with an obvious European influence. I had previously overheard Giada telling someone that the inspiration for the home was French Renaissance meets modern farmhouse and I really couldn't picture that at the time. But now, standing in front of the massive structure, I saw what she meant. The entire façade was cream with black accents and old-world charm. Giada motioned us up the bluestone steps towards an arched doorway with elegant glass doors.

Giada greeted us each with a warm smile and a hug, before motioning for us to grab a drink from the kitchen. "I'll start giving tours in a few minutes, and then there's tons of food, so I hope you're hungry."

I awkwardly lifted the package in my hands, wordlessly asking where to put it.

"You're so thoughtful. You didn't have to do that though," she said, taking the box and setting it on a card table in what I assumed was a living room. I followed her into the kitchen, not at all surprised to see custom white cabinets, creamy marble countertops, and sleek gray hardwoods. A giant farmhouse sink occupied one countertop and another, slightly smaller sink sat inside the oversized island. Since I didn't notice any mundane appliances, I assumed those were hiding in some fancy butler's pantry along with a third kitchen sink.

What captured my attention was the room just beyond the kitchen. I supposed it was the informal dining room, though nothing about the space was informal. The room jutted out into the yard, extending past the rest of the house. It boasted three walls of near solid windows offering a grand view of the greenery from outside. An elegant chandelier hung from the peak of the vaulted ceiling, but was surrounded by skylights on all sides.

My heart clutched as the memory of my first time in Giada's childhood home swept over me. She'd taken me to the sunroom, and told me how that room was her sacred space. She felt soothed by the sunlight, safe in the room of glass, and the more I'd gotten to know her, the more the irony had bothered me. The woman whose life was filled with secrecy thrived on openness.

I startled, sensing a presence beside me. I turned to see Luca. He stood beside me, a crystal highball glass in his hand, seemingly admiring the same breathtaking sight as I was. He wore a blue-gray pair of fitted chinos with a white, short-sleeved button-down shirt. I briefly wondered if his wife had dressed him, but then I remembered he was Italian. And he'd always been into fashion. The fact that his pants were rolled up at the ankles revealing his sockless feet in loafers confirmed my hunch that this was all his doing.

"I'm guessing this is Giada's favorite room," I said, without making eye contact.

"Of course," he said, tipping his glass from side to side until the ice clinked against the edge. "I thought she was joking when she showed me the designs for the ceiling, but you can't say no to the princess."

I tried to think of a response to that when he patted me on the back and sauntered off, motioning towards the slew of beverages on the island. I helped myself to a bourbon and was about to move on to the snacks when Giada came up behind me.

"Care for a tour?" she offered.

I shrugged, and followed her back to the front of the house, where Enzo, Melissa, Eddie, and Giada's old friend Gabby stood waiting. *Of course* I had to be on the same tour as Melissa. I greeted everyone, then thankfully Giada launched into her spiel without hesitation. After spending several minutes apologizing for not showing us the unfinished basement and explaining about how it would be finished in the future, when she and Luca were in Italy, she showed us the study, a bathroom, the living room, the formal dining room, and her office.

"You've already seen the kitchen, the great room, and then my favorite room. I called it the morning room in all the designs but it actually faces west and catches the sunsets and not the sunrises, so the name doesn't really fit. The timing works way better for Luca and I though, since we are definitely not morning people."

Gabby snorted. "That's an understatement."

"Off the kitchen there's also a mudroom and another powder room, a laundry room, and a butler's pantry that has an extra fridge and the dishwasher and stuff like that." Giada paused and turned to me. "My mom has been giving me cooking lessons lately. I'm nowhere close to your level of talented, Adrian, but I'm hoping that in a few years maybe I'll be self-sufficient enough to not starve if we're out of delivery range."

I smiled politely, then snuck a gaze at Melissa. She was staring at me, but looked away right as our eyes met. I bit back a grin and refocused on the tour.

"There's also a second staircase back there and an entire guest suite complete with a bedroom, bathroom, walk-in closet, and private den. For now, that's Alessio's realm, but the long-term plan is to build him his own place on the other side of the pool. He's being a little stubborn about telling me his design ideas, and Luca keeps claiming we're out of money, so who knows when all of that will happen." Giada laughed jovially and led us all up the wide, wooden staircase.

I hung back, letting Gabby go ahead of me, but then Enzo and Eddie jumped in, leaving me with Melissa.

"Gorgeous house," I said.

She nodded in agreement, then said, "You jealous?"

The question caught me off guard, and while I suspected she meant it as a joke, I wasn't positive. On the surface, anyone would be jealous. The house was immaculate and far beyond what anyone our age should logically dream of having. But if I were being honest, no, I wasn't jealous. This lifestyle wasn't for me. I prided myself on being the hardworking pull-myself-up-by-my-bootstraps type of guy. And Giada wasn't the right woman for me.

As I turned back to Melissa, I finally understood what she'd been saying, too. Melissa also was not the right woman for me.

"This place is perfect for Giada. I'm pretty content with my condo though," I finally said.

Melissa smiled. "It's a great condo."

I grinned, then heard Enzo ask something about the security features.

Giada paused on the landing and scowled, tucking her hair behind her ear. "Okay, so I wouldn't share this with just anyone, but you all probably already know that I've been a little freaked out about my safety lately."

"You have?" Eddie chimed in. "I thought Luca was the paranoid one."

Enzo glared at him, but Giada just shrugged.

"Yeah, well, neither of us are too keen on me getting killed. So, the house has a few features we both love. Lots of security cameras, digital locks, and fancy alarm system. Plus, the double staircase makes me feel like I've always got an escape route. My personal favorite feature though is the panic button."

"Uhh you said button, singular. There are multiple," Enzo corrected.

"True. There's a few, scattered throughout. So anytime I get scared, I tap the button, and it sends an alert."

"To the police?" I asked.

She shook her head. "If I just tap once, the alert only goes to my emergency contacts. If I tap three times, then it'll also call the cops."

"Three? Not two?"

"I want to be sure I'm intentional."

"Get to the good part," Enzo interrupted. "Tell him who these emergency contacts are. No wait, actually, let everyone guess."

I considered that for a moment. Luca and Alessio were obvious choices, since they lived with her, so I started there. And then Lincoln was driving her now, so he was my third guess. I spoke my conjectures aloud.

"There's one more," Giada said sheepishly.

"Marco?" I finally said.

Giada shook her head right as Enzo raised his hand. "Nope,

it's me. I get an alert every time the princess freaks out over a spider in the bathtub," he said.

"Oh my God, it was a brown recluse and that was one time. You've gotta let it go, man," Giada replied.

"It was the size of a flea and it was harmless," Enzo said, but he was grinning.

"Anyway, moving along with the tour," Giada said.

The upstairs formed a square around the open foyer in the center. Giada first showed us a beautifully decorated guestroom. A jack-and-jill style bathroom connected it to the next room, which was structurally identical to the first, but lacked any furniture or décor. A third, even larger bedroom, was adjacent from the second, and it too was empty. This room had its own private bathroom.

"We haven't really decided what to do with these rooms yet," Giada said, right as Gabby said what we were all thinking.

"This is the perfect space for the nursery."

Giada blushed, and I couldn't help but stare at her stomach. Her fitted mauve floral dress showed no signs of a baby bump, but I supposed anything was possible.

"This next room is just a rec room or loft. It could technically be a bedroom, but we'll probably use it as a playroom or craft space someday," Giada said, letting us all peer into the massive room quickly before moving on. "Here's another bathroom, a second laundry room, and then here's our bedroom."

"Where all the magic happens," Eddie crooned, in a voice that made me want to vomit. Thankfully, Enzo smacked him on the back of the head, so he shut up.

The king-sized bed was the focal point of the room, and faced a cozy-looking fireplace. The wall adjacent to the bed was lined with windows and had a set of French doors in the middle. A cozy seating area occupied that section of the room. The French doors led to a balcony overlooking the backyard. The balcony itself was shallow, extending only a few feet over the yard, but it stretched along the entire length of the room. Below, we could see the bluestone patio and the sparkling azure pool.

The closet was easily bigger than my entire bedroom, and the bathroom resembled a spa, with a massive claw-foot tub in one corner and a rainfall shower that could hold an entire family in the other.

She ushered us all back to the landing. "There's another balcony out here, and this one has a bit of space for entertaining or just quiet family meals. I'd love to have a true English garden here someday, like with fountains and a maze," Giada said, "But obviously that will take a few years."

"There's so many projects I still want to tackle, but I'm really happy with how it all turned out so far," Giada said.

We all gushed a series of platitudes about the house, then headed downstairs. I didn't have to pretend; the house was gorgeous. I could see all of Giada's touches, but I could also tell where she'd included Luca's style preference. I couldn't believe she was actually planning to live with Alessio, but Angelo had told me it had even been Giada's idea.

Back downstairs, I loaded a plate with food and braced myself for small talk with Melissa. Before I made my way to her though, Marco hopped in my path. He and Giada's uncle Leo yammered for the better part of an hour, so by the time I finally excused myself, Melissa was getting ready to leave. Oddly enough, the conversation was way less awkward than I'd envisioned, and by the time Angelo dropped me off at my place an hour later, I decided I'd been dreading it all for nothing.

CHAPTER 18

Luca

With my parents headed back to Italy in a few days, Giada and I had agreed to join them for dinner at their place. I hadn't seen them since the housewarming the previous Sunday, but Alessio had met with my papà the day before. We'd been looking into everything with Mattia and Elio, and as much as we tried to back up our suspicions about Elio with some hard evidence, we came up empty.

Despite that, I still didn't trust Elio, nor did I want him involved in my business. Alessio shared our findings, or lack thereof, as well as that message. Surprisingly, my papà didn't mind, and said he'd move Elio out to Italy with him anyway. Still, I half expected to hear more about that during dinner.

Instead, he greeted Giada and I both with a smile. He kissed my wife on each cheek, then gestured at her dress, a teal A-line she bought the day before on a shopping spree with Gabriella.

"Pretty dress," he said. "You two always manage to look so put together."

Giada and I exchanged confused looks the second he turned.

My mother echoed the sentiment, noting that I, also, looked particularly handsome, then she helped my papà prepare drinks for everyone.

"Your parents are in a good mood," Giada commented.

I nodded in agreement. They were eerily chipper. "Maybe they're just excited about returning to Italy."

We sat in the living room with our drinks, and my parents asked about some of the remaining plans for the house. I did most of the talking, even though Giada was more familiar with the plans. I wanted to spare her from as much criticism as possible, and I fully anticipated my parents pointing out some huge perceived shortcoming with the house.

Instead, they seemed excited about the landscaping and even the basement design.

Right as we were getting ready to move to the dining room, the phone rang in the study and my papà popped up, excusing himself in Italian.

"Work, work, work," Mom droned, gesturing for us to sit. "That's all he does these days."

I pulled Giada's chair back from the table then sat beside her, squeezing her hand before reaching for my napkin. Stella, my mom's latest housekeeper, delivered plates of food to the table. My mother flashed her a smile that didn't quite reach her eyes, but kept her mouth closed until Stella retreated to the kitchen.

"Really now, why would she bring the food out while your father's on the phone?" Mom shook her head, flummoxed. "Well, don't let it get cold. Sal will join us when he joins us."

Giada eyed me nervously, so I cut into the chicken and placed the bite in my mouth. The meat was savory, but dry, so I reached for my drink.

"So, what else is new with you two?" Mom asked.

"Not a lot. We've just been focused on the move lately."

"Well, now that you've got that big house, it might be a nice time to start filling it with babies."

I coughed, nearly spitting the water I'd just sipped. "Mamma!" I scolded.

"What? I'm bored with your father working all the time, and lord knows none of us are getting any younger. There are at least three bedrooms perfect for children in there. Plus room for a nanny if you kick out Alessio." Mom paused. "You two will make the most beautiful babies."

"Thank you," Giada said, avoiding eye contact.

"What's this about making babies?" My papà asked, bursting into the room looking unusually carefree.

"Mamma was just pressuring Giada and me to give her grand-children. And I was about to tell her that we just finished building a new house, and now isn't quite the right time." I smiled at Giada while I spoke, hoping she realized I wasn't backtracking on our discussions. But I also couldn't stand knowing my parents thought we were trying for a baby. Especially if it didn't happen right away, I didn't need my papà thinking I was an even bigger failure than he already thought.

"There's plenty of time for that," Papà said, waving a hand dismissively. "I'm impressed with the work you did on that house, Giada. Very tasteful and classy."

My mom nodded in agreement. Giada's jaw dropped. I tried to recall if that was the first time my papà had ever compli-mented her on anything but her appearance.

We passed the rest of the meal with small talk, and then my papà invited me into his den for drinks while Giada and my mother headed out to look at the garden.

"I really can't stay long," I reminded him. "I've got that meeting with Kelso tomorrow morning."

Papà grinned. "I can't believe you sealed that deal."

I shrugged. "It was a team effort, and we lucked out."

"Don't be modest. You're smart about these things, and you know exactly how to go after what you want. I admire that."

I opened my mouth to speak, but nearly forgot how. It

sounded like my papà had just complimented me. Luckily, he droned on to another topic before I could dwell on the praise too much. He'd just begun telling me his plans for his return to Italy the next week when Giada joined us.

She burrowed into my side, and I wrapped my arm around her, certain she needed the comfort after fifteen minutes alone with my mother. When my papà glanced at his phone, I pressed a kiss to Giada's forehead, eliciting a wide smile from my wife. I couldn't help but gaze back at her for a moment longer.

Papà was watching us when I turned back to him. I half expected a crude joke or snarky comment, but instead, he actually smiled.

"You've both done a good job of balancing your work obligations and family duty with whatever else you want in life." He turned to Giada. "If you'd asked me when Luca was seventeen or even twenty-seven, I'd have said you made him reckless and weak."

I debated whether I needed to step in to say something, to defend my wife, but my papà continued.

"I'm happy to say I was wrong. You make him stronger, and I thank you for it."

Giada and I exchanged a glance. I could've sworn my papà just admitted he'd been wrong and complimented my wife, all at once. But surely that couldn't be right. Giada's eyes were wide and her lips parted in shock, but she said nothing.

Papà leaned in to hug me then gave Giada a kiss on each cheek before stepping back and addressing me in his boss voice. "Alright, now go home and make a baby so your mother has something to play with and can stop complaining about my work schedule."

Giada's face blanched. I gripped her hand tightly and led her down the driveway as fast as we could move. When we reached the car, we both dissolved into fits of laughter.

"I'm not sure if we're in the twilight zone or what's happening, but let's just go with it," Giada said.

"Right?" I couldn't believe my luck. Not that I typically had much positive interaction with my papà, but I certainly never had any good talks with him right before one of us left the country. His parting words to me were always ridden with guilt-trips and insults. "Maybe he's finally maturing," I said.

"Maybe your mom slipped some antidepressants into his wine," she countered.

I grinned. I doubted my mom would ever do such a thing, but had to admit it was a brilliant idea.

~

Giada

When we returned home from Luca's parents' house, I stopped in the kitchen for a glass of water. I smiled as I always did when I saw our gorgeous sunroom, then noticed Alessio lounging out back by the pool.

"Meet me upstairs?" Luca asked.

I pointed to the window. "Don't you want to go tell him what your dad said?" I asked, filling a glass with ice, then water from the fridge.

Luca roped his arms around my waist, pulling my back flush against his chest. "I would love to, but I feel like I should do everything my papà said before I start to brag."

"Everything?" I repeated, frowning.

"Si, there was that bit about making them a grandchild," he explained, his lips so close to the skin on my neck that I shivered.

"You don't do everything your dad says," I countered.

"Not true. I always try, I just don't always succeed. But this is something I'm willing to try at as long and as often as necessary." He punctuated his words with a kiss on the side of my neck, applying just enough suction to make me squirm against him.

Nerves fluttered in my belly at the prospect of our lovemaking potentially serving a real function for the first time, but Luca seemed brimming with confidence. He had moved on to a new section of my neck to kiss and suck while the evidence of his desire pressed firmly against my lower back.

I sipped my water, then craned my neck to peer at him. "Okay, but we're going upstairs. I don't want to have to tell our future child he was conceived in the kitchen with his uncle looking on."

Luca snorted. "I don't think you're supposed to tell the kid anything about how they got here regardless."

I giggled, realizing he was absolutely correct. Then I started up the stairs. I set my water on the nightstand, then let Luca undress me. As much as watching him strip turned me on, letting Luca undress me was always an aphrodisiac too. He touched me with such a mixture of gentleness and eagerness, desire and love. Every brush of his fingers against my skin stoked a fire deep in my belly.

He lowered me to the bed, shucked his shirt, then kissed me like he was heading off to war. My breasts tightened, my heart raced, and my core tingled with desire.

"Why are you still wearing pants?" I whined between kisses.

Luca growled, then nipped my lip before pushing off of me. He made fast work of his pants, then stretched back over me, but went straight for my neck. I reached between us, stroking his length, and he pulled back. But before I could complain, Luca's lips closed around a nipple, sucking and teasing until I was panting and dizzy. He moved lower, spreading my innermost folds with his fingers before running his tongue along my slit.

"Oh God!" I cried.

He lapped at me like I was his favorite dessert, and my body raced to the finish line. I was breathless and overcome with the pleasure…not to mention seconds away from orgasm, when it hit me. We were trying to make a baby here, not just follow our usual trend.

"Stop!" I panted.

Luca paused, peering up at me, his expression a mixture of confusion and longing.

"If we really want to make a baby, you're supposed to make me come at the same time as you or right after. I read that somewhere. Something about the uterine contractions pushing the sperm higher and that helps."

"I have no idea what any of that meant," he murmured, still hovering over my stomach.

"Get inside me now," I clarified.

Luca complied, with one slow, smooth thrust.

I moaned at the delicious sensation, already feeling my body inching back towards climax. I needed to distract myself or I'd still come way before Luca. This was the problem with his chivalrous insistence on always focusing on my needs first. Not that I would ever complain about that in normal circumstances, but for purposes of conception, apparently it wasn't ideal.

I thought about our sex life in general. I had zero complaints in that department. Even when Luca and I were younger and were still sorting out most elements of our tumultuous relationship, the sex had been fantastic. We'd always been on the same page about sex too, and I'd loved that. I genuinely wanted him just as much as he wanted me.

What if a baby changed all that? Surely it would, at least for a little while. I'd read that sex during pregnancy was still fine, unless there were some health concerns. But I was pretty sure sex right after delivery was off limits. What if we never got back into our old groove after that? What if having a baby forever ruined our sex life?

I realized Luca's breathing had grown frantic. I knew exactly what that meant—he was close. I panicked.

I shoved him, hard, right as he groaned and came in a warm spurt all over my stomach and the bed beside me.

"Cazzo," he mumbled. "Baby, are you okay? What happened? What's wrong?"

I stared at my gorgeous husband, his sparking brown eyes now filled with concern. Suddenly, I felt like the biggest idiot alive. I rolled onto my stomach, too embarrassed to let him see my face.

"I'm so sorry," I cried against the pillow. "I'm fine. I just need a minute."

Luca didn't say anything, but I could feel him staring at me. And as I shifted to the side, I realized I needed to go clean off my stomach before I made a bigger mess of the bed. I hopped to my feet and scurried to the bathroom without another word. I switched on the faucet and waited for the water to warm up, not at all surprised when Luca came in a moment later.

"Amore, talk to me. What's wrong?"

I took one look at him, then burst into tears. "Absolutely nothing!" I cried.

Luca retrieved a washcloth from the drawer, held it under the faucet, then wrung it out. He wiped the warm cloth across my stomach and peered up at my in the mirror. "You're crying because nothing is wrong?"

"Yes. Why do you always have to be so freaking perfect?"

He frowned. "I'm really confused."

I sighed, then gave him the short version of the shitshow that had just played in my brain over the past ten minutes.

"So you don't want to try for a baby now?" he summarized.

I didn't answer.

"Okay, well, that's fine. What if we take a shower, and I finish what I started with you. You could go back on birth control for a while or we can just keep using condoms until you're ready. It's up to you," he said.

"You're not freaked out?" I asked.

Luca shrugged. "I'm sure a baby would change things, but the idea of you being pregnant is really sexy to me. So is the idea of you being a mom. And the thing is, I think everything about you is just sexy to me. I'm pretty sure I will always want to have sex with you. And I can't imagine a scenario where the sex with us is bad." He paused. "Are you worried you won't want me once I'm a dad?"

I tried to picture Luca holding a tiny baby and the image made me want to jump right on him in the bathroom. "No, dad Luca sounds very sexy to me."

"Well, I think you're worried for nothing then. But we can wait until you're ready."

I sighed, wishing I could rewind the clock. "I'm ready now," I said, nudging him backwards until he was seated on the vanity counter.

Luca chuckled but held me at arm's length. "Okay, well, you're going to have to give me a minute here to recover."

I considered that for a moment, then made my way into our closet. Luca followed, groaning the second he realized my plan. We had floor to ceiling mirrors along one wall of the closet, and an island dresser in the middle that was the perfect height. I lay my upper body on the counter, shivering as the cool marble hit my nipples. I tilted my head to the side, watching Luca's wistful expression in the mirror as he checked out the sight before him.

As I'd predicted, he had fully "recovered" within a minute. This time, as Luca thrust into me, I kept my eyes open, watching our bodies come together over and over in the mirror, and watching Luca's face as he enjoyed the same show. I didn't let my mind wander once, and when my orgasm swept over me, Luca followed suit within seconds.

We showered together, then snuggled in front of the fire and ate snacks in our bathrobes before finally deciding to go to sleep. I yawned for the hundredth time as I pulled back the covers, deeply regretting that we hadn't gone to bed earlier, and then I saw the dark stains on the sheet.

"Oh crap!"

"What?" Luca asked, coming up behind me. "Oh," he said, once he saw.

Obviously, I'd known we'd messed up the sheets earlier when I interrupted our activities, but then in the heat of the moment, well, I'd totally forgotten. And now, I was exhausted.

"Are the backup sheets in the closet?" he asked.

"Yeah, probably near the window," I said, already stripping the bed. I dumped the dirty bedding into the laundry room next door then went to the closet to see what was taking Luca so long. I found my husband standing in the middle of our gigantic closet staring aimlessly.

"Tesoro, we have so many clothes," he said.

I gazed around the room, agreeing with his observation. And more notably, I didn't see any sheets anywhere. "And no sheets," I added. We had at least one other set of sheets, somewhere. But apparently in the move, I'd misplaced them.

"Come on," Luca said, tugging my hand.

I sighed. "We can't sleep without bedding."

Luca kissed my cheek, then whispered. "We're going to the guest room. We'll figure this out tomorrow."

CHAPTER 19

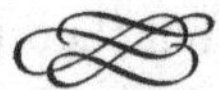

Luca

Giada left before me the next morning to meet Gabby for a workout class then coffee, so Alessio and I sprawled out in the sunroom to prep for our lunch meeting with Mr. Kelso.

"How'd the dinner with your parents go?" Alessio asked.

"Good," I said. "Like, really good." I detailed all of the unexpected compliments we'd received.

"Wow. That is crazy," Alessio agreed. "So…if everything went well at dinner, what happened to make Giada mad, if you don't mind me asking?"

I frowned. "When was Giada mad?"

Alessio winced, like he hadn't meant to make me uncomfortable. "I was looking for some toothpaste and noticed that you had, uh, slept in the guestroom. Figured something had to happen if you got banished."

I laughed, but had to admit that was a reasonable assumption. "No, just a little mishap with the sheets in our room, so we both slept in the guestroom."

"Huh?"

I stood to pour myself another cup of coffee. "Papà said he wanted a grandbaby. We were trying to make it happen, and—"

"Stop, no, stop!" Alessio covered his ears like a toddler throwing a tantrum.

I laughed, appreciating that I could still make the guy blush.

So far, the new living arrangement had been great. Granted, Alessio had only been sleeping at the house for a week, but I really didn't see any potential problems. He and Giada got along lately, but more than that, his presence comforted her. And her presence made him behave. For me, it was win-win. They were my two favorite people, and having both of them on hand at all times meant I didn't have to constantly feel torn between them.

Alessio wasn't currently in a serious relationship, and he'd been worried about bringing dates home, so that had been our only real discussion point before finalizing the arrangement. I assured him that both Giada and I trusted him. Sure, he could be a complete slut with his sexual escapades, but I didn't for one second worry he'd bring someone into our home that he didn't know. Random hookups and one-night stands could happen at his date's place, and both Giada and I would rely on Alessio's judgment about when he was ready to invite someone to stay at the house with him.

As an added precaution— at Alessio's insistence— there were alarms on the door to his suite. If he opted to invite a future partner to sleep over, he could turn on the alarm, guaranteeing he'd wake the moment his lover headed to any other part of the house.

Giada hoped Alessio would find a serious partner soon. I wasn't so sure. I wanted him to be happy, but I wasn't convinced that happiness for Alessio involved a traditional relationship. I supposed things might be different if Alessio were truly free to be himself.

As it was, Alessio openly dated women. In private, he was

often intimate with women, as well. But he was also interested in men. Alessio labeled himself as bisexual, but only to those in the inner-most circle. The label matched his behavior. But I didn't know if the label actually matched his heart.

My papà had many faults, one of which was the fact that he was homophobic. As much as he'd grown to like and even respect Alessio, my papà still wouldn't hesitate to bury him in wet cement if he learned he were gay or bi. As long as Alessio openly dated women on occasion, we figured he was safe. And if Alessio told me in private that he wasn't actually interested in any of the women he dated, that he never had been into a woman, I'd be okay with that too.

What bugged me was the worry that maybe he was afraid to tell me the truth because he didn't want me to feel guilty about what a prick I had for a father.

"Luca? You ready to roll?" Alessio asked, jolting me out of my random daydream.

I shook my head, still dazed. "Sorry. Yes."

"Did your dad mention anything about Elio during dinner?" Alessio asked as we drove to meet Kelso.

"Nothing of substance. He said he told the guy he wanted him to come with him to Italy in a few days. Apparently, Elio didn't love the plan, said he needed a little more time to get something together here. Not sure what."

Alessio turned to me, frowning. "That's odd. Don't you think?"

I shrugged. "Not everyone can pack up and leave the country with a few days' notice."

"Right, but nobody says no to Salvatore Marino. And what does Elio Randazzo have going on that he can't pick up and leave?"

I gritted my teeth. Alessio was right. This was yet another example of the shit that bugged me with this guy. We found nothing directly implicating him as a rat, but everything we did know about the guy gave us a bad feeling about him.

"What did your dad say about his reaction when he found out Matt was gone?" Alessio asked.

"He was a mess, but that's to be expected. They joined at the same time. They were close." I paused. "But there was no reaction, per se. Elio was the one who was supposed to give him the fentanyl, so he knew about it before it happened."

"Wait, he was supposed to but he didn't?"

"No. But he had a solid reason. Car accident. Some guy rear ended him on Darby Street. Whole thing's on traffic camera apparently and nothing shady about it. He told my papà he was in an accident and running late, so he had someone else do it." I paused. "I asked my papà if he thought Elio just didn't want to get his hands dirty, and he said no, that he thought the guy was going to do it, just later. Papà didn't want to fuck up our alibi and dinner plans though. Plus, how could he have planned the car accident?"

Alessio shook his head. "Okay, but if he's a cop, he can't kill someone, even if the guy is a creep like us. So maybe he stalls, planning to get back up there or bust your dad. Maybe he truly thought your dad would wait and didn't expect him to send in a replacement."

I considered that theory, but dismissed it. "If he had wanted to stop my papà, he would've tried harder to convince him Mattia was clean. Papà asked him about Mattia, and all he said was that he was an honest guy, with nothing suspicious."

"But if Elio is the dirty one, he's really got to tread lightly there. He can't convince anyone Mattia is too innocent without implicating himself."

I sighed. It was possible. I didn't like any of it. "I'll feel better when he's overseas," I said.

"Me too." Alessio agreed, pulling to a stop in front of the

restaurant where I was meeting Mr. Kelso. "Knock 'em dead, Mr. Marino."

I rolled my eyes, then climbed out of the car.

~

*G*iada

I couldn't concentrate on anything the entire day. All I could think about was baby-making, pregnancy, and babies. It didn't help that the universe seemed to be working against me. Somehow, Gabby and I wandered into a prenatal yoga class at the gym instead of our usual barre strength class. We realized our mistake and sprinted to the right class, but then I spent the entire class wondering if I'd be practicing yoga in a few months instead of alternating spinning classes with barre classes.

Next, we walked down the street to the coffee shop after our workout, but the place was packed. A group of moms had commandeered the two largest tables by the windows, and their strollers occupied most of the free space.

"Can't escape the babies today," I mumbled, gritting my teeth and trying to focus on my coffee order. Gabby eyed me warily, but said nothing.

Then, when I got home, I found a shirtless Luca standing in front of the sink, spooning cold orzo into his mouth. His bare torso glistened and my eyes honed in on his pecs.

"Hey babe, how was your day?" he asked, wiping his mouth on his forearm.

I opened my mouth to speak, but got distracted by the ridge of muscles heading downward from his hips.

"Sorry, I didn't actually eat at my lunch meeting, so I was starved. I need to head to the club this evening, but I'm free for a few hours if you want..." his voice trailed off and he stepped closer, seemingly confused by my silence and staring.

"Giada? You okay?" he asked, gripping my hips.

"Mmm hmm," I said.

"How was the gym?"

"Fine."

"Coffee?"

"Cold."

He quirked a brow, probably because I always order iced coffee after a workout. "What's on your mind then?" he asked.

I hesitated, then blurted out the truth. "Sex."

Luca's eyes widened, and a moment later my feet left the ground. He hoisted me over his shoulder and carried me towards the stairs. I shrieked until he put me down, but willingly jogged up the stairs with him.

He tugged at my leggings but I jerked out of reach. "Wait, I need a shower," I said.

"Why don't we get you dirtier, and then you shower," he suggested.

I shook my head, then switched on the shower. I stripped naked, then adjusted the center rainfall faucet and motioned for Luca to join me. He undressed and stepped beside me seconds later. I rinsed my hair, then dropped my face to Luca's, kissing him. I didn't dare touch him anywhere other than his face, less we end up fooling around too much in the shower and completely defeating the baby-making plans, although I supposed one could probably still get pregnant in the shower. I rushed through my shower routine, barely dried off, then let Luca carry me to our bed.

Luca's hands raked down my bare torso, sending jolts of electric pleasure straight to my core. His tongue lapped at one nipple, then the other, and I squealed. Already, I felt tightly wound, too close to combustion.

Luca had always made it his mission to bring me to orgasm at least once before welcoming his own release, but now I felt myself resisting, trying to hold off as long as possible. My favorite sexual endeavors with him had always been the times when we'd climaxed together, and now that we were officially trying to conceive, I had another reason to aim for that idyllic timing.

I reached for my husband, pulling him towards me. His lips crashed into mine, but he controlled the fall of his hips, hovering inches above my abdomen. I lost myself in the kiss, dizzy from the delicious swirl of his tongue. I felt every stroke of his powerful tongue inside my mouth—and also much, much lower, almost as if he were kissing me there, too. I moaned and gripped Luca tighter, needing to feel his skin against mine.

He grinned against my lips then finally reached a hand between us, spreading some of my moisture over the head of his rock-hard cock, then slowly positioned it at my entrance. I lifted my hips, desperate to take him deeper, but Luca inched his way inside, torturing me with the delayed gratification. Once he was finally fully seated, I roped my thighs around his waist, holding him tight to me.

Luca moaned his approval, then breathed a laugh a moment later when I hadn't loosened my grip. "Amore, I'm happy to stay here for eternity but if you want me to move, you'll have to give me some room."

I groaned and clenched my internal muscles in response. Luca dipped his head down and caught my nipple with his tongue, distracting me with another intense jolt of pleasure that made my thighs fall apart. Always the opportunist, Luca withdrew and thrust into me harder. I bucked my hips toward him in response, eager to keep up with his exquisitely punishing pace.

I felt myself about to slip over the edge but was determined to hold off another minute. I could tell he was close. His breathing was faster, his movements less controlled.

"Fuck, baby, just like that," I purred in his ear, certain that was just the push he'd need.

I was right. Luca thrust faster, slamming into me so hard that my orgasm swept over me with a relentless power. I felt the warmth of Luca's release filling me but I was so caught up in the rush of my own climax that I couldn't even appreciate the perfect timing. My innermost muscles contracted harder and longer than ever before, the feelings so decadent and so intense that stars filled my vision.

Suddenly, a jolt of pain cut into the pleasure.

"Ow!" I yelped, dropping my legs to the bed.

Luca jerked backwards, but I grabbed him just in time, holding him in place.

"What happened? Are you okay?" he asked, still fighting against my hands to pull out.

"Don't move," I instructed through gritted teeth. Then, I reached a hand towards my stomach, rubbing the offending muscle.

"Amore, what is it?" he asked, his face filled with concern.

"I think I pulled a stomach muscle," I admitted, struggling to catch my breath.

Luca's face fell. "Oh, baby I'm so sorry. I thought you came. I should've been less rough, and—"

"Luca," I interrupted, unable to take his pity. "I did come. I came harder than I ever have. Maybe a little too hard." I shifted side to side beneath him, lifting my legs to wrap them around him again.

Now my husband bit back a smile. "You're saying you came so hard you pulled a muscle?"

"It's not funny. It hurts."

"Then let me move. You can stretch it."

I gripped him harder as he started to pull away. "No. I'm supposed to keep my hips elevated for twenty minutes after. Do you want a baby or not?"

Luca breathed a laugh but didn't reply. Instead, he reached his hand between us and began massaging my stomach.

Luca

I wasn't sure whether to feel guilty or proud about the painful spasms in Giada's stomach, but nearly an hour passed before we both made it back down the stairs. Alessio leaned against the island, his phone clutched in his hands and a smirk on his face.

"What's so amusing?" I asked.

The mischievous gleam in his eyes told me he was debating not answering, but thankfully, he spoke. "Giovanni sent over some pictures. Apparently, Lauren wants to post one of you and Aldo on social media, you know, since you're the godfather and all."

I grimaced. I hated social media. "Why'd he send them to you?"

"Probably because he knew you'd be pissed and veto them all," Alessio said. "But some of these are fucking awesome."

"Great, more baby pictures," Giada mumbled, brushing past us both to grab a sparkling water from the fridge.

I decided not to unpack the attitude there, but Alessio apparently took the bait.

"Come on, Giada. You have to love this one," he said, angling his phone towards her.

I craned my neck to look at it, but Giada stepped in the path.

"Oh, that's terrible," she said.

"Wait, the next one is worse," Alessio warned.

Apparently, he kept scrolling. Giada giggled.

"And this one is my personal favorite," he said, roaring with laughter.

Giada laughed for a second, then shrieked in pain and grabbed her stomach. "Ow. Crap. Oh God. Ouch! Do not make me laugh!" She hobbled to a chair and gripped her stomach.

Alessio frowned. "What is wrong?"

Giada's face was now beet red.

"She pulled a stomach muscle earlier," I explained.

"At the gym?"

She shot me a look that clearly instructed me to shut up, but I couldn't resist. "No, it's a sex injury. This baby making stuff is no joke."

Giada punched my shoulder and stormed out of the room, but she clearly wasn't too mad since she only went so far as the sunroom.

"I didn't know that was possible," he admitted.

"We are learning all sorts of new things," I said.

"And it's only going to get worse when we actually have a baby," Giada chimed in. "I mean, are you sure you want to keep living here Alessio?"

He pulled a face. "Wait, I thought you brought me on as the nanny. Was that not the deal?"

I laughed, then snatched his phone out of his hands. He was right, the photos of me and Aldo were terrible. Well, Aldo looked adorable in all of them, but my expression could best be described as terrified or constipated, depending on the photo. *Super*.

"We should head over to the club," Alessio said.

I nodded. "Yeah, okay. What are you up to tonight, Giada?"

She shrugged. "If Lincoln's free, I might see if he can drive me over to Gabby's."

"Weren't you with her all morning?" I asked.

Giada's gaze darkened. "Yes, but I forgot to show her the pictures from the housewarming. Your little godfather photos reminded me. And besides, weren't you with Alessio all morning?"

I chewed the inside of my lip, silently berating myself for never knowing when to shut up. "You are right, amore. I love you so much. You two should have a relaxing wine night while you still can drink, especially since Lincoln is driving." I paused. "I won't be late, but you just come home whenever."

I leaned in to kiss her, lingering when she kissed me back more sweetly than I'd envisioned. Man, life was good.

CHAPTER 20

Giada

Alessio forwarded me the hilarious pictures of Luca and the baby so Gabby and I could giggle at those before we started flipping through the house pictures. We paused to sip our wine and chat while we did. I hadn't told her Luca and I were trying for a baby, but this felt like a good time to open up.

To my surprise, she was supportive. She thought we'd be good parents, and the closest Gabby came to any negativity was her comment that a baby might help keep Luca out of trouble. Well, she wasn't exactly wrong.

We discussed possible nursery designs, then returned our focus to the pictures from the housewarming. I scrolled through the final picture, then smiled.

"The before and after is insane. I can't believe you were able to do all that in under a year."

"I was shooting for six months, so technically I was way behind schedule."

Gabby laughed. "If you'd hired that out, it would've taken two years."

I didn't disagree, but my phone rang before I could say anything. It was Lincoln, again. I sighed just as he texted, "We need 2 go now."

"I think my driver is getting sleepy. He keeps calling and texting."

Gabby's brows knitted together. "You should answer. It could be important."

"If it were important, Luca would call me. Or Alessio. Linc is so far down the chain of command that I don't even think he'd be in charge of picking up the dry cleaning."

"They must trust him if they've got him driving you."

I shrugged. "Well, if he really wants to head home now, he could get his lazy butt out of the car and drag me out of here."

A knock on the door made both of us jump. I followed Gabby to the foyer. She peered out the door then turned to me.

"It's like you summoned him," she teased.

I laughed, confirmed it was him, then unlocked the door. I was preparing to make some sassy comment about not having a curfew, but one look at Lincoln's face stopped me dead in my tracks.

"We need to go," he said.

"What's wrong?"

He tugged my hand, and I yanked back.

"I'm coming, but I need my shoes and purse."

Gabby grabbed my phone off the coffee table and handed it to me while I slipped into my shoes. She gestured at the bottle of wine we hadn't yet opened. "Just keep it," I said.

"Call me," she instructed me as Lincoln led me out of the house.

"What's wrong?" I repeated once we were outside.

"I don't know details. Luca is okay."

"Did he get hurt? Arrested? Is someone after him?"

Lincoln shook his head. "No, he's fine."

I called him the second I sat in the car.

Lincoln peeled out of the drive and glanced at my phone. "I said he's fine."

"Well, he's not answering," I replied, hanging up then trying Alessio. He didn't answer either. "What is going on?"

"I don't know. They just called and said something happened and we needed to get to Rize right away."

"They? Who called?"

Lincoln blew out a breath and his eyes darted from side to side as he merged onto the highway. "Giovanni called. His exact words were get Giada to Rize fast. Luca needs her."

I squeezed my eyes shut, trying to stay calm. Whatever was going on, Luca wouldn't need me blowing in like a hot mess hurricane. And trying to guess what had happened would only stress me out.

I opened my eyes and glanced at Lincoln. He wasn't exactly the picture of zen, either. The guy looked like he was about to shit his pants. I realized I'd never fully appreciated the calm, cool way Alessio and Enzo handled everything.

I considered calling Enzo, but decided against it. Depending on what the issue was, Luca might not be thrilled to hear that I'd discussed the drama with people outside the family. Besides, we were surely almost there now. Traffic was light at this hour on a Sunday night.

I gazed at my phone again, then tapped out a message to Luca. "On my way," I wrote, "I love you."

A few minutes later, Lincoln's phone rang. I recognized the number as Giovanni's, so I reached over and clicked to answer the call.

"What's going on?" I asked.

"Linc?" Giovanni's voice boomed through the speakers, ignoring my question.

"Yeah," Lincoln said. "I've got Giada and we're—"

"How far away are you?" Giovanni interrupted.

Lincoln chewed his lip. "Maybe ten minutes."

"What is going on?" I asked before Giovanni could hang up. "Are you sure Luca's okay?"

I could hear Giovanni's rapid breathing. Whatever had happened was bad. "Luca's fine, Giada. I promise."

A new thought hit me, the fear ripping through me. "Did something happen to Alessio?"

My driver perked up at that, as though it hadn't even occurred to him that his own cousin might be in danger.

"No. He's here with Luca." Giovanni hesitated, then said more. "It's Sal. He's—he was shot."

I replayed his words in my head, then repeated them aloud. "Like, Salvatore Marino?"

"Yes."

"Is he okay? Why aren't we going to the hospital?" I asked.

"I can't talk now. Just…get here fast, but be safe, okay?"

He disconnected before either of us could say anything else.

"Poor Luca," I mumbled under my breath. Then, I retrieved my rosary from my purse and began to pray.

I felt calmer by the time Lincoln sped into the parking lot. He pulled right up to the curb by the back entrance, and a moment later, Giovanni swung open the door. He peered around, then reached for my hand and pulled me inside.

The club was closed, as it always was on Sunday and Monday nights, but a nervous energy filled the room.

"He's in the office," Giovanni said, pushing past several men I didn't recognize.

I sped up, but right before we reached the door, Giovanni gripped my wrist.

"Hang on," he said. "I didn't…," he paused, wincing, "I didn't want to tell you over the phone, but Sal wasn't just shot. I mean, he…"

I jerked my hand free and gestured for him to hurry up. I needed to be with my husband, not standing in the hall with his friend stammering like an idiot.

"Sal didn't make it," Giovanni said. "Salvatore Marino is dead."

Right as the words left his mouth, the door to Luca's office swung open. A handful of men filled the small space, but no one spoke. They all stood there, gathered around the desk, where Luca sat like a king on his throne.

Alessio's gaze met mine, his expression stoic as always, but I could tell a fire raged just below the surface. He and Thomas both stepped back, offering me a clear view of Luca.

As I gazed at my husband, who was just as devastatingly handsome as the day we married, I realized we'd overcome a lot together. So I knew now that whatever life threw at us, we could handle it.

To a casual onlooker, Luca likely appeared calm, maybe even bored. His button-down shirt wasn't rumpled, and not a single sleek hair from his gorgeous head was out of place. He sat upright, with his back straight and his shoulders back. Luca looked cool as a cucumber. But I could see the hidden signs—the tiny flexes of his jaw, the way his throat worked to force each swallow, and the measured, deep breaths.

My chest tightened at the thought of everything Luca must be feeling—the loss, the anger, the fear, and the sorrow. His feelings for his father had always been complicated, and I already knew this would just make everything even more fuzzy and strained.

Luca stared at me and I simply nodded, hoping that simple gesture conveyed that I already knew, that he didn't have to say the words aloud. I crossed the room and dropped to my knees at his feet right as he whispered, "Amore."

I wrapped my arms around his hips and pressed my face to his abdomen, embracing him as best as I could without knocking him backwards from his chair. Luca bent to kiss the top of my head, his warm lips lingering for several heartbeats. Then he reached beneath my arms, lifting me to his lap and burying his face in my hair.

I felt the room empty around us and heard the door click

shut, but neither Luca or I moved. We just held each other tightly, both of us desperate to ground the other in this moment rather than to think about what awaited us next.

As I breathed in the fresh, familiar scent of this hauntingly beautiful man—my husband, lover, partner, and soul mate—the realization hit me. There was something else Giovanni hadn't told me. Something else no one, it seemed, was saying aloud just yet.

Salvatore Marino's death had a far greater significance than any other simple tragedy.

With the head of the family now gone, Luca was the official boss of the Marino family.

The End

If you enjoyed this story, please consider leaving a review.

ACKNOWLEDGMENTS

I'm so grateful to everyone who has supported me throughout the entire Mafiosa Princess Journey so far. There is only one book in the series after Mafiosa Princess Family, and I promise you won't want to miss the exciting conclusion of this story!

Now…for the acknowledgements. First, a huge shout out to my editor, Sarah, and to my cover artist, JD Designs. Another big thanks to all of my proofreaders, my ARC readers, and everyone who offered feedback on early drafts of the cover art and back-of-book blurbs.

Finally, thank you to everyone who reads my stories, reviews my stories, buys my stories, and shares my stories. Recommending a Liza Malloy book to one of your friends is truly the greatest compliment you could ever give me.

I'm so excited to finish this series with all of you!

Thanks for sticking with me!
Liza

ABOUT THE AUTHOR

Liza Malloy writes contemporary romance and women's fiction. She's a sucker for alpha males, bad boys, dimples, and muscles, and she can't resist a man in uniform. Liza loves creating worlds where her heroine discovers her own strength and finds her Happily Ever After. When Liza isn't reading or writing torrid love stories, she's a practicing attorney. Her other passions include gummy bears, jelly beans, and the occasional marathon. She lives in the Midwest with her four daughters and her own Prince Charming.

Visit her website at https://authorlizamalloy.wixsite.com/lizamalloy

Join her email list at http://eepurl.com/gnuROD

ALSO BY LIZA MALLOY

Sixty Days for Love

For Love and Italian

Forbidden Ink

The Brothers' Band

The Brothers' Band: The Next Track

Hollywood Endings

Hollywood Beginnings

Supporting Roles

Legacy: The Awakening

Legacy: The Revelation

Legacy: The Reckoning

Mafiosa Princess Beginnings (Prequel)

Mafiosa Princess

Mafiosa Princess: Sacrifice

Mafiosa Princess: Honor

Mafiosa Princess: Trust

Mafiosa Princess: Omertà

Mafiosa Princess: Loyalty

Mafiosa Princess: Faith

Her Mafia Valentine (A Short Story)

Love All- A Steamy Sports Romance

The New Boyfriend

Manic Love- A Billionaire Romance

The Cowboy Assignment

My So-Called Superpower